A DUKE IS NEVER ENOUGH

❊ *The Spitfire Society* ❊

USA TODAY
BESTSELLING AUTHOR

DARCY BURKE

A DUKE IS NEVER ENOUGH

Notorious rake Marcus Raleigh, Marquess of Ripley, is gracing the gossip pages for a new reason: the rumors he may have murdered his swindling cousin. His quest for answers regarding his cousin's death leads him to an incomparable self-declared spinster, and he is—for the first time—beguiled beyond reason. Neither is what the other wants, and yet their intense mutual infatuation is inescapable.

After abandoning her philandering betrothed at the altar, Phoebe Lennox fled from London only to return an heiress who refuses to follow the ton's rules. She won't risk a relationship of any kind—until she meets the scandalous Marquess of Ripley. Swept into his seductive embrace, her resolve falters in the face of a pleasure she never anticipated. But when the truth about Marcus and the murder come to light, Phoebe could lose everything she holds dear, including a love for all time.

Don't miss the next book in The Spitfire Society series, A DUKE WILL NEVER DO, coming May 19, 2020!

Want to read what came before The Spitfire Society? Discover The Untouchables , twelve love stories featuring the most untouchable peers of the realm and the wallflowers, bluestockings, spinsters, and widows who bring them to their knees.

Love romance? Have a free book (or two or three) on me!

Sign up at http://www.darcyburke.com/readerclub for members-only exclusives, including advance notice of pre-orders and insider scoop, as well as contests, giveaways, freebies, and 99 cent deals!

Want to share your love of my books with like-minded readers? Want to hang with me and get inside scoop? Then don't miss my exclusive Facebook groups!

Darcy's Duchesses for historical readers
Burke's Book Lovers for contemporary readers

A Duke is Never Enough
Copyright © 2020 Darcy Burke
All rights reserved.

ISBN: 9781944576646

Book design: © Darcy Burke.
Book Cover Design © Hang Le.
Cover image © Period Images.
Darcy Burke Font Design © Carrie Divine/Seductive Designs
Editing: Linda Ingmanson.

❀ Created with Vellum

CHAPTER 1

London, March 1819

*A*n unsettled irritation ran through Marcus
Raleigh, Marquess of Ripley, as he rode onto
Rotten Row. The breeze cooled his face and a bit of
his ire. Until he neared the end of the track, where a
group of gentlemen were gathered to the side of the
footpath. On the periphery of that group, a familiar
face jolted him to a stop.

Marcus steered from the path and dismounted.
After securing his horse to a post, he stalked toward
the group. His annoyance grew to anger, an emotion
he rarely succumbed to.

Upon his reaching the group, the object of his ire
met his gaze with eerily light eyes. "Afternoon, Ripley," he said.

"Might I have a word, Drobbit?" Marcus kept his
tone even despite his displeasure.

No, not displeasure. He was furious for the first
time in…years. His cousin Archibald Drobbit had
apparently been embezzling money from gentlemen
by organizing investment schemes. He'd all but ru-

ined Marcus's new friend, Graham, the Duke of Halstead. Rather, Drobbit had ruined the former duke and Graham had inherited the mess.

"Certainly." Drobbit, who was short and stocky, with a thick neck, left the group and ambled toward Marcus, who then led him off the track away from the others. "It's been some time, cousin."

Satisfied they were removed enough for a private discussion, Marcus stopped and turned on the smaller man. "Spare me your idle conversation. It's boring and pointless. It's also offensive."

Drobbit had to tip his head back to look up at Marcus, his eyes narrowing with unease as his usually sly smile disappeared. He clasped his hands behind his back, perhaps in an effort to appear nonchalant, as if they conversed like this every day. As if they conversed *ever*. "How have I offended you?"

"By preying on others."

The unease in Drobbit's eyes expanded to fear, his pupils dilating slightly.

"Don't." Marcus edged forward, glaring down at the man, who was his elder by a handful of years. "I know precisely what you've done. Well, not precisely, but I know what you've done to Halstead, and you're going to tell me who else you've stolen from. Then you're going to make restitution to every single one of them."

Drobbit's face paled. He lifted his hand to his neck and pulled gently at his cravat. "I, um, none of that is true."

"Don't lie," Marcus spat. "I know it's true, and I know there are others. Perhaps you'd rather I ensure you're prosecuted for fraud."

"You can't do that."

Marcus nearly laughed. "Have you forgotten I'm a marquess? And you're...no one."

Panic leached into Drobbit's features, making

him appear feverish. "I'm your cousin!" While that was true, they weren't close. Their mothers had been sisters who'd fallen out after Marcus's mother had married a marquess. Drobbit's mother had grown to despise her sister.

"I'm sure you used that connection to benefit you in any way possible." Marcus glowered at him. "You'll return the money you stole. And don't bother protesting again. You demean what's left of your character.

"You'll also tell me about this scheme. I want to know everything—how you found your marks, how you persuaded them to trust you, what you did with the money."

Drobbit shook his head. "I have nothing to say to you."

Marcus moved toward Drobbit until he stood close enough to tower over the man. "You do, and you will."

Drobbit's lip curled, and for the first time, he didn't look like a sniveling coward. "Go to the devil."

Marcus grabbed the man's lapels and shook him. "I refuse to allow you to sully my family name or continue ruining people's *lives*." He thought of Graham's betrothed and how her family had been on the brink of bankruptcy, her father fearing debtor's prison.

"Ripley!" Drobbit shrieked, prompting Marcus to remember they were in a very public place. He let go of the man, but did so with enough force to send Drobbit stumbling backward.

The anger roiling inside Marcus simmered as he strode toward his cousin. "I will call on you to settle this matter."

"Settle it how? You don't mean to call me out?" Drobbit's voice climbed. "You'd kill me."

Marcus snorted. "You're lucky you aren't dead already. Though, if it were up to me, you might be."

Drobbit's eyes goggled, and his throat worked. He looked as if he were choking on something. Then his gaze shot to Marcus's left.

Marcus darted a look in that direction and swore under his breath. A crowd of onlookers watched them with rapt interest. As if Marcus didn't already enjoy a questionable reputation as a libertine.

Scowling, Marcus kept his voice low. "I'm not going to call you out."

Drobbit shook his head. "We have nothing further to discuss."

"Did you not hear what I said before?" Marcus asked with quiet frustration. "You'll go to prison. You may even be transported."

"Perhaps. Perhaps not." Drobbit's tone was so arrogant, so blithe, that Marcus's temper snapped.

Marcus grabbed him by the lapel once more, but with only one hand. Drobbit quickly pivoted and brought his left fist up, striking Marcus in the cheek.

Reacting without thought, Marcus hit him back, delivering a blow to Drobbit's eye. He followed with a second punch to his cousin's jaw. Drobbit's head snapped back, and Marcus let him go. The smaller man teetered, then dropped to the ground on his arse.

A few of the spectators rushed forward, but they simply stood there staring between Marcus and his cousin. Bloody hell, this was not what Marcus had intended. And yet, what did he expect? This was what happened when one surrendered to emotion. His father's voice echoed in his head: *Strong emotions never did anyone any good.*

It was one of many things the man had been right about. Marcus pushed away thoughts of his father lest one of those strong emotions rise to the surface.

Drobbit glared up at him, almost taunting him. Did he want a spectacle? Marcus wasn't going to give him the satisfaction. He'd discover the man's direction and call on him.

"This isn't over," Marcus said. He wanted to be sure Drobbit really had ceased his deceptive behavior, and he'd find out where the money had gone. There couldn't be *nothing*.

With a final curl of his lip, Marcus started to turn. Something hit him in the side of the head. The projectile connected with force, driving pain through Marcus's temple. He realized Drobbit had thrown something—a rock, perhaps.

Marcus started toward him, but Drobbit scrambled to his feet and dashed off. Stifling an invective, Marcus spun away from the crowd that had gathered and stalked to his horse. A second group, this one of ladies, stood on the footpath and stared at him.

After untying his horse, Marcus swung up onto the saddle and urged the gelding into a trot back down Rotten Row. By the time he reached the end, however, he blinked against a stinging sensation— blood had trickled into his eye.

"Blast it all," he muttered before steering from the path and dismounting. He didn't have a damn thing to wipe at the blood so he pulled his cravat free and immediately swiped the silk over his eye in an effort to clean it. Horace nudged his shoulder as if to ask if he was all right.

"I'll be fine," Marcus said, stroking his muzzle.

The sound of hooves drew him to turn toward the path he'd just left. A woman walked her horse toward him, then dismounted without assistance.

"Impressive," he said.

"Here, let me." She came toward him with a

handkerchief and brushed his hand away. Lifting her hand, she dabbed around his eye. "You're rather tall."

He saw a bench nearby. "Would it be better if I sat?"

"Yes, but what of the horses?"

Leading Horace to a nearby tree, Marcus tossed the reins over a branch. He went back to fetch her horse and slipped the reins over a different branch. "This should do."

With a faint nod, the young woman pivoted and walked briskly to the bench.

Following his angel of mercy, he sat down and removed his hat. He tipped his head back, both to give her better access and so he could study her.

She wore a pert peacock-blue-colored riding hat set atop her dark curls at a jaunty angle. Delicate sable brows crowned a magnificent pair of jade-green eyes. They gleamed with intelligence and concern. Her rose-pink lips were slightly pursed as she tended to him.

"His aim was quite good," she murmured, cleaning his temple.

He winced when she pressed on the wound itself. "You saw what happened?"

"Everyone in Hyde Park saw what happened." Her wry tone sparked with wit, igniting his curiosity about her.

"I can't believe that's true." But then he hadn't paid close attention to the size of the crowd.

"Well, perhaps not everyone. It's a rather large park." She lifted her hand briefly before applying pressure once more. "This doesn't seem to want to stop bleeding."

"It will take a minute—or ten," he said, studying her more closely. The tip of her nose turned up just slightly, and he suspected she had dimples when she smiled. "Wounds to the head are like that."

"You have experience with head wounds?" she asked.

"Once or twice," he answered absentmindedly as he took in the gentle sweep of her jaw and the graceful line of her neck, nearly hidden from his gaze by her smart riding costume. "You're very beautiful. Why haven't we met?"

Her laughter sparkled around him like a firework at Vauxhall. And yes, she had dimples. The right one was slightly deeper than the left. "I daresay we do not keep the same company."

"Pity, but I fear you are correct. You are obviously a Society…matron?" With her smooth skin and plump lips, she looked young, but that didn't mean she wasn't wed. Since she was without a companion or a chaperone, she must be married. Either way, it was odd for her to be here alone.

Her laughter was more subdued this time. "I am not a matron. I am a spinster."

Now it was his turn to laugh. "You sound quite proud of yourself."

"It's preferable to being a wife." She shuddered.

How rare to meet a woman who shared his opinion of marriage. "Is that why you're a spinster? You seem awfully young for that designation."

"It is self-declared, I assure you. I have no quarrel with being called such. Furthermore, I'm not young at all."

"Surely you can't be more than twenty-one."

"Surely I can. I am, in fact, twenty-five."

Marcus gasped in mock horror. "You're positively ancient. Whereas at thirty-one, I am at the height of my virility. It's too bad you weren't born a man."

"A sentiment I have reflected upon many times." Her wry tone and humor-filled gaze stirred a warmth inside him. The word *rare* rose in his mind again.

"So why not behave like one? Is that why you're here alone?"

"I'm not alone. My groom is waiting nearby."

"Well, that's a shame, because I was going to offer to see you home." He gave her a lazy smile. "I still could." His gaze connected with hers, and heat flickered between them. Attraction came easily to Marcus—perhaps too easily—but once in a while, there was something...more.

She quickly looked away, leading Marcus to question what he thought he'd seen. "That won't be necessary."

When she started to remove her hand, he reached up and gently clasped her wrist. "Why did you stop to help me?"

Her gaze found his once more, and color tinted her cheeks. She was more than beautiful. She was charm and grace, and there was something else lurking beneath the surface of her spinsterliness—passion. "Because you needed someone to, didn't you?"

He would argue that he didn't *need* anyone; however, in this case, her assistance was most welcome. "Apparently, and for that, I am grateful. I wish to repay your kindness."

She pulled the cloth from his head and studied the wound a moment. "I believe the bleeding has stopped. You will need to clean this up when you get home."

"If I saw you home, you could invite me in and clean it up for me."

She folded the handkerchief so that the blood-soaked part was on the interior. "There is the Lord Ripley I expected."

He exhaled and stood from the bench. "Alas, my reputation always precedes me."

"Perhaps if you ceased your roguish behavior, your reputation would change."

"Oh, I don't wish to change it." He grinned. "Like you, I am quite content with my designation. As a libertine, that is." He reached for the cloth she held. "Let me take that." His fingers grazed hers, and, despite their gloves, desire thrummed through him.

She relinquished the handkerchief more quickly than he would have liked. "Why?"

"I'll have it cleaned and then return it to you. However, I don't know your direction or even your name. Pray release me from the darkness of ignorance."

After staring at him a moment, she rolled her eyes. "You really have perfected this, haven't you? That does not require an answer. Nor does your request. Keep the handkerchief. You don't need to return it."

He blinked at her in slight surprise. He'd been rebuffed before, but seldom and not in some time. "You aren't going to tell me your name? That's rather cruel and again begs the question why you stopped to help me."

"As I said, you seemed to need it, and I am, if nothing else, a considerate person."

"Then have a care for me, dear lady, and deliver me from misery. Will you give me your name if I promise not to call?"

One of her sable brows tilted dubiously. "Will you actually keep that promise?"

No, and that she'd already discerned that about him was…intriguing. "I'm going to find out who you are whether you tell me or not. I guarantee I will be on your doorstep by tomorrow."

Her lips spread into a wide, vivacious smile, and Marcus's breath fixed in his lungs. "You're welcome to try. I bid you good day, my lord." She inclined her head, then turned to go.

"Until tomorrow, mystery lady." Marcus couldn't recall the last time he'd been so...aroused. Not just physically, though he absolutely was, but mentally. He very much looked forward to learning her identity. "You know, I could just follow you," he called after her.

She stopped, then looked back at him over her shoulder. "You could, but where's the fun in that?"

Oh, this was going to be too diverting. Anticipation curled through him as he watched her go to her horse. The groom she'd mentioned appeared from behind some shrubbery and helped her mount. Marcus should have accompanied her so he could provide assistance. What a bloody missed opportunity.

After she was gone from his view, he went back to his horse and mounted. He patted the gelding's neck, "Did you see her, Horace?" He was tempted to follow her, but he'd learn her identity without resorting to that. How many breathtaking, self-declared spinsters could there be?

Hell, he didn't know any spinsters. Perhaps his friend Anthony Colton could help him. Anthony was a viscount and, until recently, in possession of a sterling reputation. Perhaps he would know who she was. Except Marcus didn't have much information to provide. Now he regretted *not* following her.

As he rode home to Hanover Square, he felt much better than when he'd set out. Recalling his earlier agitated state, he winced inwardly. The situation with Drobbit was frustrating, and he hated that he'd allowed himself to be provoked into fighting with the man. In public, no less.

But his cousin had to answer for his crimes. Marcus owed it to his friend Graham and the countless other people Drobbit's fraud had harmed. He'd get to the bottom of things with him.

Right after he found his mystery beauty.

~

*A*t last, it was time for the break. Phoebe Lennox gathered the cards on the table and set them in a stack before rising from her chair. Sweeping her gaze across Mrs. Matheson's drawing room, she found her closest friend, Jane Pemberton, standing near the corner.

Before Phoebe could get to Jane, Lady Pemberton moved to her daughter's side. Jane stood angled toward Phoebe while Lady Pemberton's side was presented. The elder woman's mouth moved quickly as she spoke close to Jane's ear, then Lady Pemberton cast a furtive glance over her shoulder, her gaze connecting with Phoebe's. Pink bloomed in the woman's cheeks, and Phoebe had no question as to what, or rather *whom*, she was talking to Jane about.

Jane gave Phoebe a pleading look that clearly conveyed *Save me.*

Never one to abandon a friend, Phoebe continued on her path until she arrived at Jane's side. "Good evening, Lady Pemberton, Jane."

Lady Pemberton smiled broadly, the pink in her face still lingering. "Good evening, Miss Lennox. How lovely to see you."

Liar. Phoebe was undesirable in Lady Pemberton's eyes and in the eyes of plenty of other Society women of Lady Pemberton's age. Phoebe's self-declared spinsterhood and jilting of Laurence Sainsbury on their wedding day the previous Season ensured her reputation was lacking. That didn't stop Jane from being her friend, however, as much as her mother wished their friendship would cease.

"If you'll excuse me, I must speak with Lady Chadwick." Lady Pemberton took herself off in the direction of the dowager countess, who was holding court on the opposite side of the room.

Lady Chadwick was the hostess's great-aunt and the only reason Phoebe was invited to these card parties. The dowager had congratulated Phoebe on jilting Sainsbury, for she found him to be tiresome and sycophantic. Lady Chadwick's approval was the only thing that had kept Phoebe from utter ruin. That and her newfound role as an heiress. It was astonishing what people overlooked if you were wealthy.

"Your mother couldn't escape quickly enough," Phoebe murmured, moving closer to Jane and pivoting so they both faced the room.

"Thank goodness," Jane said, adjusting a blonde curl near her ear. "You saved me from another discussion about Mr. Brinkley." Her nose wrinkled slightly.

Mr. Brinkley was the Pembertons' neighbor in Shropshire. A banker, he was widowed and in need of a wife for his two young daughters. Since Jane hadn't yet attracted a title in London, her mother had begun to push for a match between her and Brinkley.

Actually, it wasn't only because Jane hadn't attracted a title. She'd also become too close with Phoebe. Lady Pemberton now feared her daughter was no longer viable on the Marriage Mart, a potential truth that pleased Jane, who loathed trying to land a husband.

"I'm glad to help," Phoebe said. "I keep waiting for your mother to say you aren't allowed to speak with me anymore."

"That shall be the day I leave and declare my own spinsterhood." Jane wanted that above anything.

"If it weren't for Anne, I would do it tomorrow. Even tonight." Anne was her younger sister in the throes of her first season.

"Anne may be wed by the end of May," Phoebe said wryly, for Anne was quite popular.

"Indeed she may. And I hope for her sake, she is."

"Why?"

"Because she's desperately in love—or so she told me last night."

"With whom?" Phoebe asked.

"That, she wouldn't say. I'm afraid she has so many suitors, I can't hazard a guess either." Jane straightened her shoulders. "Better her than me. If she marries well—perhaps even exceptionally well—I may be able to persuade my parents to let me be."

Phoebe shot her a dubious look. "Do you really think your mother will allow you to become a spinster like me?"

Jane exhaled. "No."

"Oh, Miss Lennox, didn't I see you riding in the park today?" The question sailed through the air from Mrs. Matheson. Flanked by two other ladies, she came toward Phoebe and Jane.

"You must have," Phoebe said, though she didn't recall seeing Mrs. Matheson.

"Did you see the Marquess of Ripley's altercation in Rotten Row?"

The mention of Ripley sent a ripple of awareness through Phoebe. "I did."

"I daresay he could have taken that poor man apart," Lady Faversham, the middle-aged woman on Mrs. Matheson's right, said.

"Unlikely," Lady Lindsell, from Mrs. Matheson's left, put in. "What I mean to say is that while he *could* have, he would not have. The man is his cousin."

Lady Faversham's eyes widened, and she pursed her lips. "I did not realize. I'm usually far more aware of such things."

Indeed she was. Lady Faversham was a terrible gossip.

"Well, it's easy to be blinded by Lord Ripley's... charms." Mrs. Matheson waggled her brows.

Lady Lindsell looked scandalized for a brief moment, but then her smile and the twinkle in her eye indicated her reaction was counterfeit. "Oh, but we mustn't be. He's a horrible reprobate."

"An absolute wastrel," Mrs. Matheson agreed.

Lady Faversham tilted her head. "Perhaps not that. I'm afraid we must reserve that description for the likes of Lord Colton."

The other women exchanged pitying looks, nodding somberly. Then the trio continued on their way circuiting the room.

Jane rolled her eyes. "Why did they even stop here?"

"So they could watch us listen to them blather. We failed to give them an adequate reaction, so they moved on."

Jane laughed softly. "That's probably true." She lowered her voice to ask, "You saw Lord Ripley fight?"

"I did more than that. I tended the cut on his head caused from a rock wielded by his cousin."

"You didn't! How on earth did that come about?"

"I saw that he was bleeding, and when he rode away from the path into a more secluded area—"

Jane interrupted. "Secluded?" One fine blonde brow arched in query.

"Not very," Phoebe said as if it mattered. She didn't have much of a reputation to protect. "No one saw me—or us. Together, I mean." Why did she suddenly feel hot? And slightly agitated?

"Tell me everything," Jane said, her eyes glowing with curiosity.

"There isn't much to tell." Wasn't there? He'd taken her handkerchief and promised to return it in person. Worse than that, they'd *flirted*. Phoebe might not care about her reputation, but that didn't mean she wanted to link herself to one of the most notorious rakes in England. "There may have been a bit of flirting," she murmured, her gaze drifting away from Jane's.

"*May have been?*"

Phoebe looked back at her friend. "Yes, there was flirting. What else would you expect from a man such as Ripley? Anyway, blood was streaming from his wound. I had to help."

"I would expect nothing less from *you*," Jane said warmly.

"He kept my handkerchief, promising to launder it before he returns it to me. In person."

"How gallant. That's not typically a word one hears in conjunction with Ripley. When will he call?"

Gallant wasn't a word Phoebe would use to describe him either. Vexing. Masculine. Tempting… Phoebe pushed those words from her mind. "He said he would do so tomorrow, but that's only if he can find me."

A laugh bubbled from Jane's lips. "Why wouldn't he be able to?"

"Because I didn't give him my name. Or my direction."

Jane looked at her in…admiration? "Oh, you *did* flirt. How did it feel?"

"Strange." It wasn't that Phoebe had never flirted. Since Sainsbury, however, she hadn't wanted to. She still wasn't sure she did, and yet Ripley had somehow provoked her. She didn't like that. No, she didn't like *men*, especially those of Ripley's ilk. Libertines and philanderers. Men such as her former betrothed, Sainsbury. "I don't plan to continue."

"Why not? As a spinster, you can do whatever you like."

"Not if I value what remains of my reputation."

"And do you?" Jane asked.

"We won't be able to be friends if I fall even farther."

Jane snorted in disgust. "Society is too priggish."

"And superior," Phoebe added, casting a look toward Mrs. Matheson and the others. "To some, it's amusing to imagine yourself above others."

"It's obnoxious."

Phoebe laughed softly. "And this is why we're such good friends."

Jane cocked her head to the side, her expression one of contemplation. "I find myself wondering how Lord Ripley will try to determine your identity. It's not as if he can encounter you at a social event—he rarely attends any, does he?" She snorted softly. "It's horribly hypocritical that the same people who won't invite you extend an invitation to him, all for the sake of creating a buzz in an effort to elevate their own popularity."

"I'm not sure obnoxious is a strong enough adjective to describe such people."

"Odious?" Jane offered.

Phoebe nodded. "Offensive."

"Outrageous!"

"*Obscene.*"

They dissolved into giggles for a moment.

Once recovered, Jane said, "I find myself still imagining how Lord Ripley will find you. I'm almost inclined to provide him with a clue."

"You must *not*." Phoebe briefly thought Jane was serious, but realized she wasn't, of course. "That wouldn't be fair."

"A wager, then. I'll bet him he can't find you."

"Except you contacting him would *be* a clue." Phoebe shook her head, knowing for certain her friend was in jest.

The glimmer of humor dissipated from Jane's gaze. "It occurs to me that Lord Colton has become rather close with him. Is it possible the marquess could trace you through him?"

Lord Colton's sister Sarah, now the Countess of Ware, was a friend of theirs. "I can't imagine how," Phoebe said.

"I suppose it's unlikely Ripley would describe you to perfection. Perhaps he will wander London in search of you."

"More likely he'll forget about me entirely." How could she compare to his countless paramours? And why would she want to? "Yes, I shall hope that he does." Except there was a pulse inside her saying, *no, you don't.*

"Do you? I find it curious you even stopped to help him. Your incredibly kind heart not-withstanding." Jane looked at Phoebe expectantly.

"I didn't really think about it. I just went to help." She had, however, thought about it plenty since then. She kept revisiting the moment when his fingers had grazed hers. The connection had radiated through her with heat and power. She felt it still.

"I can see that you're thinking *now*," Jane said.

"Let us speak of something else." Phoebe didn't want to discuss Ripley or her reaction to him. For if she did that, she'd think about him more than she already was, and any thoughts were too many.

"My apologies if I made you uncomfortable. I would never do so on purpose."

"I know that."

"I suppose I find it exciting to be able to flirt and engage with a man such as Ripley, if only to flaunt your independence. One of the benefits of being a self-declared spinster. Perhaps that should have been the name of our club, the Self-Declared Spinster Society."

Phoebe grinned. They'd formed a two-person alliance at the start of the Season. They were officially three people with the addition of their friend Arabella, but she was soon to become the Duchess of Halstead. "That doesn't sound nearly as dashing as the Spitfire Society."

"No, it does not. I do think spitfires would flirt, however."

Jane was probably right; however, Phoebe had no intention of seeking Ripley—or any other man—out. For flirtation or anything else. "I'll leave that to you," Phoebe said.

Jane laughed. "When I meet someone with whom I would like to flirt, you'll be the first to know." She winked at Phoebe.

The sound of a bell chimed through the drawing room, indicating it was time for the next round of cards.

"I do hope you'll let me know if Ripley finds you," Jane said as they made their way back toward the tables.

Phoebe didn't answer, for they'd joined the others and had to separate to find their seats. Of course she'd tell Jane, not that she expected it would be necessary. Ripley wouldn't find her—how could he?

Plus, she didn't *want* him to find her. Their paths would likely never cross again, and for that, she should feel relieved.

Instead, she felt more than a trifle disappointed.

CHAPTER 2

*T*he familiar sights, sounds, and smells of Brooks's welcomed Marcus as he stepped into the subscription room, his gaze moving about in search of his friend Anthony Colton. The scent of tobacco wafted in the air while Marcus nodded at dandies in their brightly colored waistcoats.

"Ripley!" someone called. Suddenly, there were several gentlemen blocking Marcus's path, all eager to speak with him.

A broad-shouldered man pushed his way to the center of the group. "Someone wagered you'd call your cousin out before dawn, if you haven't already."

"Am I a known duelist?" he asked sardonically.

The large man—Galbraith—blinked, then laughed. Another man, a smaller fellow next to Galbraith, spoke. "No, but perhaps you're looking to expand upon your…reputation."

Marcus gave them all a smile that belied his lack of patience. "I'm quite content to be celebrated as a charming libertine, thank you."

"Then why fight like that in the middle of the fashionable hour?" the smaller man asked. Marcus couldn't quite recall his name, but recognized him as one who liked to stir the pot of gossip.

"Was it the fashionable hour? I'm afraid I rarely pay attention to such things. If you'll excuse me." He flashed another smile, this one tighter than the first, and pushed through the gentlemen in search of Anthony.

Marcus finally caught sight of the viscount in conversation with another gentleman. Cutting his way in that direction, Marcus avoided making eye contact with anyone. He'd never minded being the source of gossip because it was always about his latest paramour, and many of the rumors weren't even true —but Marcus never kissed and told.

No, this was different. His cousin had embarrassed the family, and he'd provoked Marcus to behave in a manner he didn't care to. And Marcus hadn't even obtained the information he wanted or the resolution he needed.

Drobbit had stolen from people and, in some cases, had completely ruined their fortunes. Because of him, Marcus's friend Graham Kinsley had inherited a nearly bankrupt dukedom and had been forced to sell a valuable property that had been an especial part of his family's legacy. To salvage matters, Marcus had purchased it, and he would have gifted it right back if Graham's sense of honor and pride hadn't prevented him.

Marcus tossed the thoughts to the back of his mind as he arrived at Anthony and Sir Robert. Both men welcomed him with smiles and raised their glasses.

"Join us," Anthony said. "Sir Robert was just relating the most amusing tale of a duck attacking Lord Beasley in the park this afternoon. I don't suppose you saw it?"

"I did not." Marcus was relieved they weren't discussing the other spectacle of the day in the park.

Sir Robert chuckled. "He was likely too busy exchanging blows with Mr. Drobbit."

Anthony's dark brows arched briefly. "Yes, I heard about that. I'm sorry to have missed it. Do you need a second?"

Marcus gritted his teeth. "No."

"What was the cause of your disagreement?" Sir Robert asked. The question sounded nonchalant, but the eager glint in his eyes told the truth—he wanted to know the core of the matter. Likely so he could share it with all and sundry.

"It's a tedious matter," Marcus answered. Drobbit's behavior would get out. He'd fleeced too many people, and the threat of their own exposure—no gentleman wanted to be known as a financial fool or for the pitiful state of his fortune to be publicized—was no longer enough of an incentive to keep them quiet. At least, that was what Marcus suspected would happen. So far, he knew of only two of Drobbit's victims: his friend Graham, or rather the duke from whom Graham had inherited his title, and Mr. Yardley Stoke, father to Graham's soon-to-be wife.

Identifying additional victims and ensuring Drobbit made restitution was of the utmost importance to Marcus. He wasn't going to stand by while a member of his family ruined people.

"Tedious how?" Sir Robert prodded.

Anthony snorted. "Tedious means it doesn't bear discussion. Good God, man, go find something interesting to talk about. I heard Lord Fenwick's gout is acting up again, and I understand he's organizing a pilgrimage to Bath. However, everyone going must agree to take the waters in the nude. The rumor is he's already recruited Mrs. Dorris."

Sir Robert's eyes lit with this information. "Well, you would know," he said to Anthony with a chuckle. "How delicious. I must see who else is going. It may be worth the trip just to see Mrs. Dorris…"

The knight took himself off, and Marcus moved to take his place so he could turn his back to the wall and face the room. "Thank you for the diversion."

"You seemed annoyed with his interrogation." Anthony sipped his brandy. "In fact, there was a dark gleam in your eye I'm not sure I've seen before."

"This situation with my cousin is infuriating." Marcus glanced about for a footman.

Anthony was aware of Drobbit's swindling. "Provoking enough to fight with him," he murmured. "In public. It's shocking. People see you as a lover, not a fighter."

"People should mind their own damn business." At last, a footman came by with a glass of Marcus's favorite port. "Thank you," Marcus said before taking a fortifying drink. Then he looked back to Anthony. "Let us find a private place to speak."

Anthony's dark brows arched in mild surprise. He turned and led Marcus from the subscription room to an alcove off the main hall. "Will this do?"

Marcus withdrew the folded piece of parchment from his coat and, juggling the glass of port, managed to open it up so Anthony could see. "I'm looking for this woman."

Anthony's gaze barely scanned the drawing. "That's Miss Phoebe Lennox."

Victory thrummed in Marcus's chest. "I was hoping you might know of her, but you didn't even hesitate. How well do you know her?"

"Not terribly. She's a founder of the Spitfire Society with Miss Jane Pemberton. My sister, along with her good friend Lady Northam, is friendly with both of them. You may recall hearing of Miss

Lennox last Season after she jilted Laurence Sainsbury at the altar."

She suddenly sounded familiar. "Have you mentioned her before?" Yes, he had—Marcus remembered now. "You suggested her as a potential bride for Halstead a few weeks ago."

"I did. And you joked that she was more your type—because of her blemished reputation, to which I said she absolutely was *not*."

Dammit.

"Do you know where she lives?" Marcus still had to return her handkerchief.

"Cavendish Square, I think. Why?"

"You only think, or you know?"

"Why is this important?" Anthony poked his head from the alcove and waved at a footman. When the man came around, Anthony set his empty glass on the tray and asked for a fresh brandy.

"It just is," Marcus said when Anthony had ducked back into the alcove.

"You've set your sights on her, then? An unmarried miss isn't your typical quarry," Anthony observed.

No, it was not. Marcus kept his sport to paid professionals and the occasional widow. Once or twice, in his youth, he'd dallied with a married woman. He preferred his liaisons tidy and short. "She's not my quarry." Then what was she?

Intriguing. And right now, that was all that mattered.

Anthony continued as if Marcus hadn't spoken. "She *is* a self-declared spinster—which is why she founded the Spitfire Society—so I suppose she isn't like other unmarried misses. Still, please remember that my sister likes her."

"I'm not in the habit of ruining young ladies."

Marcus refolded the parchment and put it back in his coat pocket before drinking more of the delicious port.

"No, you are not," Anthony agreed. "That was quite a likeness. You drew it?"

"Yes." Marcus shared his drawings with only a handful of people—his butler and valet and most recently Anthony, who'd happened to catch him in the act one day. Many of Marcus's drawings were not fit for public consumption. They were detailed and provocative...erotic in nature. He'd been tempted to draw Miss Lennox nude, but while he could guess what she would look like, he found he didn't want to. He'd much rather discover the reality instead of rely on his imagination.

The footman stopped by with Anthony's brandy. Anthony quickly drank half the glass. "I'm for Mrs. Alban's. You're coming?"

Marcus shook his head. He wasn't in the mood for his favorite brothel. Anthony's eyes widened briefly.

"Why not?" Anthony's lips curled into a teasing smile. "Miss Lennox."

"No." The protest sounded weak, even to Marcus's ears. "I've no plans to debauch Miss Lennox." That much was true. Thoughts—and he'd had a few since meeting her that afternoon—were not plans.

Yet.

Marcus finished off his port and stepped from the alcove. "After today, I require a quiet night at home."

"Except you opted to come here in search of the identity of the woman you drew in excellent detail. Truly, I knew her straightaway—the likeness was extraordinary, as if she'd sat for you."

Marcus wished she would. Perhaps he'd ask...

"I have something that belongs to her." Marcus had made her a promise—that he'd find her before tomorrow and deliver her laundered handkerchief—and he meant to keep it.

Anthony sipped his brandy. "How in bloody hell did you obtain something of hers without knowing who she was? There's a story here, and you're being damnably cryptic."

He was and would continue to be. "Have a good evening at Mrs. Alban's." Marcus inclined his head, then turned and deposited his empty glass on the tray of a passing footman.

As he approached the main entrance, another gentleman stepped in his path. "I hear you're fighting a duel. Should we show up at Hyde Park at dawn?" He glanced toward a pair of gentlemen standing nearby.

Marcus resisted the urge to pound his fist into the man's face. "You're more than welcome to. However, I shall be warm in bed at that hour."

"Whose?" one of the other gentlemen asked, drawing laughter from everyone within earshot.

Reining in his irritation, Marcus found Anthony's gaze. To his credit, he was not laughing, but there was a glint of humor in his eyes. Along with curiosity. Because he knew there was more going on with Marcus than his idiot cousin.

While Marcus would put up with Anthony's curiosity, he found himself annoyed by everyone else. He summoned a sharp grin. "You know I never fuck and tell." The forced smile instantly fell from his lips the moment he turned his back to the group and exited the club.

He directed his mind back to Drobbit and what needed to happen next. Marcus would visit the man soon.

Marcus's driver opened the door to his coach. Before stepping inside, Marcus directed him to Cavendish Square.

The destination had spilled from his mouth unbidden. But there it was, and he found he didn't want to change it. The ride through Mayfair was short, and he was soon passing into Cavendish Square.

His coachman drove to one side and stopped. The door opened, and he asked if Marcus wished to depart.

"Yes." Marcus stepped out and surveyed the square. Which house was hers? If, in fact, any of them was, since Anthony hadn't been completely certain.

This was folly. He knew her identity. He would certainly find her location in the morning, and then he could deliver her handkerchief. Still, he began to walk around the square, sweeping his gaze over each building and wondering if she was inside.

An image of her sparkling green eyes and elegant brows came to his mind, followed by the rest of her alluring face—the small, charming tip of her nose, the lively dimples that danced in her cheeks, the inviting curve of her lips...

Yes, he'd been able to draw her exactly because he'd memorized every detail.

What in the hell was he doing? He could find her location and simply send the handkerchief. There was absolutely no need for him to go in person. Unless, as Anthony suggested, he'd set his sights on her. For seduction.

His cock stirred. And it shouldn't. She was unwed, probably a virgin, the type of woman who'd never turned his head. Even in his youth, he'd been drawn to older, experienced women. They'd taught him everything he knew, and he'd been an eager student.

He didn't have the patience or interest to do for someone what they'd done for him. Or did he?

Suddenly, the thought of tutoring Miss Lennox sent his cock into a full stand. The sound of a coach driving by prompted him to pick up his pace. He needed to get back to his coach and then home. Where he'd take the edge off his lust with the aid of his right hand. Or he could follow Anthony to Mrs. Alban's...

The coach stopped a few houses in front of him, and out stepped the unmistakable form of Miss Lennox. She walked up the steps to one of the largest houses in the square, the door opening and then closing behind her far too soon as she disappeared inside.

Marcus's heart began to pound as anticipation sparked through him. He glanced toward his coach —and sanity—before staring at her house. He knew where she lived and could now deliver the handkerchief.

But of course, he didn't have it with him. Because for all that he'd wanted to find her tonight, he hadn't expected to. Not this easily.

He waited for the thrill of the hunt to dissipate. Instead, it intensified, forcing him to again ponder what the hell he was actually doing.

Go home. Send the handkerchief. Be done with this. You've other things to occupy your mind.

Too bad none of them were this fascinating.

❧

"I trust you passed a pleasant evening," Phoebe's butler asked as he welcomed her home.

"I did, thank you, Culpepper." She removed her gloves and handed them to the man, a robust fellow in his late thirties.

"Would you care for your customary nightcap in the garden room?"

"Indeed." Phoebe enjoyed a glass of a particular port most nights. When she thought of her life now that she was an independent—and wealthy—woman, she felt incredibly grateful.

Culpepper turned to leave the hall, but a knock on the door halted him. He turned, one dark brow arching as he contemplated the door. "Are you expecting someone, Miss Lennox?"

"I am not." Who would call at this hour? Jane was the only person who came to mind, and since Phoebe had just left her a short while ago, it likely wasn't her. Phoebe supposed it could also be her parents, but they didn't call very often and surely wouldn't do so this late.

Culpepper answered the door, and right away a deep, masculine voice slid into the hall.

"Good evening. Is Miss Lennox receiving?"

Recognition caused Phoebe's heart to speed. No, it couldn't be *him*.

"It's rather late," Culpepper said coolly. "Would you care to leave a card?"

"Yes."

Culpepper responded with a note of surprise. "My lord."

It *was* him.

Culpepper looked toward her, and she inclined her head. He opened the door further so she could fully see the marquess. He filled the doorway, dressed to evening perfection in stark black and pristine white.

"May I come in?" he asked.

She should say no. "Briefly." She glanced at

Culpepper. "Two nightcaps, please." Then she tossed another look at Lord Ripley before turning and leading him into the garden room.

A low fire burned in the hearth, and Phoebe went to stand near the mantel. She pivoted to face him as he strode into the room. The space had always felt particularly feminine, with its floral wallpaper and rose-colored furnishings. Now, however, there was a distinctly masculine air. It was surprisingly...pleasant.

Pleasant? No, stimulating.

"You found me."

He removed his hat and set it on a table beside the settee. "I did, and it is my distinct pleasure to formally make your acquaintance, Miss Lennox." He came toward her and took her bare hand. Sadly, he still wore gloves.

Sadly?

He pressed his lips to her knuckles, allowing his flesh to touch hers. A shiver tripped up her arm and through her, settling somewhere in the vicinity of her belly. Or perhaps just a tad lower.

Reluctantly, she withdrew her hand. "I must ask, how did you find me?"

"Luck."

Phoebe rolled her eyes. "Hardly." A terrible thought occurred to her, and she was rather furious with herself for not thinking it sooner. "Did anyone see you?"

He rested his forearm on the mantel. "No. It may not seem like it, but I am quite discreet when the situation warrants."

Culpepper returned with a tray bearing two glasses of port. Phoebe took one and indicated Ripley should take the other. The marquess did so, and Culpepper retreated from the room.

Ripley raised his glass. "A toast to your divine hospitality."

"A toast to your ingenuity. I didn't think you'd find me by tomorrow, let alone this evening."

He gave her a confident smirk that should have been annoying but instead only added to the awareness pulsing through her. He sipped his port, and she did the same.

Phoebe decided some space between them was necessary. She pivoted and sat down in her favorite chair. That way, he couldn't sit next to her. He did, however, perch on the small settee near the chair—as close to her as possible without sitting on her lap.

"I appreciate your discretion," Phoebe said. "Still, you should not have called."

"And yet you invited me in." He relaxed into the settee, his posture one of comfortable nonchalance, as if he called on women in this manner and at such a late hour all the time. "To my great benefit. In any case, are you concerned about your reputation? I would think a spitfire like you wouldn't care."

"Just because I don't wish to follow Society's rules doesn't mean I want to make myself the center of attention. You are the notorious Marquess of Ripley. A visit from you at this hour—at any hour—would surely set the tongues wagging."

"Apparently, everything I do elicits such a response."

She heard the weariness in his tone, as well as a touch of irritation. "You're speaking of something in particular?"

"Just what happened at the park today."

For a brief moment, she thought he referred to their encounter, and her stomach dipped toward the floor. Of course he meant his altercation. Suddenly, she recalled his head and was angry with herself for not asking about it straightaway. "How is your wound?" She looked at his hairline but couldn't see the injury.

"Much better, thank you. I am not suffering any ill effects."

She noted he specified the physical hurt, but she recalled his earlier tinge of annoyance. "From the gossip, then, I take it?"

"There was a wager at the club this evening that I would call my cousin out."

"Because he injured you this afternoon?" He nodded after sipping his port, and she couldn't resist pointing out his hypocrisy. "Why should you care about such things like that wager, particularly given your reputation?"

He chuckled. "Touché. Like you, I prefer not to be at the forefront of *ton* gossip. However, I do not mind my reputation at all. Do you mind yours?"

She wondered what he meant, what he knew. "That depends on what it is."

"A spitfire with the courage to jilt an unwanted betrothed."

He knew everything, then. Well, everything that could be known by way of gossip. "You've been very busy since this afternoon—learning my name, where I live, and my personal history. I wonder how you managed it." She purposely said this with the tone of a question.

Frustratingly, he said nothing. He took another drink of port instead.

"You're being frightfully secretive about how you found me. I think you owe it to me to explain."

His gaze locked with hers. "I wanted to find you, and I always get what I want."

Again, she shivered. Just from a look. From him. She refused to fall prey to his charm. "Your flirtation won't work on me. Either tell me how, or I'll snatch your port away."

He clutched his glass, drawing it close to his chest in mock alarm. "But it's delicious. I do love a good port. Fine. Lord Colton told me who you are." He reached into his coat and withdrew a piece of parchment. "I showed him this." He handed her the paper.

Phoebe set her glass down on the small table next to the chair. Opening the folded parchment, she sucked in a breath at what she saw. There, staring back at her in exquisite detail, was herself.

She lifted her gaze to his. "Where did you—"

He hesitated the barest moment. "I drew it."

She looked back at the drawing, amazed at how completely—and accurately—he'd captured her like-ness. "It's extraordinary."

"Keep it."

"Indeed?" She didn't want to deprive him of such a fine rendering, and yet, why should he want it? Furthermore, he could simply draw another. "How enterprising of you to use this skill to find me."

"One does what one must."

"Yes, one does," she murmured, staring at the drawing another moment before setting it on the table and picking her port up once more.

"Such as refuse to marry a scoundrel, as you did with Sainsbury." He even knew whom she'd jilted. "In my opinion, that only elevates your reputation. I admire a woman who knows what she's about."

It was hard not to feel flattered, so she did, even as her mind was screaming at her to keep this dan-gerous man at bay. Dangerous? Did she think he would take advantage of her as Sainsbury had? A wave of apprehension rose over her. She barely knew this man, and his reputation was one of scandalous behavior. But was there more to it than that?

"You called Sainsbury a scoundrel," she said, probing. "Why?"

He shrugged. "I scarcely know him, but I've always thought him a braggart with an exaggerated opinion of himself. He seems the type to be a scoundrel, and since you threw him over, I can only assume there is something hideously wrong with him."

Phoebe delighted in his insight. She took a long sip of port, both to steady her nerves and to mask her unwanted reaction to him. It was time to draw this interview to a close. "Did you bring my handkerchief?"

He winced slightly, his eyes crinkling. "I must apologize for I did not. I'm afraid I'll have to call another time." He smiled broadly, and she wondered if that had been his plan.

"If you're seeking to prolong our acquaintance, I must disappoint you."

He held up his hand. "Please don't. Pray, tell me what is wrong with our acquaintance?"

She was a spinster, and he was a rakehell. "It serves no purpose."

He sat forward, scooting toward her. His dark cobalt eyes gleamed with intensity. "I disagree. You served me a great purpose this afternoon when you tended my injury."

She looked at her port and then at the fire—anywhere but at him. "I do not regret it. However, it was not my intent to encourage any sort of…association."

"Do I make you nervous?"

She snapped her gaze to his. "No."

"Good. I should never wish to do that. I liked you immediately this afternoon, and not just because you saved me from ruining more than my favorite cravat." He flashed her a smile. "I'm joking. I don't have a favorite cravat."

If he was trying to put her at ease—and that seemed his intent—he was finding success. To put him in the same class as Sainsbury was so ludicrous as to be almost laughable. She'd thought about Ripley several times since that afternoon, in a pervasive and anticipatory manner. She'd never done that with her former betrothed. With him, she'd felt relief to finally have an offer of marriage and an eagerness to manage her own household. Then he'd begun to make her feel an altogether different way: uncomfortable, anxious, and ultimately repulsed.

She frankly couldn't imagine feeling disgusted by the marquess. He was an exceptionally handsome gentleman, with his broad, muscular shoulders and piercing blue eyes. But it was more than that. It was the easy way he smiled and laughed. Or flirted.

Yes, he was quite good at that. And what's more, he made her want to flirt in return.

Dangerous hardly sufficed to describe him. He was an absolute threat to her peaceful, autonomous, *solitary* life.

Phoebe finished her port in one long drink, then stood. "As I told you this afternoon, it isn't necessary for you to return my handkerchief. I have many others."

Ripley rose. "What's more, I'm certain you can buy any handkerchief you desire." He looked around the garden room, which she'd refurbished entirely after purchasing the house. "This is a beautifully appointed room, and I assume the rest of the residence is as well. You are either a woman of means or in debt up to your magnificent eyebrows."

She arched a brow. "It's gauche to speak of financial matters."

"Is it? I've been accused of much worse." He finished his port and deposited the empty glass beside hers. Doing so brought him close, and she was awarded with the scent of sandalwood and spice.

Phoebe had to prevent herself from swaying even closer. Steeling herself, she expected him to move away. He did not, however. On the contrary, he leaned closer and spoke near her ear.

"I'll return your handkerchief. I'm afraid I can't resist another opportunity to bask in your company."

"You're a rogue."

"Unquestionably. And you...you smell divine. Oranges and cinnamon? An unusual but distinctive scent." He inhaled, and Phoebe feared her speeding heart might leap from her chest.

He adjusted his position so that he could look at her. His dark, seductive gaze bored into hers. "I wonder if I might kiss you."

Again, her body threatened to betray her and move toward him. "No, I shouldn't want that."

"An interesting choice of words." His lips spread into a sly smile.

"I *don't* want that."

He tipped his head slightly, regarding her with an expectation that curled her toes. "I'm not sure that's true, but let's not debate it tonight. There will come a day—soon, I'd wager—when you'll ask me to." He straightened. "Or, because you're a spitfire, you'll take the matter into your own hands and kiss me. You are that kind of woman, I think."

She wasn't. He'd said she was a woman who knew what she wanted, but that was only since her great-aunt had left her a fortune. And so far, it included just a house in Cavendish Square with a garden room she adored. There were many things she hadn't considered, not the least of which was what this man seemed to be offering.

"Are you suggesting I'll want to embark on a liaison with you?" She hated how breathless she sounded, as if she could hardly wait to do so. And while she was attracted to him—shockingly so—she was not at all ready to do anything about it. Furthermore, she might never be.

Surprise flickered in his gaze, followed by a flash of something deeper, darker. "I hadn't gone quite that far, but I can certainly hope."

She wanted to berate him, but she'd brought it up! "Why do I feel manipulated?"

"Do you? That is not my intent, nor would it ever be. I like you. I want to kiss you. I'll wait for you to feel the same."

He'd wait? Nothing else he'd said that night had affected her so deeply. "What of your other paramours?"

"I have none."

She found that hard to believe, but he'd given her no reason to doubt him. Not yet. "I do like you," she admitted. "But I don't want to kiss you, and I doubt I ever will." Kisses were horrid and led to other, more horrible things. At least with Sainsbury they had.

"As I said, I'll wait. And I daresay it won't be that long. Since I said I'd wager… If you can last a fortnight, I'll give you a hundred pounds."

She swallowed her surprise. "I don't need your money."

"Then name your favorite charitable endeavor, and I'll deposit it there."

"You're going to lose a hundred pounds."

"It will be the best loss I ever endured. But it won't happen. You'll kiss me before then."

She would do everything in her power to *not*. "If I do, I'll give *two* hundred pounds to that charity."

His eyes widened briefly, and he chuckled. "Are you certain?"

She *was* a woman who knew what she wanted. Or she was at least determined to be. "Never more."

He held out his hand, and she took it, giving him a firm shake. She was grateful he still wore his gloves. Skin-to-skin contact might have forced her to forfeit the game before it had even begun.

Was this a game?

Oh yes, and she meant to win.

CHAPTER 3

*M*arcus stood from the wingback chair in his study as the Bow Street Runner walked in. "Thank you for coming, Harry."

Tall, with impossibly broad shoulders, Harry Sheffield was not the sort of man one wanted to encounter on a dark night—or any night, for that matter. However, it was that physical intimidation that made him perfect for his chosen career.

"Always a pleasure to see you, Rip," Harry said with an easy smile.

"Have a seat." Marcus gestured to the chair across from his and sat down once Harry had done so. "Brandy?" A low table bearing a bottle and two glasses sat to the side and between their chairs.

"Thank you."

Marcus poured and handed the libation to his old friend. "Keeping busy?"

"Always." Harry took the brandy and raised his glass in a toast. "To Christ Church."

"To Christ Church." They customarily toasted their Oxford college, where they'd met fifteen years before.

Marcus got right to the point. "I'm looking for my cousin, who seems to have gone missing."

Harry rested his arm on the chair and held his brandy glass in his fingers. "When?"

"He hasn't been to his lodgings since early Wednesday." Marcus had called on him yesterday to tell him how things were going to be—that he'd stop swindling investors and return the money he'd stolen. However, the landlord had informed Marcus that Drobbit hadn't come home the previous night.

"It's only been two days," Harry said. His dark auburn brows pitched over his tawny eyes. "Not even, since it's only afternoon. You think a man is 'missing' after such a short time? He could be curled up in his mistress's bed. That's where I'd look for you."

Marcus let out a short laugh. "I don't keep a mistress."

Harry gave him a knowing smirk. "Too permanent for you." The fact that mistresses weren't necessarily permanent at all was not lost on Marcus—he understood the jibe. "Are you concerned he's met with foul play?"

"Perhaps." Not really, but Marcus couldn't discount the notion given what Drobbit was up to. However, he didn't want to disclose all that to Harry. Not yet. Marcus would give his cousin the opportunity to make amends. Yes, he'd let Harry think he was concerned. "I'd just like to find him as soon as possible."

"I'm afraid I don't know your cousin." He tipped his head to the side. "How is that when I've known you for so long?"

Because Marcus had never spoken of him. "We aren't close, but he's the only family I have left, so I feel a need to look after him. His name is Archibald Drobbit. He lives on Suffolk Street." Marcus went on to describe him.

Harry nodded here and there. "Do you think he's gone missing of his own choice?"

Marcus considered the question. Since he didn't want to divulge Drobbit's scheme, he said, "It's possible, but I suspect he's trying to avoid me in particular."

"Why is that?"

Marcus should have anticipated such a question from a Runner. "A family disagreement. We had a bit of an altercation in the park the other day." Harry would surely learn this in the course of his investigation, so Marcus mentioned it now.

"I take it you'd prefer to keep the subject of the disagreement private?"

"For now." Marcus realized it might be helpful for Harry to know about Drobbit's thievery in order to find him, and if Harry wasn't able to track him down, Marcus would reconsider what to reveal. Not that it would be hard—if Drobbit chose to avoid doing what Marcus had demanded at the park, Marcus wouldn't protect him from anything. In fact, Marcus would be the first to see him punished.

Harry finished his brandy and set his empty glass on the table before standing. "If you discover anything else I need to know, please inform me as soon as possible. I'll get started."

Marcus deposited his glass next to Harry's and rose. "Thank you. Keep me apprised."

Inclining his head, Harry turned and left.

Marcus frowned after him. Perhaps he should have told him everything and just allowed Drobbit to hang. Or suffer whatever justice he deserved.

Picking up his brandy glass, Marcus hoped Harry would find him quickly. Then Marcus could see how deep this scheme went. And what it would cost to at least make partial amends.

"My lord?" Dorne, Marcus's butler, came into

the study. "His Grace, the Duke of Halstead, is here."

"Show him in." Marcus picked up Harry's empty glass and took it, along with his own glass, to the sideboard. He turned just as Graham walked in. "Welcome. Would you care for a brandy?"

"No, thank you." Tall, with long legs and an athletic grace likely due to his fencing skill, Graham strode to the middle of the room. "I don't have much time. So much to do with the wedding on Tuesday and planning to vacate Brixton Park. That's why I've come. Your offer is too much."

Marcus had been expecting this. "It's a beautiful estate. I'm looking forward to hosting many scandalous events there."

Graham cracked a small smile before straightening his features into a more serious expression. "I asked you for a loan, not a gift." With the mortgage due on Brixton Park and Graham's inheritance stolen by Drobbit, Marcus had loaned him money to pay the mortgage. Graham had planned to repay Marcus when Brixton Park sold.

"I'm not giving you anything" *Yet.* "I'm buying an estate."

Graham's dark eyes fixed on him, his mouth twisted into a half frown. "You're being far too generous."

"Am I? I really want the estate. Furthermore, I want you and your bride to stay there as long as you like."

"How can we do that amidst all your scandalous events?"

Marcus chuckled. "I'll postpone them for the time being. Actually, if you don't mind, I'd like to host a masquerade there to celebrate your nuptials. Consider it a wedding gift."

"I think you buying Brixton Park is gift enough,"

Graham said wryly. "And allowing us to stay. We will be traveling to Huntwell soon to visit David and Fanny. She's due to deliver their first child any day." The Earl of St. Ives was Graham's closest friend as well as his former employer, so it made sense he would go to visit.

"Then you definitely need a celebration before you go. How about next Saturday? And I mean it— I'm funding the event."

Graham laughed. "So you can sneak in some debauchery?"

"Always," Marcus answered with a grin.

He immediately thought of Miss Lennox and how close that would be to the end of their wager. If he hadn't kissed her by then, debauchery would be required.

No. He'd said she would initiate it, and he would wait for her to do so. But a scintillating masquerade at the lovely Brixton Park couldn't hurt...

Graham smoothed his hand down his jaw. "Well, I can't thank you enough for all you've done."

"It's the least I can do given my cousin's actions and how they've affected you. Brixton Park should still be yours." And if Marcus had any say, he'd gift it right back to Graham. However, he knew the man's pride wouldn't allow it. There would be another way to transfer the property back, and Marcus was patient. "Regarding my cousin, I'm working to ensure he doesn't steal from anyone else. And that he returns whatever money he can."

Graham blinked in surprise. "He told me he has none."

"I mean to determine whether that's true. I can't say I'm inclined to take his word."

"Nor am I," Graham said darkly, his gaze simmering with anger. "I appreciate you trying to squeeze whatever you can out of him. I heard you fought with him at the park the other day and that a duel may be forthcoming. I assumed the latter was a fantastical rumor, particularly since you persuaded me not to call him out."

"You're correct. I simply tried to speak with him at the park, and he became defensive."

"It's no wonder. If there's anything I can do to help, please let me know. He nearly ruined Arabella's family." The fire in Graham's eyes intensified as he spoke of his betrothed and her parents.

"Which is why I'd like to know who else he's nearly ruined—or perhaps entirely ruined. To think we share blood…" Marcus shook his head. "I prefer not to think of it, actually." He smiled at Graham, adopting a more pleasant tone. "Do not concern yourself with any of this, not while you're planning your wedding. How shall we arrange the masquerade? Shall I send my secretary to Brixton Park to organize the details?"

Graham shrugged. "I didn't manage such things when I was David's secretary, but, then he didn't host masquerades. Let me speak with Arabella. Perhaps she'd like a hand in things."

"Of course." Marcus hadn't ever hosted this type of event either—his parties were of a different nature. They were smaller, more private, and not for Society. This would be different. "I truly want it to be a celebration of your marriage."

"Thank you. I know Arabella will be thrilled." They spoke for a few more minutes and then Graham took his leave.

As soon as he was gone, Marcus went to his desk and pulled Miss Lennox's handkerchief from the top drawer. He ran his thumb over the delicate embroidery—a purple flower and a yellow butterfly hovering just above it. Had Miss Lennox done this? Perhaps he would ask her when he returned it.

Which he would do presently. Anticipation gathered in his chest as he tucked the handkerchief in his pocket. He pushed all thoughts of Drobbit from his mind and focused entirely on Miss Lennox. Hopefully, she was at least half as eager to see him as he was her.

He couldn't wait to find out.

~

"*I*s that a Gainsborough?" Phoebe's father asked as he entered the garden room. Phoebe glanced at her newest acquisition, a vibrant landscape that continued the garden theme of the room.

"Yes, welcome, Papa."

The center of her father's forehead pleated and formed a small divot directly between his brows. "You spend too much money."

"You have no idea how much money I spend," she said with a laugh, hoping to dispel the dark cloud in his gaze.

"No, we do not," Mama said as she moved into the garden room. "You've decided to be independent."

Phoebe stiffened. Someday, she hoped her parents would understand her choice to remain unwed. At least for now. And maybe forever. "I've decided to be happy, and I should think that would make you happy too."

Papa made a low disgruntled sound. "No, making a good marriage and enriching our entire family would have made me happy."

"I still hold out hope…" Mama smiled weakly before going to look more closely at the Gainsborough.

Gritting her teeth, Phoebe said nothing. There was no point in having the same argument.

Papa, however, had no problem doing so. "You should've married Sainsbury."

"No, I shouldn't have." Phoebe's insides shriveled as ice coated her skin when she thought of the future she might have had.

"His father has ten thousand a year, and his cousin is Lord Haywood. Sainsbury was an excellent match. I understand he's still looking for a wife. Perhaps he would consider renewing your betrothal."

Phoebe worked to keep herself calm—at least outwardly. The thought of marrying Sainsbury sent her into a near panic. "I would not consider such a thing."

Mama went and put her hand on Papa's arm. "My dear, there is no going back to that."

"I suppose not. She all but ruined herself with her conduct."

Her conduct? Sainsbury had been the one seen kissing another woman. Then there was the other behavior. The things her parents didn't know and never would. The things almost no one knew—and even if they did, she would still be the one who was ruined. Society was grossly unfair to women.

Mama gave Papa a pleading look. "Let us not dwell on the past."

Phoebe welcomed a flash of relief. It seemed Mama was at last ready to move on. The fact that they'd come to visit was a good sign. This was only the third time they'd come since Phoebe had taken up residence the previous fall.

Papa made another aggrieved sound deep in his throat, but said nothing more on the subject. Instead, he turned from Mama and walked toward the doors that led to the garden. "You installed these when you refurbished this room?"

"Yes. I call this the garden room now."

"I can see why," Mama said, her gaze roving about the room with interest.

"I recall what this looked like before you spent what has to be a ghastly amount of money. It was fine. You needn't have wasted a small fortune."

Phoebe ignored his disdain. It was her money to spend, and she didn't do so mindlessly. "Papa, I am capable of managing my funds."

Papa glanced at her with derisive skepticism.

Phoebe tamped down her irritation. Sometimes her father made it difficult to love him, let alone like him.

"It's a bloody travesty that you have all that money." He looked at his wife. "Your aunt should have left that money to me to manage for Phoebe until she wed. It's unconscionable. Better yet, she should have left it to *you*."

Mama's cheeks grew pink. "Well, she didn't."

For the first time, Phoebe suspected her father might be jealous. There was more than just anger at Phoebe disregarding expectation. "Papa, I know you're still bitter about me not marrying Sainsbury, and apparently, you're angry with Great-Aunt Maria, but is there more than that?"

"Of course not," Mama answered. "You know your father can be difficult." She pursed her lips and sent him a stern look before softening her expression toward Phoebe. "You know we love you, dear, and your happiness is all that matters."

"Thank you, Mama."

"But we would be remiss if we weren't concerned. You may think you're happy now, but a fancy house and *independence*," Mama said the word as if it carried poison, "won't make you happy in the end. You'll be lonely someday. You should have a husband and children. I trust you'll come to that conclusion. I just hope it won't be too late." She gave Phoebe a warm smile of encouragement, but it didn't soothe the sting of her condescension. She simply couldn't imagine that Phoebe *could* be happy alone. Or that it was really none of their concern at all.

"You wouldn't be remiss, actually," Phoebe said tightly. "In fact, I absolve you of such worry, if that helps." She offered a bright smile.

Mama came forward and touched her hand briefly. "Of course we will, whether you want us to or not." She laughed, but it was high and false.

"Besides, I want grandchildren. It's awful enough that I will have no grandsons to carry on my name, but to have no issue at all?" Her father shuddered. "Another travesty."

Despite his behavior, Phoebe felt for him. Her older brother had died of illness in the war in Spain eight years ago. The loss had affected her father most profoundly.

"I didn't say I would never marry, Papa," she said softly. "I'm just never marrying Sainsbury."

He responded with another low grunt, then turned toward Mama. "Let us depart."

Phoebe invited them to return any time. She hated being at odds with them, but accepted there was nothing she could do. They would accept her as she was or not. She refused to change herself to appease their desires. This was *her* life, not theirs.

Going to the front sitting room, she watched through the window as they climbed into their coach and drove away. Scarcely a moment later, another coach arrived in place of her parents'. This one was larger and far more expensive. The door opened, and out stepped the Marquess of Ripley.

Phoebe's breath hitched. If decadence were a man, it would surely be the marquess. He was the sweet you mustn't eat or the expensive gown you didn't need, a luxury one desperately craved but acknowledged you probably couldn't—shouldn't—have. Like her new Gainsborough. Evidently, she liked unnecessary things.

He glanced up at the façade of her house before climbing the three steps to her front door. She watched him move, the tails of his coat brushing against his legs, long and muscular, encased in superbly fitting breeches and glossy boots, polished to a near-mirror shine.

She heard Culpepper open the door and hurried into the garden room, where she always received guests. Heat flushed her skin, and her pulse thrummed.

The butler stepped in to announce the marquess. And then he was there, taking up the space and making the room feel much smaller than it really was.

He bowed. "Miss Lennox."

She dipped a curtsey. "My lord."

Culpepper retreated, and Phoebe was keenly aware of the impropriety of being alone with the marquess. Improper and yet infinitely exciting.

"I brought your handkerchief." He withdrew the cloth from his coat, reaching beneath his lapel. "Though I'm loath to return it."

"Why?"

"It's rather pretty. Is the embroidery your hand?"

She laughed softly. "No. My needle skills are utilitarian. Design, I'm afraid, is beyond my ability. Unlike you."

"I may be able to draw, but don't ask me to stitch it into fabric." He gave her the handkerchief. It was warm in her hand, reminding her that it had nestled against his chest. Or nearly, anyway.

"Thank you." She sounded a tad breathless, which wouldn't do. Lowering her gaze, she saw that the cloth was quite clean. "There's not a trace of blood. Your maids are to be commended."

"I'll tell them." His cobalt gaze held hers, and they fell into a charged silence. The room seemed to shrink even more until she wasn't sure they were still *in* a room. All she could see, all she could sense, was him.

She forced herself to speak. "Now that you've returned this, how will you contrive to spend time with me?"

He took a step toward her so that they were just a couple of feet apart. "Is that hope I hear in your voice?"

She ignored his question. "You can't keep paying visits. My parents only just left. If you'd arrived ten minutes earlier, they would have seen you."

His eyes glinted with humor and dark provocation. "Would that have been a problem?"

"You know it would," she said with a measure of exasperation. "You are *you*."

"And I shouldn't be visiting you, a self-declared spinster? Where's the fun—or point, really—in being a self-declared spinster if you can't receive whomever you want whenever you want?"

Damn, he made a solid argument. Every defense turned to ash on her tongue. Really, what *was* the point? In this instance, the point was entirely her parents. It was one thing for her neighbors to see the marquess calling and quite another for her parents, who were already displeased with her, to do so. However, at least one of her neighbors would presumably gossip about Ripley's presence, and that would surely reach her parents' ears. Or her mother's, anyway.

She seized on the only protest she could possibly make. "Just because I am a self-declared spinster doesn't mean I wish to tarnish my reputation by entertaining rogues and scoundrels."

"I'm afraid I am both of those."

"Precisely."

He smiled slowly, like a cat who'd cornered a mouse. "And since you entered into a wager with me about kissing, I must submit that you are too. A rogue, certainly."

He'd neatly turned that around on her. Her heart fluttered as it began to pick up speed once more. "I am not a rogue. I'm…enterprising."

A laugh leapt from his too-seductive mouth. "So this is merely an investment?"

She nodded. "I have several."

"What an intriguing notion, investing in your own ability to withstand temptation. You must have an extremely high opinion of yourself."

She sucked in a breath because he couldn't be more wrong. Until she'd left London after refusing to marry Sainsbury, she'd believed herself to be nearly worthless. She couldn't attract a husband, and when she finally did, he was of an exceptionally loathsome caliber. Going to stay with her great-aunt had been the wisest thing she could have done. Great-Aunt Maria's kindness and encouragement toward independence had gently but firmly set Phoebe on a path to improved self-esteem. But to say she had a high opinion of herself, extremely or otherwise, was laughable.

"Hardly. What I do know is that men are not to be trusted, particularly those who seek to flatter and beguile with the intent to seduce."

"You think seduction is my ultimate goal."

"What else could it be?" Angry with herself for playing this game with him, Phoebe turned and went to the glass doors that led out to the garden. She kept her back to him as she worked to regain control of her emotions.

It was a long moment before he spoke. "I'm not

going to seduce you," he said quietly. "Not unless you ask me to. The same as the kiss."

She heard him move, and her body tensed—with anticipation and apprehension. But she didn't feel him nearby. Pivoting, she saw that he'd gone to the settee near the fireplace and settled himself in the corner. With his arm draped along the back, he looked utterly comfortable and, somehow, commanding. She couldn't look away from the line of his arm, the breadth of his shoulders, the tightening of his breeches over his crossed legs.

"Have you ever been friends with a man?" he asked.

"No. Why would I be?" It was silly when you thought about it, that young unmarried women were not really allowed to even be friends with a man. And why not? They were half the population.

"Will you allow me to be your friend? I am forever in your debt for stopping to tend my wound, so it really would be easier if we were friends. Don't you agree?" His lips curled into a placid, nonthreatening smile. Even so, she couldn't help but wonder at his ulterior motive.

"I'm afraid I will always be wondering when you plan to pounce." She nearly flinched when she said it. He wasn't behaving like a predator. However, she refused to be naïve.

He withdrew his arm from the back of the settee and uncrossed his legs. Fixing his gaze on her with powerful intensity, he said, "I will never pounce. Not unless you invite me to. I will repeat that to you as many times as necessary to gain your trust. Not all men are awful."

She wanted to remain unmoved, but it was difficult in the face of his earnest concern. "Thank you."

He settled back, once again adopting his nonchalant posture. "Now, tell me, will you be at the Duke of Halstead's wedding on Tuesday?"

His abrupt change of topic would have been jarring if it wasn't so thoughtful. Assuming he realized how agitated she'd been. He had an astounding ability to put her at ease.

"I will—and at the breakfast at Brixton Park."

"Excellent. I will see you there. I must admit I like weddings, provided they aren't my own."

"I had my own wedding once." Everything had been planned to the last detail—the ceremony, the breakfast...the rest of her life. Turning her back on all of it had taken more courage than she'd thought she possessed. "Rather, I would have."

"Do you wish you'd gone through with it?" he asked with utter candor and without a hint of pity.

Phoebe was entranced. She moved away from the window and sat in her favorite chair. "No, not with that bridegroom." She didn't hide her contempt. "My dress was quite beautiful." Her great-aunt had paid for the expensive silk as a wedding gift. Phoebe had apologized profusely for wasting it. Great-Aunt Maria had insisted she wear the gown to dinner on Sundays when Phoebe lived with her. Now the garment held happy memories instead of bitterness.

"You should wear it to the masquerade at Brixton Park a week from Saturday."

"There's to be a masquerade? Arabella hasn't mentioned it." And Phoebe had just paid her a call yesterday. Arabella's parents' back garden bordered Phoebe's. That was how they'd met and become friends.

"It just came about this morning."

"I've never been to a masquerade." She thought of Ripley in his evening finery—and a mask. She expected she'd recognize him even with his face partially covered.

"You've plenty of time to procure a mask. And I'll look forward to seeing the gown your idiot bridegroom didn't deserve."

That he cast Sainsbury in the role of villain nearly made her grin. "I'll think about it—wearing the gown, I mean. I'll be at the ball."

"That will be day thirteen."

Of their wager. "And you will be no closer to winning then than you are now."

"That's possible, unless I'm able to see you more than at the wedding." The side of his mouth curved up. "Or are you afraid you'll find me irresistible after all?"

"I can and will resist. A fortnight is nothing."

"Particularly if we rarely see each other," he mused with a smile.

"I will win even if we see each other every day. To prove it, let us take a picnic to Richmond on Sunday."

His eyes widened slightly with surprise, then lit with admiration. "Why not tomorrow?"

"I already have plans. And apparently, I need to purchase a mask." She found it alarmingly easy to flirt with him. Perhaps she didn't need to be alarmed, not after today.

"Sunday…after church?"

"I don't attend church."

"Indeed? Me neither. Seems like I would be cast out." He winked, and she smiled in response.

"I haven't been able to go since… Never mind." Since she'd left Sainsbury at the altar.

He nodded as if he understood. And maybe he did. He rose. "Sunday it is. Noon?"

Phoebe stood, smoothing her pale green skirts. "I'll bring the picnic."

"I'll drive my curricle. It won't bother you to be seen with me?"

She hadn't fully considered that. The things he'd said today—asking her the purpose of being a self-declared spinster if she couldn't choose who to spend time with and whether she'd ever had a male friend —took root in her mind.

"No," she said firmly. "We're friends, and I don't care who knows it." A tremor passed through her, but she ignored the sensation. She'd wanted to leave her old self behind, and it was time to move forward and embrace who she was going to be. Who she *wanted* to be.

"I'm delighted to be your friend, Miss Lennox. Until Sunday." He bowed, then turned and left.

After he'd gone, Phoebe lifted the handkerchief and inhaled his singular scent—sandalwood and a dark spice. Clove. Plus something indescribable. Something that sparked an awakening inside her. An…arousal.

Where that would lead, Phoebe didn't know, and that was fine. It was maybe even exhilarating.

CHAPTER 4

The morning had been overcast, but now, as they were on their way to Richmond, the sun had begun to peek through the clouds. Marcus likened it to the way he kept casting surreptitious glances toward his curricle mate. He didn't want to be caught looking just as the sun perhaps didn't want to be caught shining.

But it was incredibly hard not to. Miss Lennox presented a most alluring figure—from the tip of the jaunty feather in her stylish hat to the curve of her jaw leading to the lush shape of her mouth down her graceful neck to the fetching costume adorning the body he ached to explore. And didn't that make him the most wretched of scoundrels?

It would if he acted upon his desire, which he refused to do. There was trepidation and distrust in her gaze if he drew too close. She was content to keep their relationship to a light flirtation—for now —and he would be too.

Besides, he was having a hell of a good time. Miss Lennox was smart and wry. They'd laughed several times since starting out from Cavendish Square —about learning to drive (her) and getting lost in London (him).

"I've only been to Richmond twice," Miss Lennox said. "It's not terribly far, but not close either."

Nearly two hours west of London in their current vehicle, Richmond Park was a vast parkland founded centuries earlier. Deer and all manner of wildlife roamed free. "It's a welcome respite from the city."

Miss Lennox turned her head to look at him. "Is that why you purchased Brixton Park? As a respite from the city?"

He hadn't considered that, but it was as good a reason as any. He wouldn't get into the actual specifics with her. She didn't need to know about his cousin's malfeasance or how it had affected Graham. Although, since she was friendly with Graham's betrothed, she might already be aware. "Indeed. Have you been there? The maze is spectacular."

"I have—for a picnic. We played hide-and-seek in the maze."

He envisioned finding her in a secluded nook and ending their wager…if she so chose. "Perhaps we should do that at the masquerade."

"In the dark?" She'd gone back to looking ahead at the road. "That could be rather scandalous, but then you're hosting this party, aren't you?" Her mouth twitched as if she were trying not to smile.

He resisted the urge to chuckle, enjoying her company. "No, Graham and Arabella are. Rather, the new Duke and Duchess of Halstead."

"But you're funding the event. Don't deny it— Arabella told me."

"As a wedding gift."

"You're incredibly generous." She said the next words softly, so that he had to strain to hear. "I know how much you've helped them, by loaning Graham money and purchasing Brixton Park."

"Arabella has confided quite a bit to you."

"We've become close friends." She paused, sending him a grateful smile. "Thank you for doing that. I wish I'd known of her family's difficulty. I would have helped. But I understand why she didn't ask."

It had taken Graham being pushed to the brink of disaster before he'd asked for the loan. Marcus understood pride and dignity. "You sound like a good friend."

"I've tried to be. They can be difficult to find."

"Can they? You and I have found each other. And friendship." For now. He acknowledged he wanted more, but how much? If she did allow him to kiss her, would he be satisfied? His cock stirred, and he shoved any thoughts of a sexual nature into the farthest reaches of his lurid mind.

"I lost many friends when I decided not to marry Sainsbury."

It was the opening he'd hoped for. He was curious about Sainsbury and why she'd chosen social devastation over marrying him. Put that together with her general apprehension when he came close, and his curiosity became suspicion.

"Since we *are* friends, I hope you don't mind my asking, but why didn't you marry him?"

The sound of the wheels and the horses grew louder as he waited for her to answer. At last, she said, "He demonstrated an incapacity to be faithful."

Marcus realized he'd been holding his breath. Blowing it out, he glanced over at her stoic profile. "Many husbands are—unfaithful—unfortunately. As are wives."

"I don't plan to be, and I expect my husband to behave the same. I certainly don't want to see him locked in an embrace with another woman at a ball."

He heard the hurt and anger in her tone and

wanted to plant his fist in Sainsbury's gut. "He was a fool."

"Because he didn't take more care?" she asked with a touch of acid.

"No, because he lost you. He won't ever do better."

She exhaled, her posture relaxing slightly. "Your flattery isn't necessary. I took his actions personally, but he will be a terrible husband to whomever he weds." She composed herself, clasping her hands in her lap. "Men like that shouldn't marry. If a man knows he won't be faithful, he shouldn't take a wife."

"Except men, especially those of my station, are often raised with a sense of duty. We're expected to wed and provide an heir, at least. And some men simply can't be faithful."

"Does that include you?" she asked, pinning him with a challenging stare.

"Because of my reputation?"

"Because you aren't married. As you pointed out when we met, you are thirty-one. Surely you should be wed with an heir and a spare by now."

He shrugged. "Some men wed later."

"Is that your plan? Or are you one of the men you mentioned who can't be faithful?"

"I don't really have a plan. I haven't been moved to take a wife, and so I haven't." Hearing his words come back at him gave him pause. As Harry had said the other day, Marcus didn't do anything permanent. Faithfulness had never been necessary. Furthermore, he avoided permanence because he desired spontaneity.

You avoid connection.

The small voice whispered in the recesses of his mind, where he kept distant memories and truths he preferred to ignore. Like that one.

"That is my plan precisely," she said, straightening in her seat. "I'll marry when—and if—I'm moved to do so." She flashed him a smile. "We were clearly destined to be friends."

Marcus couldn't help laughing. Unmarried friends who were undoubtedly attracted to each other and who shared the same outlook on marriage. If that wasn't a recipe for an affair, he didn't know what was.

Because that's what you want.

That goddamn voice again, seducing him. Yes, he wanted her. But when he'd suggested they be friends, he'd realized he didn't have any woman friends either. Mrs. Alban didn't count—her brothel provided a service for him. Why didn't she count? He dined with her regularly and they shared enjoyable conversations. Wasn't that a friend?

Hell, he didn't want to think about her or her bloody brothel while he was with Miss Lennox. Phoebe. He didn't want to keep thinking of her in such a formal manner.

"Since we are friends, may I call you Phoebe? I'd be honored if you called me Marcus or, if you prefer, Rip, which most of my gentleman friends—particularly those from school—call me."

"I prefer Marcus, I think."

His name on her lips sounded utterly delicious. He wanted to kiss her as she said it, see if it tasted the way it sounded. Oh, he was going to be in a mess if he didn't stop thinking of her like that.

"You may call me Phoebe," she continued. "But only when we are alone."

"That's reasonable. Phoebe." He slid her a smile as he drove into the park. They'd arrived faster than he'd imagined, or perhaps he'd simply been lost in her company.

Other vehicles were parked along the road, and people picnicked here and there. Richmond was a popular destination given its beauty and relative proximity to London.

Marcus drove farther into the park. "Where shall we picnic?"

"Up on the hill?"

He took them up and stopped the curricle. "How's this?"

A sweeping vista of the parkland and the Thames stretched before them.

"Lovely," she said. "Though I imagine Pembroke Lodge has an even better view. Have you seen it?"

"I have not."

Phoebe laughed softly. "I don't imagine Lady Pembroke would invite someone like you."

He gasped in mock outrage. "I am not faithless, as we've already established. Or perhaps we didn't." He climbed out of the curricle and went around to help Phoebe down. As he took her hand, he extended his leg. "Unlike Lord Pembroke, I would take my wedding vows most seriously."

Would he though? His father had been utterly faithful to his mother and only became an inveterate libertine after her death. Marcus had done the opposite by starting out in that fashion. Perhaps he wouldn't be able to be faithful. A ripple of unease shot through him.

That was a thought for another time. Or maybe never.

"Then your future marchioness will be most fortunate," she said smoothly as he helped her out of the vehicle.

Marcus fetched the picnic basket and blanket while she walked out over the grass in search of the perfect spot.

Turning, she swept her arm to the left. "Here, I think?"

He joined her and set the basket down. "Spectacular." He diverted his gaze, lest she thought he was referring to her. And he was.

Marcus spread the blanket upon the grass and placed the basket on the edge. Phoebe set about unpacking the picnic, which seemed far more food than the two of them could eat.

"I'm famished," she said. "What is it about travel that makes one hungry? It's not as if it's exerting. By vehicle, I mean. Riding is a different situation, of course."

He reached for a small pastry. "This is enough food for a battalion."

"Those are pork," Phoebe indicated. "May I pour you some ale?"

"Is that the only beverage?"

"Yes. Would you have preferred something else?"

"No, I'm just surprised. Wouldn't *you* prefer something else? Lemonade or ratafia maybe?" He bit into the pie and savored the succulent pork and flaky pastry.

She laughed. "No, I happen to like this ale very much. My cook's husband is a brewer." She poured two cups and handed him the first. "I definitely prefer it to ratafia."

He sampled the brew, then licked his lips. "Delicious. I may have to plead for a keg of my own."

"Don't bother. He only makes small batches for a handful of households, and I don't believe he's taking on new clients."

"Pity." He raised his glass in a toast. "To excellent ale and friendship."

She inclined her head and lifted her ale before taking a drink. Surveying the items she'd unpacked, she said, "This really is too much food. My cook has outdone herself."

"You don't eat like this at every meal?" He devoured the rest of his pork pie.

"Heavens, no." She spread peach jam on her roll, focusing on her task. "It's just me."

That sounded lonely, and yet that was precisely how Marcus took his meals. "We have much in common," he observed. "Not the least of which is our solitary existence and the fact that we are unbothered by it."

She finished with the preserves and looked over at him. "I try to think of myself as independent. Solitary sounds so…sad. I'm not sad. Are you?"

As she took a bite of her roll, a bit of jam smeared against her lip. Her tongue darted out to catch it and sweep the fruit into her mouth.

He directed his attention to the conversation instead of her tongue. "No, I'm not sad either." Especially not right now. "Relationships are messy. Complicated."

"What sort of relationships? Family? Friends? Romantic? No, not those, because you don't have those."

"Because they're messy!" He laughed. "Friendships are easy."

"I don't know that any relationship is *easy*, particularly family. Do you have any family at all?"

Drobbit came to mind. He wasn't family. Marcus would consider his retainers family before he thought of Drobbit in that way. "No."

She'd finished her roll and now sipped her ale. "What about your cousin? The one who wounded you in the park."

Of course she would have learned who he was. "We may be related by blood, but I don't count him as family. Our mothers—they were sisters—were estranged."

"I'm sorry to hear that. And that you have no other family at all. My parents are difficult, but they are still here." She served them ham, salad, and stewed plums on plates, then handed him one.

Setting his ale down, he took the plate. "How are they difficult?"

"They don't like that I'm unwed. Or that I didn't marry Sainsbury, particularly that I didn't decide not to do so until our wedding day. And that I live alone. Also that I'm a self-declared spinster and have settled myself on the fringe of Society." She shook her head." I could go on." Instead, she took a bite of salad.

"Please do. I happen to like all those things about you."

She finished chewing and eyed him skeptically before continuing. "They don't like that I spend money on refurbishing my house or buying things like a Gainsborough."

He adopted an expression of mock horror. "What must they think of your investments?"

She giggled, and he was enchanted. Women giggled around him all the time, but it was an affectation. This was real and...charming. "They don't know about them," she whispered, as if she were imparting a dire secret.

He laughed, and they ate in silence for a few minutes. In those quiet moments, he watched her—covertly—his gaze straying to her mouth and wondering what it would be like to kiss her, someone he counted as a friend. Would the sensation be richer? Or would it be somehow less?

He should call off this wager and just pay her the hundred pounds. But he wouldn't, and he also wouldn't press her. He made a wager with himself that he wouldn't bring it up again.

She pushed her plate away. "I'm afraid I can't eat another bite. We'll have to save the cakes for the ride home, I think."

Marcus was delighted at the prospect of the return journey. There were still so many things they hadn't discussed. "Did you get a mask yesterday?"

She began to pack the picnic items back into the basket but slid him an enigmatic glance. "Maybe."

He laughed. "Is it a secret?"

"No. And yes. I got a mask, but I won't tell you what it is."

"You don't think I'll be able to discern who you are?"

She lifted a shoulder. "Why not?"

"Your hair, for one."

She laughed. "It's nondescript brown."

She couldn't be more wrong. "It's a brilliant sable with threads of oak and deep mahogany. And here in the sunlight, there's a tawny strand here and there, like hidden gold. I would absolutely recognize it."

A faint blush suffused the edges of her cheekbones, and she busied herself with her task. "Then I'll have to cover it, I suppose."

"That will be a clear signal," he said. "I'll know precisely who you are."

She looked up at him. "No one covers their hair?"

"No one under the age of fifty. Are you planning to wear a turban?"

Her eyes lit with mirth as she packed the bottle of ale into the basket. "Perhaps I will."

"Please, I beg of you, don't. Don't deprive us of the glory of your hair." He stopped himself from saying me, don't deprive *me*, because he didn't want unease to drive the cheer from her gaze.

"I'll think about it," she said dryly.

He picked up the basket and moved it from the blanket, then came back to help her stand. "Don't you want to know what my mask is?"

She shook her head.

He extended his hand, and she clasped it. Neither of them had put their gloves back on, though she clutched hers in her other hand. The connection of their bare flesh wound through him like a river rushing downhill. The sensation gained velocity as it moved, racing through his chest and much lower. "Why not?"

"Because I don't need that information—I'll know precisely who you are."

Her words were a punch to his gut—without the blistering pain. Instead, there was a flush of arousal, of shared secrets. The two of them in a ballroom of masked people, everyone hiding their identities, and yet they knew exactly who the other was.

"Is it my hair?" he teased, reluctantly letting her go.

She laughed. "No. Other...things."

He bent to retrieve his gloves, then set them atop the basket so he could help her fold the blanket. Squatting down, he clasped the edges of the fabric.

After donning her gloves, she picked up her side. "Shall we have another wager?" she asked, surprising him. "Who recognizes the other first?"

"Does this mean you're going to try to disguise yourself from me?"

"Perhaps." Her grin was sly and so seductive—perhaps unintentionally so—that he nearly dropped the blanket as they folded it in half. "Thirty pounds."

They walked toward each other, and he gave her his edge of the blanket, his hands lingering against hers. He stared down into her eyes. "The game is on."

She didn't look away, and he was overwhelmed with a desire to kiss her. So he took a step back. "Perhaps you should drive back to town."

"I couldn't." She finished folding the blanket,

and he plucked up the basket. Offering her his arm, they walked back to the curricle.

"You absolutely could. It would be my honor to instruct you. You don't have to drive the whole way, but you did say you were learning."

She looked horrified. "You'll see how bad I am at it."

"Everyone was bad at it once, including me. I promise to be kind and patient." He stowed the basket in the curricle and took the blanket from her to do the same.

"All right."

A burst of delight shot through him. Over something so...mundane. But it wasn't. She trusted him to teach her, to allow herself to be vulnerable with him, even if it was just about driving.

It was an excellent start.

CHAPTER 5

"*T*hank you for coming," Graham, Duke of Halstead, said loudly as he raised his glass of champagne. The drawing room at Brixton Park was full of Graham and Arabella's family and friends following their wedding that morning. "A toast to my beautiful bride, the Duchess of Halstead." He beamed at Arabella, whose smile was equally incandescent.

The guests lifted their glasses amid cries of "hear, hear" and "huzzah." Joy radiated from Arabella—and Graham—permeating the room and everyone in it. Phoebe couldn't have been more thrilled for her friend.

Marcus walked to her as conversation broke out around the room. "They look very happy."

Phoebe tried not to look overlong at Marcus. He was exceptionally handsome in a cobalt waistcoat that made his eyes appear even more piercing. "Yes. Arabella can't quite believe how lucky she is."

"Nor can Graham. It's a bit nauseating, really."

Phoebe turned and stared at him, aghast. "It is *not*."

He grinned. "I was joking. I may not understand

the allure of a permanent union, but they do, so that's all that matters."

She wasn't sure she entirely believed that he was in jest, but didn't have time to debate the issue since Lavinia and her husband, Beck, were coming toward them.

Beck spoke, "Ripley, may I present my wife, Lady Northam."

Marcus made a gallant bow. "A pleasure to make your acquaintance, Lady Northam. I'm sorry we haven't met before now."

Phoebe wondered why not, but then recalled that she'd only just met him herself, what, a week ago? And purely by chance. However, Lavinia had been a marchioness for some time now. Wouldn't she have met him?

Lavinia offered Marcus a smile. "It's good that I don't need to curtsey, for if I did, I'd never be able to lift myself back up." She was, of course, referring to her very round belly. "Indeed, this is to be an abbreviated outing. I shouldn't even be about, but I didn't want to miss Arabella's wedding—and Fanny made me promise to come if I could, since she and David are gone from London awaiting the birth of her child." Fanny's husband was Graham's former employer as well as his best friend.

"You preferred to remain in London?" Marcus asked.

Lavinia nodded, then adjusted her spectacles. "I love London in the spring. We'll remove to the country in summer." She looked to Phoebe. "I just wanted to come speak with you before we go. I hope you'll call soon. This is to be my last excursion until after the babe comes. If he—or she—takes too long, I shall be hideously bored."

Phoebe laughed softly and took her friend's hand, giving it a squeeze. Lavinia had been there for

her after the Sainsbury debacle. She'd been kind, understanding, and, most of all, supportive. Phoebe
glanced at Beck, who was actually to blame for Sainsbury's attentions in the first place.

Lavinia and Beck took their leave. After they
were out of earshot, Marcus edged closer to Phoebe.
"Didn't Beck write a poem about a Miss Lennox
when he was drafting his Duke of Seduction tripe?
By God, I didn't put that together until now."

Thank goodness for that. Phoebe preferred to
forget about that entire period. "Tripe?" She sniggered. "It *was* tripe, actually."

"It was *supposed* to help unmarried women gain
notice, I believe."

She nodded. "His ballads were lovely—as poetry.
But as a means for attracting men, they were woefully misguided. Thankfully, Lavinia set him
straight." Just as soon as he'd set his sights on helping
her. She'd somehow deduced his identity and put a
stop to his "assistance." Then she'd shocked everyone
and married him.

"That's how Sainsbury found you, isn't it?"
Marcus asked softly.

His concern clashed with her distaste for Sainsbury, and she flinched. "Yes."

"Shall I call Northam out?" he asked. "Or Sainsbury? Or both?"

He was joking again. Except he wasn't smiling as
he was before, and there was an underlying steel to
his tone.

She turned, and her hand brushed his arm. They
both reacted, pausing just long enough for their
gazes to connect, then moved apart so they didn't
touch. "Neither. Northam has apologized. His letter
of regret was even more beautiful than his poetry.
Sainsbury isn't worth your effort."

"I'll be the judge of that," Marcus murmured, his

gaze settling on her briefly before moving about the room. He finished the last of his champagne. "I'm in need of more wine. You?" He glanced at her half-full glass. "Just me, then." He flashed her a smile and took himself off.

Phoebe watched him go, her insides in a turmoil. She'd thought of him too much since their picnic. She'd driven more than halfway back to London, and she had to admit he was an excellent teacher. He was also delightful company. Especially when he threatened her former betrothed.

She sipped her champagne and made eye contact with Jane across the room. They moved toward each other, meeting somewhere in the middle.

"Flirting with Lord Ripley?" Jane asked with a saucy smile.

"No." Phoebe *had* flirted with him before, but she wasn't sure that was what had just happened. Still, *something* had happened. Something deeper than their previous interactions. She realized she was in real danger of kissing him. No, of *asking* him to.

No, no, no. She didn't want that.

"I'm teasing," Jane said. "Though you looked rather…friendly."

"Because we're friends." Phoebe felt a pang of guilt because she hadn't yet told Jane about their picnic. And why not? Because it was scandalous?

Yes, because he was the Marquess of Ripley.

"You're *friends*?" Jane asked dubiously.

"Yes. What's the point in being a spitfire spinster if I can't have male friends?"

Jane laughed. "Indeed. I'd ask you to introduce me, but my mother would suffer a fit." She cast a glance toward Lady Pemberton, who stood near the windows talking with Arabella's mother, Mrs. Stoke.

"Then definitely don't tell her that we took a picnic to Richmond the other day."

Jane's eyes widened, and her jaw dropped briefly before she snapped it closed. "You didn't." Her voice was low and urgent.

Phoebe nodded. "You don't think I'm being naïve, do you?"

"Why would I think that?"

"Because Ripley is not all that different from Sainsbury." She stole a glance at Marcus and saw the many ways in which he was *vastly* different from Sainsbury. It was the way he carried himself—with self-awareness and confidence. He exuded a masculine ease, while Sainsbury always seemed to be on edge. Furthermore, he was exponentially more handsome. Still, they did share a few things in common. "They're both philanderers, and you know how Sainsbury behaved."

"Has Ripley behaved in the same manner?" Jane also darted a look in Marcus's direction. Thankfully, he wasn't paying attention, or he was bound to know they were talking about him. "I can't imagine he has. You wouldn't have taken a picnic with him, and you certainly wouldn't be talking to him and smiling with him today." She had a point. A good one too.

Phoebe ought to trust herself. However, that was hard when she'd believed Sainsbury would be a good husband only to discover how very wrong she'd been. She suddenly felt fiercely angry at him all over again. He'd made her doubt herself, and that was unforgivable.

"Did I say something wrong?" Jane asked with concern.

Summoning a smile, Phoebe rushed to reassure her dear friend. "Not at all. You said exactly the right thing." Of course Marcus was different from Sainsbury, and she'd do well to remember that.

"How was it?" Jane asked, her eyes alight with interest. "The picnic."

"It was lovely. He's actually very kind. And amusing."

Jane blinked. "So he's...normal?"

They laughed and then Arabella joined them. The conversation turned to the wedding and then the upcoming masquerade. "I'll scarcely have a chance to catch my breath," Arabella said, "but we're so thrilled to host a ball before we leave Brixton Park." There was a tinge of regret in her tone.

"You don't really want to leave, do you?" Phoebe asked.

"It's not that. I just know how important this estate is to Graham and his legacy." His ancestor had helped to design and build the property and had laid out the gardens, including the maze. Then the duke, his older brother, had cast him out for a perceived transgression—an affair with his wife that had never happened. "I think reclaiming it was what he'd most looked forward to when he suddenly became the duke." His inheritance had only come after the other line had died out without issue.

"Well, I'm looking forward to the masquerade," Jane said. "I've never been to one."

"Neither have I," Arabella said, grinning. "I've the most cunning mask—it's a swan."

"That sounds beautiful." Jane sent a pouting expression toward her mother. "I wasn't allowed anything elaborate. It's just a simple mask with a few flowers. I swear, I'm growing closer and closer to declaring my own spinsterhood and moving in with you, Phoebe."

"You know you are always welcome."

"You may find true love yet," Arabella said. "I did."

"I'm afraid you landed the last decent gentleman," Jane said. "Just look around. There are only two unwed men here, and neither one qualifies."

"What's wrong with Lord Colton?" Arabella asked, notably leaving Marcus out of the question.

Jane shook her head gently as she looked toward the viscount. "His reputation is almost as bad as Ripley's this season."

"Isn't he excused because of his parents' demise?" Phoebe tried to keep the edge of irritation from her voice. Men had different standards. They could suffer loss or heartache and behave like imbeciles with relative impunity. Women, however, couldn't decide not to marry a scoundrel after he revealed his true character without being shunned. Or at least suffering a grave loss of status. Colton would probably be able to wed just about anyone he chose anytime he chose, whereas Phoebe would be incredibly lucky to receive an offer from a country vicar with a humble living.

"Hardly," Jane said. "My mother says he's not as desirable as he once was—which is what happened to Ripley several years ago. Not that either of them cares. Or so it seems." She turned to Phoebe. "Is that true? Does Ripley care about not going to Almack's or attending balls?"

"I'm sure I don't know," Phoebe murmured, her gaze finding Marcus across the room where he stood with Colton. His eyes were on her, sending a tremor of awareness down her spine. She finished her champagne. "Pardon me for a moment."

She turned and went to one of the doors, where a footman stood with an empty tray. Depositing her glass with him, she asked for the direction to the retiring room.

Making her way there, she took a few minutes to reset her equilibrium. Marcus was unsettling her in a way he hadn't before. She wasn't sure what to do except avoid him. Perhaps she wasn't really equipped for friendship with a man. Or a man like *him*.

Phoebe checked her reflection in the glass. She

tried to see the beauty in her hair that Marcus had described. His words could have been mere flattery, a pretty, vocal seduction, but they weren't. Not when she compared them with those of the vile Sainsbury. His words had been empty, disgusting promises.

No, they weren't at all alike. Marcus hadn't accosted her, despite ample opportunity, at any point during their picnic the other day. He'd been the consummate gentleman, actually. Not at all what she might have expected before she'd come to know him. Before they'd become *friends*.

Her lips curved back at her from the glass. She felt better, more at ease, ready to return.

She left the retiring room and ran straight into Marcus. Or would have, if she hadn't stopped short.

"There you are," he said.

"Were you looking for me?" Phoebe glanced around and saw they were alone.

His mouth slanted in a roguish smile. "Always." He stepped toward her and offered her his arm. "Might we take a turn?"

In answer to his question, she curled her arm around his sleeve. "Where?"

"Back to the drawing room?"

Then it would look as if they'd had a rendezvous. Or that they'd encountered each other outside the drawing room. She wasn't entirely sure which these particular guests would assume, but she guessed it was probably the latter. However, at least a few, particularly Jane's mother, might think the former. "We shouldn't arrive together."

"I see." He steered her into another room and closed the door.

That wouldn't look scandalous.

"This is worse than arriving together," she said.

"Just give me a moment." He sounded so earnest and his gaze was so serious that she withdrew her hand from his arm and faced him expectantly. "I want to cancel our wager. About kissing."

Words failed to form on her tongue. She stared at him in shock.

"I can see that's the last thing you expected to hear," he quipped.

At last, she was able to manufacture speech. "Why?"

"We're friends now, and I think my…flirtation makes you uncomfortable. I never want to cause you unease."

A swoon threatened to pitch her toward the floor. Not really, but her knees had grown a bit watery. "I'm not uncomfortable. I'm just not used to it." Except she *was* a trifle uncomfortable. When she thought of where it might lead. "I don't like kissing."

The admission tumbled from her lips without thought. As soon as it was out there between them, she wished she could haul it back in.

His eyes flickered with surprise. "Then you've actually done so before?"

She nodded, again unable to speak.

"*Sainsbury.*" It wasn't a word so much as a growl. Marcus's eyes darkened to that pitch-black place between midnight and dawn.

"Yes."

Marcus looked away, then inhaled deeply. When he turned his gaze back to hers, he appeared more like the man she'd come to know. "Tell me where to deposit the hundred pounds."

"I—" She wanted to protest, but he was right. When she thought about taking their flirtation… anywhere, a cold apprehension swept through her. Despite that, there was also the faintest hint of anticipation. And loss now that the wager was over.

"The Foundling Hospital."

"Done." He started to offer her his arm once more, but she held up her hand.

"What about the other wager—the masquerade?"

"We can cancel that t—"

She interrupted him. "No, I don't want to. I've already organized my costume."

He narrowed one eye briefly. "All right. You sound rather confident in your ability to win."

"Because I am."

He moved closer to her, but not too close. Near enough, however, that she noted the faint lines around his eyes and the curl of his long, dark lashes. "Are you afraid you'd lose the other wager?" he asked softly.

Yes. "You're the one who called it off."

"So I did. I'd still be delighted—honored—to kiss you if you ever want me to. Whatever was done to you before wasn't good or right. I won't ask about it, but don't take that as my not wanting to know. I want to learn every last thing about you. What you eat for breakfast, if you rise early or stay up late, how you prepare for bed, what you dream about. And everything in between."

Phoebe couldn't look away from him, nor could she move. She was enchanted by the passion of his stare and the seductive timbre of his voice.

"A kiss isn't a weapon or a tool, it's a shared desire made manifest," he continued. "A joining borne of urgency or emotion or bare need—or all those things. A kiss should make you tremble and catch flight, like a leaf breaking free from the tree and skipping on the breeze. More than that, the anticipation is akin to a cold winter night when the fire is just starting to blaze. You hold your hands up, eager for the warmth, knowing it will give you everything you need, that you will feel safe and whole and content. As the heat finally settles in, you twitch and laugh, your body welcoming the joy and bone-deep satisfaction it brings. For that moment, everything is right and perfect."

Phoebe made a sound she didn't recognize. It was part sigh and part…longing. She didn't care about any wager. She wanted to feel the way he described.

He took her hand, his fingers warm against hers. "You deserve that and nothing less." He lifted her hand and pressed a kiss to the space between her thumb and forefinger, his gaze never leaving hers.

Then he let her go and presented his arm. "We should return."

Yes, they should. Her body was trembling, just as he'd described. Except she wouldn't take flight. Not today.

And that left her profoundly disappointed. What remained was what she planned to do about that. Right now, she didn't know.

&

"*A* note arrived for you, my lord," Dorne said, handing Marcus the missive as he stepped from the stairs.

"Thank you." Marcus continued to his study, glad for the black coffee he'd drunk upstairs after his relatively sleepless night. That was two in a row. Two nights of dreaming of Phoebe and waking up frustrated. Because those dreams were all he was ever going to have.

He glanced down at the note and immediately recognized the handwriting. Opening the parchment, he quickly scanned the note from Mrs. Alban.

She wanted to know if he would come for dinner tonight.

He'd regularly dined with the brothel owner, at least once a fortnight. In addition, he paid more frequent visits to her establishment, but not to see her. They'd never shared a bed—she left that to her employees—but they'd shared many meals, conversations, and laughter. She was the only female friend he'd ever had.

Until Phoebe.

His focus had been almost entirely on her this past week and a half. A delightful, pleasant interlude —a sort of respite from his rakehell life. Now it was over.

He sat at his desk and dashed off a note to accept Mrs. Alban's invitation. As he was folding the parchment, Dorne returned to announce the arrival of Harry Sheffield.

Marcus handed the butler his response to Mrs. Alban. "Have this delivered, please. Send Harry in."

Harry entered a few moments later. "Morning, Rip. Hope I'm not disturbing you too early."

"Not at all." Marcus gestured for Harry to sit. "I hope your visit means you have good news to share."

Frowning, Harry took the chair next to Marcus's desk. "I'm afraid I don't. Drobbit has proven to be difficult prey. It's almost as if he's vanished."

"Damn." Marcus knew that if Harry couldn't find him, it *was* as if Drobbit had disappeared from the earth.

"I do have news, however." Harry narrowed his eyes slightly as he rested one arm on the chair. "Drobbit may have been up to some shady behavior. I don't suppose you'd know anything about that?"

Marcus wondered what Harry had learned. "What sort of shady behavior?"

"I'm not certain, but my search for him has led me to some unsavory individuals. Criminals, to be frank. Underworld moneylenders." Harry's brow darkened. "I suspect he owes someone money."

Bloody hell. That would explain why he was

stealing—and why he was broke. "I can't get into specifics, but I believe he may have swindled someone. He took money for an investment, then said it went poorly and the money was lost."

"You—or the someone—think he lied and stole the money?" Harry asked.

"It's possible. That's why I want to find him."

"If you think of anything, anything at all, that would help me, I'd appreciate it. In the meantime, I'm going to follow where this leads." Harry stood and gave Marcus a grim stare. "Your cousin may face arrest."

"So it appears." Marcus wanted to put a stop to Drobbit's criminal behavior, and that seemed the best way to do it at this point. Still, he wanted a list of who his cousin had cheated and how much he'd stolen. It bothered him to think that Drobbit had ruined, or come close to ruining, any number of people.

Harry departed, leaving Marcus in a pensive mood. Where the hell had Drobbit gone? Had something happened to him?

Marcus swore under his breath. *Osborne.* Drobbit's assistant in crime. He'd invited Graham to a pub in Leicester Square to discuss investing with Drobbit. Marcus was thoroughly vexed with himself for not recalling that sooner and blamed his fixation on Phoebe. He'd go to the pub tonight.

First, however, he needed to pick up his custom-made mask from Bond Street. They'd delivered it the day before yesterday, but it hadn't covered enough of his face and head. The goal was a *disguise* so he could win the bet with Phoebe.

At least he had that to look forward to. Not winning, though he wanted to, but having something with her. Because after that, he wasn't sure what would sustain their friendship. Unless they could truly continue on as friends. That would be damned difficult when he wanted to know her in ways that transcended friendship. He wanted intimacy with her. On every level.

Fuck, man, pull yourself together.

Marcus made the short walk from his house in Hanover Square to Bond Street. As he turned south, his mind was still very much on Phoebe. Their current wager, the wager he'd forfeited and paid two days ago, potential wagers he could make when this one was finished. Anything to stay in her orbit.

Instead of wagers, perhaps he could convince her to allow him to continue giving her driving lessons. She was an excellent student. So good, he doubted his services would be necessary for too long. Still, it was better than nothing.

As if conjured from his desires, Phoebe was coming toward him. He recognized the precise moment she saw him. The dimples he loved flashed briefly. His gut tightened.

"Good afternoon," he greeted as he came upon her. She was not alone. Miss Jane Pemberton accompanied her, and it seemed a maid trailed them, for the woman paused when they did.

"Good afternoon, my lord," Phoebe said, dropping into a curtsey.

Miss Pemberton followed suit.

He could just have continued on. Probably should have, but he was captive to Phoebe's presence. "What are you shopping for today?"

"I just picked up the last piece of my costume for the masquerade," Phoebe said, her gaze dipping to the box she carried.

"I wonder if you were at the shop where I am headed. Imagine if we'd shown up at the same time." He suppressed a smile but looked at her with mirth. Her gaze responded in kind, glowing with humor.

"Then I suppose things would have been spoiled."

"I'm pleased they are not," he said. He looked to Miss Pemberton, lest he forget entirely that there were other people who weren't Phoebe. "Are you looking forward to the masquerade?"

"I am, though I had to persuade my mother that we should go." She blushed slightly. "Forgive me."

Marcus arched a brow, then glanced at Phoebe in question.

"She's referring to the news that is newly circulating—that you purchased Brixton Park."

He'd been a bit concerned about his reputation dampening the attendance of the ball, but he also knew people were eager to visit Brixton Park. Close to London with grand and extensive gardens, the house hadn't hosted an event in over a generation. "I assumed people's curiosity would win out."

"It did with my mother," Miss Pemberton said with a light laugh. "Thank goodness."

"Excellent. It's going to be spectacular." He leaned forward—to impart a secret but also to hopefully catch a whiff of Phoebe's spicy feminine scent. "Don't tell anyone, but there's to be hide-and-seek in the maze, followed by fireworks."

Miss Pemberton sucked in a breath. "It's a surprise?"

"Yes, for the Duke and Duchess of Halstead. To celebrate their union."

"That *will* be spectacular." Miss Pemberton grinned at Phoebe. "I'm so glad I'm allowed to attend!"

"Me too." Phoebe sent a smile toward Marcus, and he wanted to take it very personally—that she was glad to be going to an event at his house to see him.

Christ, he'd never hung on a woman like this.

Past time to go. "I'll look forward to seeing you both Saturday." He bowed, then continued on his way, taking care to walk as close to Phoebe as he dared.

She turned her head as he did the same, their gazes connecting for the briefest moment. "See you Saturday," she murmured.

Knowing nothing he wanted would come of it, he'd count the minutes nonetheless.

CHAPTER 6

*P*hoebe's gaze lingered on Marcus for a moment as he walked away. She couldn't help but appreciate his smooth, confident gait or the way the tails of his coat brushed against his muscular thighs. Reluctantly, she turned her head back and started walking.

She felt Jane's attention before she said anything. "What is going on with you and Ripley?"

"Nothing," Phoebe answered. "We're just friends."

"Friends who picnic in Richmond, give each other driving lessons, and who flirt."

Phoebe glanced toward her. "There was no flirting."

"If you say so." Jane didn't sound convinced. "You should do what you like, what makes you happy." Meaning, even if she *had* been flirting, there was nothing wrong with it.

Except there was, because flirting with the Marquess of Ripley would leave her with nothing but heartache. He might not be the reprobate Sainsbury was, but he was still a philanderer.

What's wrong with that exactly?

Phoebe ignored the tiny voice in the back of her head.

You don't have to be heartsick. Take what you want.

"What are you suggesting, Jane?"

"Only that if you want to flirt with him, you should. There's no harm, and no one will judge you."

Phoebe let out a sharp laugh. "The hell they wouldn't."

"All right, they probably would, but who would know? I don't mean offense, but no one pays attention to you. Or me, for that matter."

"Perhaps not, but they pay attention to Ripley." At last night's card party, someone had asked if she'd taken a picnic in Richmond. They hadn't come out and asked if she'd been with Ripley, but the question had been clear. "People know we took a picnic to Richmond."

"And?" Jane pressed her lips together as they neared Phoebe's coach. "You don't have to answer to anyone. Unlike me." She glanced toward her maid, whom her mother had insisted accompany them.

"The time may be coming very soon that your mother won't allow you to visit or shop with me anymore. And I may be disinvited from Mrs. Matheson's card parties."

Jane's fair brows bunched together. "I can't control the latter, but I will not permit the former. If it comes to that, I *will* declare myself a spinster and come to live with you. Then they can focus all their attention on Anne."

They climbed into the coach and, since the maid sat opposite them, changed the topic of conversation to their shopping excursion. A short while later, they arrived at Jane's house. The coachman opened the door, and Jane indicated the maid should depart first.

Then Jane turned to Phoebe. "Don't let Sainsbury ruin anything for you. Not all men are like him. I don't know Lord Ripley at all, but you seem to like him, and that's enough, isn't it?"

Enough for what? "I wasn't flirting."

Jane sighed in exasperation. "But you *can* if you want to. And you can drive to Richmond. Or dance with him at the masquerade." She laid her hand atop Phoebe's briefly. "Do what I can't. *Please.*" With a parting wink, she left the coach.

Phoebe thought of her friend's advice as they drove to their next destination. Unfortunately, they arrived far too quickly. Looking out the window at the house in which she'd grown up, she took a steadying breath.

The coachman helped her out, and she was warmly greeted at the door by her parents' butler, Foster. "Welcome home, Miss Lennox."

"Thank you, Foster. But you know this isn't my home anymore." She smiled.

"Doesn't stop me, and everyone else, from wanting it to be." His light blue eyes twinkled with warmth.

Phoebe wasn't entirely sure "everyone" wanted her to return. She was beginning to think her father was too angry with her independence to find their way back to their father-daughter relationship. A burst of sadness spread through her. They'd once been close, but he'd changed after her brother had died in Spain. She'd understood his despair, but she realized now that he'd never fully recovered.

"Well, everyone that's left," Foster amended, his expression pained.

"What do you mean?"

"Harkin, Wick, and Meg were let go last week." He shook his head. "They'll be fine, I suppose. It was just a shock."

"Indeed." Phoebe was quite surprised to hear that

several of the retainers had been terminated. "Have they found new positions?"

"Wick has. He was ready to become a butler, and so he has."

Phoebe heard the pride in Foster's voice. "That's wonderful. What about Harkin and Meg?" Meg was one of the maids, but Harkin had been her mother's personal maid.

Foster shrugged. "I haven't heard from them since they left. Harkin went to stay with a friend, and Meg returned to her mother, though she said she couldn't stay there long."

"I'll see if I can help." Phoebe made a mental note to ensure both women found employment. Perhaps she could at least hire Meg.

"I hope I haven't spoken out of turn," Foster said. "I thought you'd want to know."

She gave him a warm smile. "Of course. I appreciate you telling me."

They went toward the back of the house, and Foster announced her at the entrance to the small sitting room. Phoebe greeted her mother, who stood from her chair, where it looked like she'd been embroidering. She'd been the one to stitch the delicate flower and butterfly on the handkerchief Marcus had returned. The one that smelled like him and that Phoebe had kept on her nightstand since he'd delivered it. Next to his drawing of her, which she looked at every night before she went to sleep and every morning when she awakened. She wished she had a drawing of him, actually.

Mama came and kissed Phoebe's cheek. "It's good to see you."

"I thought Papa would be here." Phoebe glanced around at the otherwise empty room.

"He'll be in soon, I imagine. He knows you were coming."

Was that why he was avoiding the sitting room? Phoebe bit her tongue before she could ask. She didn't want to fight with him. She loved him and wanted things to be different. To be…easy. Or at least *easier*.

Phoebe decided to take advantage of her father's absence. After gesturing for her mother to sit, she took a seat on the settee facing her chair. "Did you really let Harkin go?"

Mama's mouth tightened briefly. "Foster told you? Yes."

Silence reigned for a moment as Phoebe waited for an explanation. When none was forthcoming, she blurted, "Are you and Papa having financial difficulty?" It seemed the only logical explanation, especially considering her father's outburst at her house the other day.

"Not at all." Mama's voice was smooth, but she didn't make eye contact with Phoebe. "We just don't need so much help, not with just the two of us."

"You need a lady's maid. Why would you let Harkin go?" She'd been with their family for as long as Phoebe could remember.

"I don't *really* need my own maid. Lettie is excellent at dressing hair, and she's been helping Harkin with my clothing of late." Lettie was another maid, younger and less experienced than Harkin.

"I'm sure she's fine—"

"She's more than fine, and really, none of this is your concern," Mama said firmly. "What is your concern, however, is with whom you picnic in Richmond. Is it true you accompanied Lord Ripley *alone*?"

Since the rumor had surfaced at the card party last night, Phoebe had expected her mother might ask.

"Yes." While Phoebe saw no need to explain herself, she added, "It was a lovely day. I enjoy the marquess's company. He is quite intelligent. Erudite, really, which might surprise you. Plus, he gave me driving lessons."

Mama's eyes narrowed slightly. "He is not known for being intelligent, erudite, or an excellent driver. He's a scoundrel."

Phoebe shrugged. "He isn't to me."

"How on earth did you even meet him?"

"I don't recall," Phoebe lied. She recollected, and delighted in remembering every moment of their acquaintance. "We've become friends."

"Friends? With *him*?"

"With whom?" Papa chose that inopportune moment to enter the sitting room.

"The Marquess of Ripley." Mama said the name with considerable distaste and a curl of her lip.

Papa looked toward Phoebe with enthusiasm. He didn't appear to share Mama's unrest. "Dare we hope it becomes something more? She could do far worse than marriage to a man of his rank."

Mama sent him an irritated glare. "It's *Ripley*."

Again, Papa was not moved by her agitation. "He's a *marquess*."

Mama sat back in her chair with a disgruntled sound deep in her throat. She crossed her arms, looking thoroughly vexed.

Papa turned his expectant gaze on Phoebe. "Well? Will your connection to him become something more?"

"No. We're only friends."

"Men like him aren't friends with women. Hell, unmarried men aren't friends with women period."

Annoyed with both of them for meddling, Phoebe shot back, "And you, as a married man, have so many female friends?"

Papa grunted. "This isn't about me, it's about

you. You can't be friends with the Marquess of Ripley, not unless you want to be *completely* ruined. But given your behavior, perhaps that's your ultimate goal."

Phoebe forced herself to remain calm. "No, my goal is to lead a happy, fulfilling life. I find the marquess interesting, and he's teaching me to drive." That somewhat skimmed their relationship, which she believed had far more depth, since revealing the truth would only encourage her father's assumptions.

And maybe your secret desire.

That voice in her head needed to *die*. Violently.

Standing, Phoebe realized her visit was not going to be pleasant, not with them badgering her. Nor was she going to get any answers as to why they'd let three retainers go.

"Buy any Gainsboroughs this week?" Papa asked. He sounded nonchalant, but there was an edge to the question that fed her irritation.

"No. I'm looking at a Reynolds, though." She wasn't really, but she'd *thought* about it. The Foundling Hospital, which she'd visited yesterday to take some things to the children, displayed many beautiful paintings by Reynolds as well as Gainsborough and Hogarth, who'd donated their work to the institution.

She didn't wish to taunt her father. There was something wrong here, and she wanted to help. If she could. And if Papa would let her.

"Papa, if you ever need anything, I hope you'll ask."

Something dark—alarm, perhaps—flashed in his gaze. "What could I need from you?"

"Probably nothing." She didn't hide her exasperation. "Still, the offer stands."

Mama rose from her chair. "Phoebe, I beg of you to have a care for your reputation."

"What's left of it," Papa muttered.

"Please cease this...*friendship* with Ripley," Mama went on. "He's not worth your time. Or your standing."

Phoebe gave them both a frosty stare. "Since my standing isn't what it once was and may never be again, I don't see the point in following all of Society's stupid rules. If I want to go for a picnic with a friend—a *male* friend—I shall."

They both gaped at her in horror. Shaking, Phoebe bid them farewell and took her leave.

Inside the coach, she fought to put the unpleasant visit from her mind. She'd meant what she'd said: she saw no point in following rules that made no sense given her current path. And she was *not* on her way to becoming a respected member of Society with a husband and children.

Instead, she was linked to Marcus. People were even now likely gossiping about them, about their relationship. Phoebe laughed, but it wasn't really amusing. It *was*, however, ridiculous since she'd done nothing *truly* scandalous. Besides take a picnic alone with a friend who happened to be a notorious rake.

Her gaze fell on the box sitting on the opposite seat. Inside was the final piece of the disguise she would wear at the masquerade. Marcus wasn't going to be able to tell who she was. She, however, would ferret him out, and then she'd find the right moment to claim her victory.

~

*H*osenby's was a small but somewhat elegant pub located on the corner of Cranbourn Alley near Leicester Square. Marcus had first come here somewhat recently, when Graham had arranged to meet Osborne,

Drobbit's apparent assistant in crime. Marcus wished he'd thought to look for the man sooner.

He'd been too distracted. By Phoebe.

"Ho there, Rip."

Marcus turned to see Anthony swaggering toward him, a tankard in his hand. "What are you doing here?" he asked.

Anthony lifted his mug. "Drinking their fine ale. And seeing what comes up next." He waggled his brows. "Glad you stopped in. Shall we find a table?"

"So you came here for the ale? I don't remember it being remarkable when we were here a few weeks ago."

"Eh, the ale is fine, but I recall a particularly pretty serving maid."

They wove their way to the corner, and Marcus took a seat that allowed him a view of the large room. A serving maid came upon them immediately, her dark curls bouncing as she stopped at their table. Marcus wondered if she was the one Anthony was after.

"Evening, gentlemen," she said, her rouged lips pulling into a saucy smile. She fixed her gaze on Marcus. "You need an ale?"

"I do."

"Anything else?" She slid her hip toward him so that she grazed his shoulder.

"Not right this moment, but I'll let you know when you come back." He winked at her, and her eyes lit with hope.

When she left, Anthony slammed his tankard on the table with a grin. "You aren't here five minutes, and the women are already throwing themselves at your feet. Maybe I'm sorry you came. When I'm alone, I don't have competition."

"I didn't come for that, actually, so she's all yours."

"Excellent. She's not the one I was thinking of, but she's quite pretty too." Anthony was turning into a regular lothario.

"Remember that you need to soak the French letters before you use them. No quick fucks." Marcus deemed it his responsibility to protect the younger man, especially since he felt wholly responsible for his decline into hedonism.

"Yes, Father." Anthony's eyes darkened just before he tipped his hand down and lifted the tankard to his lips, draining it.

The maid returned with Marcus's ale, depositing it on the table, and gave him an expectant look. "Another ale for my friend," Marcus said.

She hastily took herself off once more.

Marcus hadn't meant to provoke Anthony's melancholy. That was the true reason for his slide into debauchery—Marcus had just provided the path.

"I didn't mean to lecture," Marcus said softly.

"I know." Anthony looked up, then sat back in his chair. "I just… I like to feel good. Is that bad?"

"No, so long as you're careful, and I'm sure you are."

"Because of your guidance, which I appreciate. Now, if you aren't here for the maids, why are you here?"

"I'm looking for Osborne."

"That tall fellow with the cane?"

Marcus nodded. "I'm hoping he can tell me where Drobbit's hidden himself."

The maid returned again with another tankard. She set it in front of Anthony, then gave Marcus an openly suggestive stare. "How can I help you, my lord?"

"I'm looking for a rather tall gentleman with a

walking stick. Goes by Osborne. Have you seen him of late?"

Her full red lips drew down into a pout. "That's what you wanted?"

"Yes." He took a coin from his pocket and slipped it into the bodice of her gown, letting his fingers linger against her flesh, not because he wanted to, but because he knew *she* wanted it. And he needed information.

She licked her upper lip in blatant invitation. "Haven't seen him in over a week. He does that sometimes—disappears for a bit."

Damn. It sounded like he'd gone underground around the same time as Drobbit. "Do you know where he goes?"

"No, but I could ask." She cocked her head to the side. "For a price."

Marcus pulled another coin from his pocket and pressed it into her hand.

She closed her fist around it, then dropped her gaze to his crotch. "Not what I was hoping for." When she didn't immediately leave, Marcus worried she wasn't going to help him. And he wasn't going to shag her for information.

Anthony stood and wrapped his arm around the maid's waist. He leaned down and spoke softly, but loud enough that Marcus could hear. "Come, we'll see what we can do to get you what you want. I may not be a marquess, but I'm a viscount and you'll still be able to boast to your friends."

Marcus opened his mouth to object, but Anthony gave his head a shake before spiriting the maid away through a doorway into the shadows. Hell and the devil, he didn't want Anthony shagging her for information either. Not that Anthony appeared to mind.

Scowling, Marcus drank a good portion of his

ale. He looked around the room and instantly made eye contact with a well-known prostitute. She was a celebrated entry in the *Ladies of Covent Garden* circular. Apparently, she'd moved on to Leicester Square.

He quickly averted his gaze and finished his ale, then moved on to Anthony's. Even so, she appeared beside his table a moment later.

"Lord Ripley. What a delight to see you here."

Normally, he would exchange pleasantries with her, perhaps even a light flirtation, but he wasn't in the mood. He'd come for one thing: information. And then he was going to Mrs. Alban's.

"Evening." He dropped his attention back to his ale.

"Oh dear, when a gentleman is more interested in his cup than me, I fear I may be on the decline."

Marcus gave her a faint smile. "Not at all. Don't let me keep you."

She exhaled with regret. "I wish you would keep me."

Thankfully, she took herself off, and Marcus focused his energy entirely on the ale and keeping his head down. Dammit, but Anthony was taking his time.

Perhaps he'd taken Marcus's counsel about soaking the letter to heart.

Shaking his head, Marcus finished the ale just as Anthony returned. He sat down with a smug expression.

"Damn it, Anthony, you can't have soaked it long enough to use."

Anthony laughed. "I didn't tup her. I did, however, learn that if you leave a particular word with the barkeep here, he'll notify Osborne that one of his associates is looking for him."

Marcus edged forward in his seat. "What word?"

Anthony shrugged. "He won't tell her, said it defeats the purpose of having a special word."

Marcus slapped his hand on the table. "Fuck." He stood up and stalked toward the bar.

But Anthony followed, clasping his arm and pulling him to a stop. He swung around to see Anthony grimacing. "Don't ask. She wasn't supposed to tell me any of that. You'll just get her in trouble."

Groaning, Marcus threw an irritated glance at the bar. Then he changed course and stalked toward the door leading to the street.

Anthony followed him outside. "Where are you going in such a hurry?"

"Mrs. Alban's," he clipped.

"Indeed?" Anthony sounded...overjoyed. He clapped a hand on Marcus's shoulder. "Excellent! Ripley is back to form, ladies and gentlemen!"

The people passing by cast them looks, and one fellow grinned and applauded. Marcus rolled his eyes.

"Mind if I join you?" Anthony asked. "Mrs. Alban's always has soaked letters on hand."

Yes, they did, which was why it was typically Marcus's destination of choice when he was in search of female companionship. Her establishment was the closest thing he'd ever had to a mistress. But tonight, he visited for a different reason.

As they walked toward Covent Garden, Anthony asked, "I was there the other night, and Mrs. Alban asked when you planned to visit."

"She invited me to dinner this evening. I'm sure you could join us."

Anthony shook his head. "I wouldn't want to intrude. You and Mrs. Alban have a...special relationship."

Marcus paused and turned to face Anthony. "What do you mean by that?"

"That you have a special relationship. I don't know of anyone else she invites to dinner, do you?"

No, but then Marcus had never asked. "I'm sure I'm not the only one."

"You're the only one who puts that light in her eye and the lilt in her voice. Surely you've noticed."

Hell. "No." He started walking, moving quickly across St. Martin's Lane. The brothel was just two streets ahead on the right. "Listen, there is nothing special about our relationship. We are friends, which I know is odd, but that's all we are."

"Truly?" Anthony sounded quite surprised. "I assumed you shagged her when we visit. Is that not the case?"

"I've never taken her to bed." And he never would. That would be wrong somehow. They were friends.

Yet, he considered Phoebe a friend, and he would take her to bed tonight if she invited him.

Instead, he was going to a brothel, to ask Mrs. Alban if she had any contacts who might know of Osborne's or Drobbit's whereabouts. But in the back of his mind, he'd expected to go upstairs to one of her most expensive ladies. Or two.

Suddenly, the thought of it repulsed him. His steps slowed when they neared the brothel's door. As Anthony went up the steps, Marcus lagged behind.

The door swung open, and the wide footman, Barclay, greeted them by name. Anthony disappeared inside while Marcus stood with his foot perched on the bottom step.

"Coming in, Lord Ripley?" Barclay asked.

"Yes." Because he needed information and was expected for dinner. He was many things, but rude was not one of them.

Barclay turned and spoke to another footman, who inclined his head, then hurried away. "I've informed Mrs. Alban that you're here. Go on to her private sitting room."

Anthony was already on his way upstairs, and he didn't look back. Marcus steeled himself for what he hoped wouldn't be an uncomfortable evening. It shouldn't be, and yet now Anthony had him wondering if Mrs. Alban had developed a tendre for him. And how the hell hadn't he noticed?

Maybe he could continue in his ignorance. Surely she would have said something if she wished to pursue a liaison. She hadn't risen to her position of wealth and independence without confidence, grace, and steel.

Yes, he would pretend he hadn't heard a word Anthony had said. It was entirely possible Anthony was wrong anyway.

Marcus moved into her sitting room only to find it empty. She kept him waiting sometimes, and that was fine.

A few minutes later, she swept in, her indigo skirts brushing the doorframe. Her ink-black hair was piled high atop her head in an elegant style dotted with sparkling jewels. She wore cosmetics, but never to excess and always to advantage, highlighting the delicate arch of her cheekbones and lush curve of her lips. "Good evening, Ripley. How delicious you look." She said the same thing every time they met.

And he repeated his part of their ritual, taking her hand and presenting a perfect leg. "Good evening, Mrs. Alban. You are far more delectable than I."

She gave him a saucy smile. "Indeed I am. Come, let us enjoy a feast that pales in comparison to us both."

He offered her his arm and escorted her into her private dining room. Once they were settled and he'd sampled the excellent madeira, he wasted no time broaching the topic uppermost in his mind.

"I wonder if you might be able to help me find someone. I'm looking for Archibald Drobbit, my cousin. He frequents this area—in gaming hells mostly." Where he preyed on gentlemen who were down on their luck and eager to recoup their losses by making a risky investment.

"I don't know of him, but I will see what I can discover. Anything to help you." She lifted her wineglass in a silent toast.

He returned the gesture, then took another sip. Setting the glass down, he continued, "I'm also looking for his associate, Mr. Osborne."

"That name sounds familiar. Isn't he exceptionally tall? Carries a walking stick with a raven's head?"

"Yes, that's him precisely. If you can find him, he should be able to direct me to Drobbit."

A footman served turtle soup. "And why are you in search of your cousin?"

Marcus didn't wish to explain the specifics. If Drobbit thought he was telling everyone about his misdeeds, he'd likely stay hidden. "A delicate family matter."

"I see. Well, as I said, I am glad to be of service." Her eyes glimmered briefly before she picked up her spoon to try the soup. Was that the light Anthony had spoken of?

Marcus ate a bit of the soup, then, disregarding his earlier plan to continue in ignorance, set his spoon down. "We're friends, aren't we?"

She looked over at him, her lids flickering in slight surprise at his question. "Certainly. Why would you ask?"

"Some—many, probably, say men and women can't be friends. I think they can. We are."

"I agree. Though I suppose it is quite novel."

"Have you no other male friends?"

She shrugged. "One or two. Have you other female friends?"

"Until recently, no." Hell, why had he answered truthfully? His relationship was no one's business, least of all Mrs. Alban's.

But she was clearly intrigued by his answer. "Oh, do tell. If you don't mind," she added demurely.

The footman removed the soup and delivered a course of salad and ham.

"There's nothing to tell, really."

"I think there is. You asked me about friendship between men and women and admitted that I've been your only woman friend. I suspect your new-found friendship is causing consternation. Is it yours or someone else's? The consternation, that is," she clarified with a sly smile.

It was causing *him* frustration. Because he wanted more. "Truly, it's nothing. She's a friend, and I've no problem with it."

"She's a lady, isn't she? A member of your *haute ton*."

He wasn't sure she was, not anymore. "She's a friend. Let us leave it at that."

"I think she's more than a friend, but I will leave it. Since you asked. You can always come to me—for help with finding someone, for advice with women, for anything you desire."

He wanted to understand her expectations. If she felt something for him, he owed it to her to set her straight. "Is that a specific invitation?"

She smiled briefly, and it was tinged with sadness. "It probably shouldn't be. Forget I said anything. I don't like competition, and I think your lady friend is more than you admit. I'm glad for you."

"She's not. At all. Don't you agree that moving beyond friendship would ruin the friendship?"

"I do, actually, which is why I ask you to forget my brief indiscretion." She took a bite of ham. "Oh, this is divine."

And that, Marcus knew, was the end of the conversation. He breathed an inward sigh of relief. Yes, moving beyond friendship would be awkward. Especially when things ended, as they would inevitably do.

Which was why he couldn't ever think of Phoebe as more than a friend. He'd be grateful for their flirtation and nothing more.

CHAPTER 7

"*T*his is an absolute crush," Graham said with a tone of disbelief.

Marcus grinned at the throng of people in the ballroom. They spilled out through the doors leading to the brick patio and the garden beyond, where large torches flamed at intervals. Not that everything was brightly lit—Marcus had ensured there were plenty of places for private interludes. "Of course it is. Everyone wanted to come to Brixton Park." He recognized people here whom he hadn't seen socially in years.

The only problem with so many attendees was that Marcus had yet to find Phoebe. She'd taken their wager *quite* seriously, so he'd expected difficulty. Except he was also beginning to grow frustrated.

"Thank you," Graham said. "Arabella is absolutely delighted. This was an exceptional gift."

"It's my pleasure. Your ancestor designed this estate to be enjoyed, so it should be, especially with you as the host. Someday, you're going to buy it back from me."

Graham chuckled. "Yes, and for a reasonable sum, not the ridiculously low price you offered it to me for."

Marcus shrugged. "The offer stands. When are you heading to the country?"

"Thursday. We will take a meandering journey to Huntwell."

"As you should. Enjoy your newly wedded bliss."

"I intend to." Graham grinned, and his gaze found his bride. Adorned with a swan mask, she was easy to spot, which Marcus had done all night in the hope that Phoebe would speak with her. However, no one Arabella had spoken with had resembled his quarry.

Suddenly, a brunette walked up to the duchess. Marcus's pulse quickened, then tempered. She was perhaps a little too short.

"Ripley?"

Marcus realized Graham was speaking to him, and he'd missed it entirely. "Sorry, what was that?" He didn't entirely pull his attention from Graham's wife and the mystery woman she was talking to.

"I wondered if you'd made any progress with Drobbit."

"Sadly, no. It's a growing frustration. I've enlisted additional help in searching for him, however. Hopefully, something will turn up this week." Marcus thought of Mrs. Alban and their dinner the other night. After their brief period of uncomfortable conversation, the evening had progressed as it normally did, with humor and camaraderie.

With one marked difference: Marcus kept finding himself comparing her to Phoebe and the time he spent with her. While he enjoyed Mrs. Alban's company, he didn't think about when he would see her next. He certainly didn't *pine* for that moment. Which was precisely what he was doing now. He was positively consumed with finding Phoebe, and it wasn't just so he could win the bloody wager.

The woman with the dark hair speaking with

Arabella pivoted, and Marcus could finally see that she wasn't Phoebe. *Blast.*

Her hair. She must have changed her hair after what he'd told her. He should perhaps look for a blonde woman.

Parting from Graham, Marcus went on a meticulous circuit of the room, taking his time to look closely at every woman with light hair that he encountered, including those wearing powdered wigs, of which there were several. People studied him, clearly trying to determine his identity and finding it difficult. Good, that meant his elaborate golden eagle mask, which he'd designed to cover as much of his head as possible, was effective.

Anthony stood near the doorway to the gaming room, a glass of wine in his hand. From the dilation of his eyes and his too-easy laugh, Marcus deduced he was already drunk.

Marcus paused in his search and sidled close to his friend. "Having a good time, I see."

"That *is* you. I wasn't sure. And yes, I'm having a marvelous time," Anthony said. "It's a hell of a party."

"Just remember this isn't our usual venue. Try to behave." Marcus clapped Anthony's shoulder before catching sight of pale blonde hair.

Moving after the woman, Marcus increased his pace. He caught up to her near the doors to the patio where she turned. A simple ivory mask decorated with pink and orange flowers adorned her face. He knew from the mask and the young woman's mouth that it was Miss Jane Pemberton. He quashed his disappointment.

On the other hand, perhaps there was no reason to be dismayed. Miss Pemberton was, in fact, Phoebe's closest friend…

"Good evening, Miss Pemberton."

"I'm sorry, but—"

He heard the uncertainty in her voice and suffered a moment's conflict. If he told her who he was, she could, and likely would, tell Phoebe. "If I tell you who I am, do you promise to keep it secret?"

She hesitated. "Lord Ripley?"

He exhaled. "How did you know?"

"I didn't. It was purely a guess, though your size and breadth match his, even if your head is almost entirely covered with that mask. It's stunning."

"Thank you. I'm still shocked you guessed correctly. You're the first this evening."

"To be fair, I had a *bit* of help. I knew you were trying to disguise yourself beyond recognition."

"Miss Lennox told you." Which meant Miss Pemberton was aware of their wager. What else did she know?

She nodded. "You're the only two people who are taking this masquerade so seriously."

He laughed. "Wagers are serious business."

"Indeed they are, and Phoebe plans to win. Don't bother asking me how she's disguised."

He exhaled again. "I suppose that was too much to hope for."

"Don't give up, my lord," she said encouragingly.

"Oh, I shan't. That she hasn't yet found me out gives me great hope."

"How do you know she hasn't?" Miss Pemberton asked slyly. "Perhaps she's waiting for the right moment to strike."

Diabolical. He loved it. "Do you know that for certain?"

"Not at all. I just know that's what I would do. In all honesty, I haven't spoken with her this evening. She's been very careful to keep herself from people she knows."

Very diabolical. Marcus hadn't been so careful.

He'd spoken to Graham, of course, and then briefly to Anthony. If Phoebe had been watching, she likely already knew he was the golden eagle.

"I'm glad you've become friends," Miss Pemberton said, drawing his curiosity.

"Why is that?"

"I think you're good for her esteem." Her mouth pulled for a brief moment. "Forget I said that."

He wouldn't. "Is it too much to ask that you don't tell her how I'm dressed?"

"Yes, but don't worry. Since she's avoiding me, you needn't be concerned." She smiled, and Marcus bowed before taking his leave.

A table of refreshments stood near the door to the patio. Marcus swiped a glass of wine and took a sip before stepping out into the warm spring night. They'd been most fortunate with the weather. The hide-and-seek in the maze and the fireworks would be well attended.

He looked out over the torchlit garden. It wasn't as crowded as the ballroom, but there were a great many people strolling along the paths. To the left lay the maze. Surrounded with torches, the outer reaches were illuminated, while the center was rather dark. The perfect place for a tryst, especially given the number of slim nooks built into the shrubbery. Marcus had memorized the layout—it was good to be prepared.

Not that it seemed to matter, for he was without anyone to take into the maze. Oh, he could likely find any number of women who would be willing, but he wanted only one.

He finished his wine and gave it to a footman on the patio, then walked down onto the main path. He looked for fair-haired women, but those he saw were not Phoebe. He began to despair of finding her. They hadn't planned for not coming into contact with each other at all. He hadn't even contemplated such a travesty. To think he could go this entire splendid night without seeing her carved a hollow of disappointment in his chest.

The majordomo came out onto the patio and announced that it was time for hide-and-seek in the maze. As the hosts, Graham and Arabella would find as many people as they could in fifteen minutes. Guests had ten minutes to enter the maze and find their spot. When the bell rang, they had to stop where they were, whether they were hidden or not. People who moved would be disqualified. The last guest to be found would win the honor of being the Master or Mistress of the Masquerade.

People flowed out from the ballroom. Some walked straight for the maze, while others, most of them, actually, lingered on the patio to watch.

Marcus swore silently. He should have found her by now. He'd hoped they might hide together. Now there was no reason to even bother playing the game.

"Aren't you going to hide, my lord?"

His blood went cold, then instantly heated as a shiver of desire danced across his neck. He knew that voice.

He turned to see a woman gliding quickly away, her sparkling dark green skirts swirling over the path. Her pale blonde hair caught the light, as did the peacock feathers attached to her mask.

A bloody peacock. He wasn't surprised that she'd dressed as the male of a species. She wasn't content with her lot as a woman, and by damn if that wasn't one of the most attractive things about her.

Marcus took off after her, nearly running to catch up to her. She dashed into the maze, and he just caught her veering to the right. Good, that was the way toward the center. Toward darkness and privacy.

In his haste, he ran into another woman. She wavered on her feet, and Marcus steadied her.

"Oh my." She giggled, looking up at him from behind a small red silk domino. Some people had no imagination, no sense of fancy. Or, perhaps more accurately, no wager with another guest. "Thank you."

"Excuse me," he murmured, hurrying past her. Damn it, he'd lost Phoebe.

He continued toward the center, looking every which way. He came upon the first nook and looked inside. "This is taken," came a deep voice.

Marcus put his hand out to the right, feeling along the narrow passageway of leaves until he found the next opening. That alcove was also occupied.

Fearing he might not find her, he searched three more nooks, two of which were occupied and one of which was empty. Now he was in the darkest part of the maze. Faint light helped him make out the shape of the walls around him and figures up ahead, but nothing that would identify them. He paused, and a hand clasped his, pulling him around a corner.

"Looking for me?"

$\sim$

*P*hoebe's heart beat fast and hard in her chest, both from her hurrying to the center of the maze and the anticipation of Marcus following her. She'd lost sight of him and worried he wasn't coming. And now she was worried she'd grabbed the wrong man.

Except he smelled like Marcus, that arousing spice-and-sandalwood scent that identified him as precisely the man she was looking for. Still, she'd lowered her voice to disguise herself in case it wasn't him. Not that some random gentleman would recognize her voice, she realized.

He tipped his head up just enough that she saw his golden eagle mask. Yes, it was him. She grinned to herself.

"I *am* looking for someone." He didn't sound as though he knew who she was.

Oh, this was too wonderful. She kept her voice low. "Who?"

"Maybe you. I'm not sure. Who do you think I am?"

They were playing a game. Excitement curled in her belly and spread lower, igniting a delicious sensation. "The man I'm going to kiss in this maze."

He steered her into a narrow space tucked behind the hedge wall. "Unfortunately, the woman I'm looking for doesn't like kissing."

"That's too bad. Do *you* like kissing?"

"Immensely. I think I would like kissing her most of all."

Phoebe's breath caught. Tucked into the small space, she pressed against his chest. He swept his mask off, and she could just barely make out his features when his head was tipped up.

"Does this mean I win?" she asked, pulling up her own mask to expose her face. If she removed it entirely, she might dislodge her wig.

His lips hovered above hers. "I don't know. I am beginning to feel like I'm winning."

"Maybe we can both claim victory."

"Do you really want that kiss?" Now he was the one who sounded a bit breathless.

Phoebe put her hands on his chest as the bell sounded. "As it happens, we're stuck here. Can you think of anything better to do?"

"No." The single word was low and deep, reverberating in her chest like a thunderclap.

"Tonight, I'm a bird," she whispered. "Help me take flight."

With a sweet groan, he pressed his lips to hers. Instinctively, Phoebe tensed. The only other time she'd experienced this, things had gone very, very badly.

Marcus's arms swept around her, his hands pressing softly into her back as he held her close. She'd no idea where his mask had gone once he'd removed it, but she wasted no time thinking about it.

Not that she had the capacity to think of much beyond the gentle caress of his lips moving over hers. Kiss after kiss, each one lasting just a bit longer, wound her into a keen state of desire. This was exactly what he'd promised. She felt weak and quivery —in the most delightful way—her body poised for what came next.

He trailed a hand up her spine and brought it over her shoulder so that she moved her arm beneath his. His fingers traced her jaw.

"Are you ready to fly?" he whispered.

"Yes. Please."

He pressed his thumb against her chin. "Open for me."

Then he angled his lips over hers and licked into her mouth. She went rigid, for she'd experienced this before. No, she actually hadn't. There was no revulsion, only delight. No fear, only longing.

Phoebe clutched at his coat and then moved her hand up around his neck. She pressed her body against his as he expanded the kiss. His tongue glided against hers, and she floated into the air.

Or would have if she wasn't holding on to him as if her life depended on it. Or, more accurately, as if she couldn't get enough of him.

He curled his hand around her neck, cupping her nape, tilting her head to the side so he could lick deeper into her mouth. He kissed her with a gentle persuasion, stoking the passion that had ignited the minute she'd approached him outside the maze.

She'd chosen her advance on him with meticulous care since spotting him almost two hours ago. She'd waited on the fringe, watching for him to go outside, for that was where she'd planned to make her move.

Kissing, however, hadn't been part of her scheme. But now that she was here, locked in his rapturous embrace, she knew there was no avoiding it. Nor did she want to.

His fingers dug into her back as he tipped her back, cradling her against him. She clung to him, her hand on his neck and cravat. How she wished she wasn't wearing gloves so she could feel his bare flesh with her own.

He held her easily in one arm while the other skimmed down her back and along her side to clasp her waist before gliding backward to press his hand on her lower back. The movement brought her against him, their hips colliding.

Sensation exploded in her core, and for the first time, she understood the appeal of an affair. She sensed not just the ability to take flight, but the chance to fly around the world and touch the sun.

He pulled his lips from hers but didn't leave her. He kissed along her jaw and then her neck, his tongue leaving a delicious trail of want. Phoebe shivered and clasped the back of his head, her fingers twining in his hair.

"Phoebe." He murmured her name like a plea. "Phoebe." A prayer. "*Phoebe.*" An urgent demand.

He skimmed her waist again, moving his hand forward to her rib cage and bringing it up to the underside of her breast. He lingered there, barely cupping her. The caress sent another shock of desire through her.

Suddenly, she was upright, and he turned her, pressing her against the hedge and blocking her from the narrow entrance.

"Someone's coming."

Phoebe saw the light coming through the maze, and it was almost upon them. She quickly pulled her mask down over her face. Marcus completely obliterated her view of the passage. Good, that meant no one could see her either.

"Found you! Number thirty-four. Remember that, if you please," came Arabella's voice before the light moved on.

Another light followed, and this time, a man spoke, but it wasn't Graham. "If you've been found, you must leave the maze."

"Of course," Marcus answered. The light dimmed, and it seemed they were alone once more. "We need to go." He bent, and she realized he'd dropped his mask. When he had it back in place, he offered her his arm. "Now we can say we encountered each other as we left. If anyone asks," he added.

Phoebe curled her hand around his coat, eager for more of his warmth, not because she was cold but because he felt divine. Particularly pressed up against her. "It's almost as if you planned this rendezvous." She walked closely beside him as they left the nook.

"You're the one who found me."

Phoebe grinned. She couldn't help herself. A giddy excitement tripped through her. She wanted to dance out of the maze. Take flight, indeed. "I did. I suppose that means I win."

"I thought we decided we both win."

She heard the humor in his voice. "Someone has to pay thirty pounds."

"I already paid a hundred," he said with a laugh. "Fine, another thirty. Same place?"

"If you please."

He escorted her from the maze, turning her along the path that led to the patio. "Your disguise was superior. I didn't recognize you at all. And even when you approached me, I wasn't entirely certain."

"When did you know?"

"Absolutely? Not until you mentioned kissing me."

Phoebe laughed gaily. "You assume you're the only man I would invite to do so?"

"I *hope* so." He slowed his pace and turned her onto a side path. "Do you mind taking a detour?"

"Where to?"

"Heaven?" When she sucked in her breath, he amended his answer. "Richmond, maybe?"

This provoked her to laugh again. "My lord, you've plied me with exceptional kisses. I may allow you to take me anywhere."

"*Phoebe.*" He groaned her name. "Please, have a care for me. You are sorely trying my self-control."

That sounded dangerous. Deliciously, wonderfully, tantalizingly dangerous. Even so, she needed to be cautious. Otherwise, she *would* allow him to take her anywhere.

"Your mask was also excellent," she said as they walked to a darker part of the garden.

"How long did you know who I was?"

"As soon as you walked toward Graham."

"Damn. You were far smarter about this than I was."

She wasn't sure that was the only reason for her victory. "Perhaps less arrogant."

He let out a loud laugh, then quickly quieted himself to a chuckle. "I'm not the one who swore I would win."

"Did I do that?" she asked innocently.

"Maybe more than once."

"I like winning, apparently. I didn't know that

about myself." She also hadn't expected to like kissing. "Thank you," she said softly, stopping on the
path. Though they were in shadow, there was a clear
line of sight to the patio.

He turned and tipped his head down. It was hard
to tell if he was looking at her, but she assumed he
was. "For what?"

"I wish I could see your face." She reached up
and touched the underside of his jaw. "For showing
me what kissing can be. I don't dislike it anymore. At
least not with you."

"Good." He moved closer, so that their clothing
touched. He brushed his hand along her forearm
down to her hand, his fingers briefly tangling with
hers. "I wish I could see your face too."

Her heart fluttered, as if it too wanted to fly. She
still held his arm, her anchor to the earth—to him.

"I'd be happy to repeat the demonstration any
time you find yourself doubting the pleasure of
kissing."

"I'm not sure I could ever do so again. Not after
tonight. But I appreciate your offer and will keep it
in mind." She'd think of little else.

Their masks covered most of their faces, but their
mouths were exposed. She swayed toward him.

Yelling sounded from behind her. They both
turned. Marcus swore. "It's Anthony."

At that moment, a loud boom rent the air, followed by light exploding in the sky. The fireworks!

Marcus paused to look up. Then he looked at
her. She grinned at him. "They're magnificent."

Pulling his gaze from hers, he started back along
the path. She hurried alongside him, periodically
glancing up at the display as she went.

In the middle of a patch of lawn between their
path and the patio, Anthony rolled on the ground
with another gentleman. Spectators had gathered.

They looked from the fight up to the sky and back again. Wagers were exchanged amidst the light and sound.

Marcus withdrew his arm from Phoebe's hand and strode into the fray. He bent down and hauled Anthony off the other man, nearly toppling backward with the effort. Managing to keep his footing, Marcus kept hold of Anthony's arm. It was a necessary thing, for Anthony tried to pitch forward.

The other man scrambled to his feet. "I ought to call you out, Colton!"

Anthony responded by bending over and casting up his accounts all over the lawn. The crowd gasped and made sounds of disgust before beginning to dissipate. The other man snorted in derision before taking himself off the lawn.

Marcus cast a quick glance at Phoebe, and she knew their evening was done. Anthony required his assistance.

"I'll send a footman," she offered.

Marcus winced as Anthony vomited again. "Thank you."

Phoebe started toward the patio but didn't have to find a footman. A pair of them were already rushing to provide aid.

It was a rather ghastly end to their lovely interlude, but probably for the best. She was certain they'd been about to kiss again, and right where anyone could have seen them. Except would anyone have known who they were? The peacock kissing the golden eagle would surely escape notice.

"Good evening, Miss Peacock," Jane said as Phoebe stepped onto the crowded patio. The ballroom had emptied to watch the fireworks. "I see you found Mr. Eagle."

Phoebe was glad for the mask, for she blushed rather profusely. At least one person would have known who they were. "You saw us walking together?"

Jane tipped her head back as white lights speckled the inky sky. "I did. Did you win the bet?"

Phoebe nodded, her eyes on the stunning show above them.

"Did you win anything else?" Jane teased with glee.

"No." Except she had. Phoebe didn't know what she'd won, only that she felt victorious. Like a conqueror. Perhaps because she'd overcome her fear. She looked over at Jane. "Maybe."

Jane grinned, then looped her arm through Phoebe's. "Good. I won't ask for the details, because I suspect you won't give them to me. But when you change your mind, I can't wait to hear them. I'm glad you took my advice."

To do what she wanted.

Phoebe had done exactly that, and she wanted to do it again. She wanted more of tonight. More kissing. *More Marcus.*

Smiling to herself as the fireworks concluded, she let her joy fly free. She'd never felt more alive.

CHAPTER 8

*P*hoebe took a deep breath as she followed her coachman and footman into her parents' house. Foster held the door and gave Phoebe a quizzical look.

"We're taking this to the sitting room for now," she said to him. "Will you let Papa know I'm here?"

"Right away." Foster closed the door after her and took himself off toward her father's study.

Phoebe motioned for her retainers to follow her to the sitting room. "Lean it against that chair." She pointed at a sturdy piece of furniture in the corner.

They did so and straightened, the coachman asking if she required anything further.

"No, thank you," she said. "I won't be long."

They inclined their heads and departed to await her in the coach.

Phoebe went to the package and removed the paper. As she stood back, her father entered.

"Foster said you'd come for a visit." He turned toward her, and his jaw nearly hit the floor. "What the hell is that?"

She thought it was rather obvious. "It's your very own Gainsborough."

"Mine?" He looked from the painting to her.

"Yes."

"It's not my birthday," he said, returning his gaze to the landscape and then frowning. Deeply.

Phoebe tensed. Was there no pleasing the man? He'd seemed so agitated at her having bought one, she thought he might like to have one for himself. "You don't like it?"

"I don't understand why you're giving it to me."

"Because I wanted to." She wondered if she'd made a mistake.

The frown remained. "You shouldn't have."

"Nevertheless, I did." She noticed he didn't answer whether he liked it. "If you don't want it, you can sell it."

He turned on her, his eyes sparking with anger. "I don't need your charity."

She suspected he did. "It's not charity. I bought you a painting." And yes, she did so knowing he could sell it and use the funds if that was what he really needed. She didn't think he would have reacted well to an explicit offer to give—or loan—him money. "It's a gift, Papa."

"It's charity, and I don't want it."

She'd had enough of his obstinance when it came to her. "But do you *need* it? I have the impression you are in financial trouble, and I can help."

He opened his mouth, but the next words were from Mama, who'd come into the sitting room. "Don't lie to her, Stewart. She's not stupid." She gave Phoebe an apologetic stare. "Yes, we are in financial trouble, which is why we let those retainers go. We can pay Lettie less than we paid Harkin."

Phoebe had guessed as much. "What happened?"

"Your father made a bad investment."

Papa glared at her. "Augusta, don't."

Phoebe's insides roiled. She hated her father's

shame as much as she hated the anger he directed at her mother. "How much did you lose?"

His face turning red, Papa blew out a breath and quit the room. Phoebe watched him leave, her heart twisting.

Mama walked toward the painting. "What's this?"

"A Gainsborough. I bought it for Papa."

"I heard him say something about charity." Mama pivoted toward her. "Is that what this is?"

"Not specifically. But yes, I thought that if you were in need of funds, he could sell it. It was the only way I could think to offer him money without hurting his pride."

"I think it's far too late for that," Mama said softly. She went to the settee and sat down, then patted the cushion beside her.

Phoebe perched next to her, still taut with agitation after clashing with her father. "What do you want me to do?"

"Marry a wealthy duke?" Mama smiled, but it was brief, and the light in her eyes dimmed. "Give your father some time. He feels very foolish about the investment, and he thinks he's failed as a parent."

Phoebe's insides coiled. "Because I refused to marry Sainsbury and bought my own house."

"Yes. And because of your brother. Your father misses him every day."

"I know," Phoebe said softly. She missed him too, but it was different. She'd been young when he'd gone off to school and then purchased a commission. "I can't do anything about Benedict, and I can't change who I am."

"I know, dear, and your reputation may be permanently tarnished, so there really is no going back." Mama's tone was matter-of-fact but ragged at the edges with sadness.

Permanently tarnished.

"Do you believe that?" Phoebe asked quietly, almost afraid of the answer.

"Probably. Invitations for your father and I have trickled to a small number. I know that weighs on him too."

Papa didn't give a fig about attending Society events. So long as he was welcome at his club and within his group of friends, he was content. Mama, however, didn't like being excluded. While it pained Phoebe to be the cause of that, she wouldn't regret her choices. She couldn't—to do so would be to ignore her own pain and to make herself feel less. Insignificant. As if she only existed to provide a desired outcome for others.

"Mama, do *you* believe that I'm tarnished? If I weren't your daughter, would you give me the cut direct?"

Mama stared at her, her lips parting. She glanced away, and Phoebe's chest squeezed. Then she reached over and patted Phoebe's hand. "No, I wouldn't. Of course not."

"I think you would. Because in your opinion, I humiliated Sainsbury for no reason. Furthermore, you believe I should have married him regardless of his behavior."

"I don't think—"

"You do," Phoebe said firmly. "Perhaps if you knew exactly what he did to me, you would understand."

Mama stiffened and looked away. "That isn't necessary. What's done is done, and discussing it further won't change anything."

"Yet you and Papa can't keep from bringing it up." Phoebe realized they were a large part of why she'd felt trapped, why she hadn't felt truly free since striking out on her own. And why she'd felt…less. She needed to move on.

Phoebe reached over and took her mother's hand, then gave her a reassuring smile. "I need to tell you what happened, and I need for you to listen. It's going to be all right, Mama." And she realized it was. She'd been too afraid to share the truth, too full of shame, as if what Sainsbury had done had been her fault. She didn't want to feel that shame anymore.

As she rode home in the coach a while later, Phoebe felt lighter than she had in some time. Mama had sat stoically as she'd listened to Phoebe's story. Then she'd bade her never to repeat it, for if her father ever learned the truth, he might inflict bodily harm on Sainsbury.

Then Mama had cried.

Phoebe hadn't expected her to demonstrate such emotion. Because of her surprise and the sheer relief of unburdening herself, Phoebe had cried too. Then Phoebe had reiterated her commitment to never being a man's pawn or property. Mama, to her credit, hadn't debated her.

The buoyancy lifting Phoebe reminded her of how she'd felt at the masquerade with Marcus. She'd been busy the past few days with purchasing the painting for her father, but she'd thought of Marcus endlessly. The thrill of surprising him when he hadn't known who she was. The anticipation of going into the maze and knowing he was behind her. The rush of excitement when they'd moved into the dark nook. And the kiss…

She shivered as the coach stopped in front of her house. Yes, she was ready to move on. And she knew exactly what she wanted to do.

～

*T*he scent of spring blossoms filled the air as Marcus made his way along Cavendish Square toward Phoebe's house. Her invitation yesterday had come as a bit of a shock, albeit a wholly welcome one. He'd responded immediately and without begging to move the appointment up. He'd wanted to drive to her house at once and show her how much he'd missed her since the masquerade.

Indeed, the past several days had been torture.

He'd considered writing her a letter. Or paying a call. Or sending flowers. Instead, he'd done nothing. Thankfully, she was smarter than him and had taken the initiative.

Marcus had wanted her to. No, he'd needed her to. It was one thing to kiss him amidst the excitement of a game of hide-and-seek in a darkened maze, and another to want to see him in the light of day.

He dared to hope…for what, he wasn't sure. But he was about to find out.

Taking the steps two at a time, he was on her doorstep before her butler had the door open.

"Good afternoon, my lord," the butler said, welcoming him inside. "May I take your hat and gloves?"

"Thank you." Marcus handed him the items and then followed the man to the garden room. The moment he caught sight of Phoebe standing near the windows, his breath left him in a whoosh.

Her hair was dark once more—good, he preferred it that way—and swept atop her head, save for a pair of curls that grazed her temples. He could see every detail of her face, especially the hint of her dimples, which had been impossible to detect in the dark of the maze.

"Where is the peacock?" he teased.

"It was a good costume, wasn't it?"

"Very." He perused her from head to toe, appreciating the curve of her neck as it transitioned to her shoulder and the swell of her breasts beneath the dark yellow bodice of her gown. "Though I prefer you like this."

He hadn't heard the butler leave, but assumed he had. Turning his head, he saw that the door was closed. They were quite alone. His blood heated. He cautioned himself—he would assume and expect nothing.

"Thank you for coming today. May we sit?" She indicated the wide settee on the opposite side of the room from the windows, where he'd sat on his last visit.

"Certainly." He pivoted and waited for her to walk past. Following her, he sat down, angling himself toward her as she did to him.

She sounded—and looked—rather serious. The hope he'd arrived with withered and died. This was not the behavior of a woman who wished to discuss the joys of shared kisses or the potential for more.

"How is Lord Colton?" she asked.

Marcus blinked as his brain worked to change direction. He hadn't expected that question. "He's fine. I think." Marcus had taken him upstairs to one of the rooms at Brixton Park, where Anthony had slept late into the next day. He didn't recall the fight at all. Despite that, he'd written a note of apology to the other gentleman at Marcus's behest.

"Oh, good. He's lucky to have a friend like you." She clasped her hands in her lap.

Anthony might not agree. Marcus had tried to talk to him about curbing his alcohol consumption the other night, but Anthony hadn't wanted to hear it. They hadn't spoken since.

He noted that her hands looked tense, as if she were squeezing them together. Was she nervous?

Afraid? Damn, he'd hoped she wouldn't be anymore. Not after the masquerade.

After a pause, she continued. "I wanted to thank you again for kissing me at the masquerade. It wasn't at all what I expected, and I'm glad you persuaded me to try. Again."

Marcus tried to relax and reminded himself not to assume. "Did you enjoy it?" She'd said so at the masquerade, but the light of day and the absence of masks and urgent desire and fireworks could have a sobering effect.

"I did. More than I could ever have imagined." She unclasped her hands and flattened them against her lap. "I wanted to talk to you about that—about why I didn't expect to enjoy it."

Now he was curious as hell. He turned more fully toward her and rested his arm against the back of the settee. "About Sainsbury?" Just saying the man's name made him angry.

She nodded.

"You don't have to," he said softly.

"I think I do. While I've decided I like kissing —*you*, to be specific—I'm not sure about the rest. And I would like to be. But I think I need to understand what that entails. When you explained kissing to me, it changed my perspective entirely. I don't know if what I've done, what he made me do, will ruin things." She blushed, dark pink flooding her neck and face.

Marcus wanted to kill Sainsbury for causing her this pain. He closed the distance between them so that his arm was behind her head. "Tell me as much, or as little, as you want."

"I told my mother the other day. That was difficult." She let out a short, nervous laugh. "I thought today would be easier."

He put his free hand on one of hers. "What can I do?"

"Just listen." She took a deep breath. "We were betrothed. Sainsbury asked if he could kiss me. He said we were as good as wed, which I supposed we were. Breaking an engagement is ruinous." She added sardonically, "Which I later learned.

"So I said yes, and he took me for a promenade —we were at a ball. We stole into an empty chamber. It was rather dark, with only a few candles burning. As soon as we arrived, he put his arms around me." She looked away from Marcus, directing her attention toward the garden. "Then he kissed me, but after kissing you, I'm not sure I would call it that." She tossed him an uneasy smile before looking back at the windows.

"I remember wetness, and his tongue shoving so far down my throat that I wanted to gag. He was rather inebriated. I pulled away and said I didn't like it. He laughed and said I was too inexperienced to know, that I would get used to it." She turned her head back to Marcus, her eyes wide and without guile. "I believed him."

"Of course you did." Why wouldn't she? Fury built in Marcus's muscles, turning him into an animal ready to spring. "You did nothing wrong."

"So I let him kiss me again. And again. He was wrong. I didn't get used to it. But he was to be my husband, so I let him continue and prayed it would improve. That's when he pushed me onto the chaise."

Marcus wasn't sure he wanted to hear what happened next. But he would because she'd asked him to. "What happened?" He barely recognized the husky rasp of his voice.

She took a breath and blew it out, then clasped his hand between hers. Her warmth and softness soothed him, which was ridiculous and wrong. He should be the one comforting her.

"He laid me back and asked if we could do just a bit more—to prepare for the wedding night. That way, I wouldn't be so afraid. That made sense to me, so I said yes."

He'd said all the right things to her to force her acquiescence. "The man's a scourge."

"He said he wanted to look at my breasts, that if I showed them to him, I wouldn't feel embarrassed on our wedding night. I opened my gown for him. He—he thanked me. Then he said that he should show me part of himself too." The color reentered her cheeks, and her grip tightened around his hand. "So he unbuttoned his fall and pulled out his—"

"Phoebe, you don't have to go on." Marcus cursed himself. This wasn't about his discomfort. If she wanted to tell him this, he owed it to her to listen. "I shouldn't have interrupted. Continue. Please."

"Do you think less of me?"

Marcus's insides twisted. He wanted to flay himself for his insensitivity. "Never." He took his hand from hers and cupped her cheek. "I think so highly of you, more right now than ever before. What you're doing—what you did—takes courage."

"Most people would think less of me. They do since I threw Sainsbury over."

"I'd like to throw him over a damn cliff." And he might yet.

She smiled softly, briefly. "Can I help?"

"Of course. I'll drag him there, and you can push him." He clung to the humor and gratitude in her gaze. "Continue. If you want to."

She nodded once, and he put his hand in hers once more. "He showed me his penis. It was long, hard, and…pasty."

Marcus stifled a snort.

"He said we should touch each other. I told him I didn't know how, so he showed me how to stroke him. When he was satisfied that I was doing it correctly, he touched my breasts. He...hurt me. I asked him to stop, and he said he would soon. Then he told me to move my hand faster, that if I did that, he would stop."

Marcus really was going to kill him. "So you did."

"Yes, and he stopped touching me. But then...he said he wanted to put himself inside me, that it was fine since we were shortly to be wed." She paused to take a breath. "I didn't want to. Not then, not ever. I started to panic. I tried to move away, but he grabbed me. He...threatened me. He said if I didn't let him do what he wanted that he would call off the wedding and I'd be ruined. I realized right then that I would prefer that."

Marcus's chest squeezed beneath the combined pressure of pride and fury. "You were very brave."

"I wasn't. I wanted to be. A footman came in then, interrupting us. Sainsbury went...soft. I scrambled away from him and called for the footman to hold the door open for me. If he hadn't come in..."

Sainsbury would have raped her. Goddamn, Marcus could scarcely believe she'd allowed him to flirt with her, let alone kiss her. He felt like such a beast knowing what he now knew.

He gripped one of her hands and stared into her eyes. "I am so sorry."

"Later, after I spent a considerable amount of time in the retiring room, I saw him in the ballroom. He told me I shouldn't have left, that in a few days I'd be his anyway.

"The wedding was two days later. I couldn't go through with it. Not after that. I knew our marriage would be a series of battles in which I would never prevail. But I imagine that's how most marriages are."

Marcus didn't know but couldn't disagree with her, particularly when he thought of some of the men with whom he was acquainted. "Men are selfish blackguards."

"Are you sure you don't think less of me?"

"God, no. I think less of myself. When I think of how I behaved toward you… Why didn't you toss me out that night? The day we'd met."

She pondered his question for a moment, her thumb tracing circles on his hand. "I liked you. You were—are—different from Sainsbury. In every way. He never made me laugh. He never made me feel beautiful. He never made me think I was special."

"I'm going to kill him."

Her eyes widened, and she clutched at his hand. "No, you mustn't."

His gaze locked with hers for a long moment, but he eventually nodded. "I want to, however."

"And I appreciate that more than you can know. Almost as much as you listening to me and not running away as soon as I finished my story."

"Is that what your mother did?"

"No, but I was slightly less graphic in my description." She flinched. "I wanted to be completely open with you because I don't know if I can do… Are those normal things that men and women do?"

Marcus exhaled heavily and readjusted his weight on the settee. "Mostly, yes. It's generally pleasurable for a woman to have her breasts fondled, and it's absolutely pleasurable for a man to have his cock stroked." He watched her reaction, but there was nothing negative. She was listening raptly. He could be discussing anything of interest—the latest hat styles or the horses for auction at Tattersall's last week or the constellations that would be in that night's sky.

"I can't imagine having my breasts touched would feel good. As for the other, I couldn't begin to say, since I don't have a penis of my own."

"And thank God for that." He cracked a smile.

"However, I didn't think kissing would feel good either, and you demonstrated how wrong I was."

"No, I demonstrated how inept and pathetic Sainsbury is. It doesn't sound as if he could pleasure a woman if his life depended on it."

"Can we put Sainsbury from our conversation now? I'd rather focus on what you did for me. And what you can do next."

Oh God. Now he understood her purpose in telling him this. "What's that?" he asked cautiously, his heart thudding.

"I want to have an affair. With you."

Marcus's blood roared in his ears. He wasn't sure he'd heard her correctly, and what's more, he couldn't hear a damn thing at the moment.

"Marcus?"

He'd been silent too long. "My apologies. Did you say you wanted to have an affair? After everything you just told me?"

She turned toward him, shifting her thigh farther onto the cushion. "Yes. I don't want the memory of Sains—the Blackguard is what I will call him from now on—to be all that I have. I'd like you to erase it by creating something new. With me." She put one hand on his knee. "Will you?"

That she would trust him with this… Not just the tale of what she'd endured, but with helping her to move past it was the most humbling thing he'd ever been asked. "Are you certain?"

She nodded. "Never more. Can you come Saturday night?"

He wanted to flirt with her, to say he hadn't even agreed yet. But was there ever a question? She knew there wasn't. "Yes. I take it you have a plan?"

"I have many." Her answer intrigued him, but then everything about her was so damn fascinating and remarkable, he was continually astonished. "You'll come around midnight. Everyone but the footman should be asleep." She smiled, and her dimples came out in force. He had to stifle the urge to kiss her right then and there. "And me. I'll be waiting. You'll come in through the garden doors and then through there," she pointed toward the door the butler had closed, "then up the stairs. My chamber is on the second floor at the back, overlooking the garden."

"You don't have a trellis or tree I can climb to your window?" he asked with a grin.

"Alas, I do not. Shall I have one installed?"

"Perhaps wait to see if you want to invite me a second time."

"Lord Ripley, where is your arrogant confidence?" Her tone was saucy, her eyes sparkling. "Now, as to my other plans. I've researched how to prevent a pregnancy and—"

He gaped at her as her request finally sunk in. She wanted to have an affair. With him. "You've what?"

"I've purchased sponges."

"I'm impressed." And completely and irrevocably shocked.

"I suppose you could also use a French letter. I assume you know what those are?"

He coughed. "Er, yes. I can bring one. Actually, they need to be soaked prior to use, so I could send it over."

"Ah, yes, I'm aware of how to prepare them. I've done quite a bit of research." And there she went astounding him again. "Which do you think we should use?"

Marcus's cock was growing hard. His brain tried to catch up, but he was still grappling with the fact that *she wanted an affair*. "I don't know. Maybe neither. We may not have intercourse on Saturday."

Really? He'd postpone that when he wanted nothing more than to bury himself inside her?

Yes, really. He wanted to take this slow. She deserved nothing less.

He caressed her face again, stroking his fingers along her temple and down her cheekbone. "I want this to be special."

She smiled, her gaze bold and confident. "It will be. I have no doubt you will make it that way." She tipped her head to the side. "Perhaps we should use the sponge. The woman who sold it to me said the French letter may dull your pleasure a bit."

He shook his head in amazement. "That you would give my pleasure any concern after what you suffered…"

She put her finger against his lips. "Shhh. No more about him."

He kissed the pad of her finger and lightly sucked the tip. Her eyes widened, and her lips parted.

"There are many things we can do that aren't intercourse."

She put her hand back in her lap. "Show me."

"Now?" He glanced toward the door behind her.

"We won't be disturbed. I saw to that."

"Another plan?" At her nod, he went on. "Well, there's kissing, as you know."

"Yes, I *do* know. Show me something new."

His cock lengthened as arousal pumped through him. "May I touch you?" She nodded again. "You must tell me at any moment if you're uncomfortable or if you want me to stop. Tell me *everything* you're feeling."

"Everything?"

"Yes." He wanted so badly for this to be right for her. No, not right: *perfect.*

"May I touch you?" she asked tentatively.

"God, yes. Anyhow and any way."

"You'll also tell me how it feels?"

"Yes." The word came from his mouth sounding like gravel pouring from a bucket. "I know you said it was repetitive, but I'm going to kiss you now because I simply *must.*"

"I didn't say it was repet—"

He silenced her with his mouth, cupping her face with his hands as he moved his lips over hers. Tasting and teasing, tugging and tantalizing. She gasped, and he slid his tongue inside, claiming what she offered and asking for her to give in return. She did so, meeting his gentle thrust with one of her own.

He moved one hand to her nape and the other down her side. Sliding to the floor, he knelt beside the settee. Then he moved her legs onto the cushions and eased her back until she reclined.

He ached to touch her breasts, but he didn't think that was the best place to start. Not after what she'd shared with him. He swept his hand from her nape down over her front, lightly skimming one breast on his way to her belly. Then he moved lower and pressed his hand over her mound.

Drawing back from their kiss, he whispered, "Open your legs. Tell me what you feel here." He pressed again.

"A...quickening. I want...something."

He smiled against her mouth and kissed her again, losing himself for a moment in the rapture of her lips and tongue. Then he began to pull at her skirt, gently tugging it up her calves to her knees, where he reached for the hem. Grasping it, he exposed her thighs, eliciting another gasp from her lips.

He pulled away again. "Do you want me to stop?"

"No, it was just a bit cold. Don't stop, please. I promise I'll tell you if I want you to."

Her trust filled him with awe. And maybe apprehension. He needed to get this right for her.

Keeping his gaze on hers, he slid his hand along her thigh. She twitched softly as he moved between her legs. He left the gown over her hips so she was covered. Given how exposed she'd been last time... Fury rippled through him, and he had to shove it away.

Later, there would be a reckoning.

He lightly stroked her flesh as her eyes took on a sheen of wonder. "Open your legs more," he whispered.

She did as he asked, giving him greater access. He bent his head and kissed her again, softly at first, his lips and tongue mimicking his gentle ministrations on her sex.

Cupping her head, he slanted his mouth over hers as he found her clitoris. She made a noise, and he drank it in, wanting everything she had to give. More than that, he wanted to give her everything.

He went slow, coaxing and teasing her until her hips began to move—slightly at first. He kissed her cheek, her jaw, her ear. "Tell me what you feel."

"I can't explain it." Her words were breathless. "Where you're touching me... It's like starting a fire. The flames are there, but I need it to catch."

He grinned. "Let's see if I can stoke it." He snagged her earlobe with teeth. She gasped, her body rising slightly from the settee.

Marcus slid his fingers down and felt the moisture there. "You're wet," he said against her. "As you should be."

"Why?"

"To ease the way for my cock when I come inside you. But not today." He stroked his finger into her, moving slowly. She was tight and hot around him. He let out a ragged breath.

He kissed her neck, licking over her skin. She arched, and he savored the beauty of her face—her eyes closed, her lips parted, her cheeks flushed with desire. He moved down, finding the hollow of her throat.

She had one hand on his shoulder and the other on his nape, her fingers tangling in his hair. Now, as he thrust his finger deep into her, she tugged, moaning softly.

He wanted more of her, all of her, to give her an ecstasy she would never forget. But for now, this was enough. It had to be. He felt her muscles tightening as they searched for release.

"Let go," he said, trailing his mouth back up her neck and then kissing her once more. He claimed her with a savage intensity. Everywhere he touched her, he poured himself into her.

Withdrawing his finger, he focused on her clitoris once more, pushing her to the edge. "Can you let go?" he asked huskily.

"I don't…know." Her voice was tight, coiled, like a hunter about to strike, but the prey was moving very fast.

Her hips arched, and he drove his finger into her pussy again, using his thumb in fast circles on her clitoris. She clenched hard around him, and he worked his hand over her sex with rapid movements to expand her orgasm as much as he could.

She cried out, and he watched her expression dissolve into rapture. It was the most beautiful thing he'd ever seen. And it was almost enough to make him come too.

He eased her down from release, kissing her again and whispering words of calm and reverence. When at last she opened her eyes, she asked, "Was that *normal?*"

He grinned. "Quite. At least it should be. Sex is not just for men. In fact, sex is better when a woman not only enjoys it but craves it."

Her gaze was dark and cloudy with satisfaction, but she fixed it on him nonetheless. "I think I might be one of those women. I didn't think I was. Thank you."

He pulled her dress down and sat back on his heels. She came up to a sitting position, swinging her legs off the couch. Her cheeks were flushed, her chest still rising and falling steadily as her pulse worked to right itself.

Marcus's heart was also working quickly, and his cock positively throbbed. He'd take care of that when he got home. And what a memory he'd have while he did so.

Had that really just happened?

Yes, and she wanted him to come on Saturday. Did he dare take her all the way then? He wanted to go as slowly as she needed.

"That was quite lovely," she said. "What else can we do that isn't intercourse?"

He chuckled. "Nothing today."

"Saturday, then. And I want to prepare for intercourse. I find I'm quite eager to try it. With you."

He groaned as he got to his feet. "You're going to kill me, Phoebe. Saturday is two days from now."

She rose from the settee, calmly smoothing her gown as if she hadn't just come apart in his arms a short while ago. "Perhaps you should come tomorrow night. I was going to attend a soiree, but that sounds dreadfully dull now."

"What time will you be home?" he answered so quickly that she laughed.

"Let's say one o'clock—come then."

"Done." He closed the distance between them and pulled her into his arms, kissing her hard and fast. When he withdrew, they were both breathless. He rested his forehead against hers. "Dream of me."

"I couldn't do anything else."

Grinning, he caressed her cheek, then turned and left. The butler handed him his coat and gloves on the way out and wished him a good day. Marcus had to think the man knew and gave him credit for acting, convincingly, as though he didn't.

Outside, his joy ebbed slightly as Sainsbury reinvaded his mind. Rage spilled through Marcus as he thought of what the blackguard had done to her. Yes, there would be a reckoning.

CHAPTER 9

*D*reaming of Marcus had made it difficult to sleep.

Yawning, Phoebe stood from the small table in her sitting room that adjoined her bedchamber and padded back to her room to get dressed. Her maid, Page, had already laid out her gown.

"Actually, I plan to go out."

Adjusting course, Page brought a different costume and set about helping Phoebe dress. Then Phoebe sat down at her dressing table so Page could style her hair.

As Page worked, which always seemed to lull Phoebe into a state of relaxation, Phoebe's thoughts turned to the several times she'd awakened in the night, her body warm with desire. She was desperate to know what he had in store. So much so that she was contemplating going in search of a book somewhere. There had to be something that detailed sex.

Telling him about Sainsbury had been easier than she'd imagined. Easier than telling her mother. But then Marcus had been incredibly caring and sensitive. The difference between him and Sainsbury was cavernous. It was as though they were different species.

An idea struck her. Perhaps she could call on Lavinia. As a married woman, and as Phoebe's friend, she would probably answer her questions. And maybe even tell her where to find such a book. She had to believe Lavinia's husband, the renowned Duke of Seduction, would know all about the written words of sex.

Phoebe blushed. Marcus had turned her into a complete wanton in the space of a day. And she couldn't be more thrilled. *This* was what it meant to be independent, to be free of stupid rules and expectations. This was what it felt like to be a man.

She snorted.

Page paused in her work. "Miss Lennox? Did I hurt you?" She was young—younger than Phoebe— and sometimes a bit skittish. That trait had drawn Phoebe to hire the young woman as her personal maid after meeting her in her great-aunt's household. Page had relaxed in the months that she'd been with Phoebe and had started to gain confidence.

"Not at all. My apologies, I was just thinking of something frustrating."

Nodding, Page finished Phoebe's hair and went in search of a hat and gloves while Phoebe put on her walking boots. Phoebe glanced outside at the gray day. "I hope it doesn't rain."

Not that she truly cared. It could thunder and rain, and she'd still be giddy.

Page brought her accessories as Phoebe stood. "You look lovely, Miss."

She smiled at the maid. "Only because of you."

Eager to visit Lavinia, Phoebe hurried downstairs, then came to a hard stop when she arrived at the entry hall. Standing inside as Culpepper closed the door, her mother looked pale and distraught.

"Mama," Phoebe said, depositing her hat and gloves on a table. "What's wrong?"

"It's your father. We had a terrible quarrel."

So much for visiting Lavinia. Phoebe took her mother's gloves and hat and set them next to her own. "Culpepper, we'll have tea in the garden room." Then she linked her arm through her mother's and guided her toward the back of the house.

Mama sank down on the settee. The one Marcus had pleasured Phoebe on the day before. Phoebe tried not to think about that. She took a chair nearby and asked what happened.

"He sold the painting."

Phoebe could see she was upset and sought to soothe her. "That's all right. I said he could."

"He's using the money for another investment." Mama's dark brows pitched over her eyes as her mouth tightened. "I asked him not to do that, but he has no concern for my wishes."

"It might not be so bad," Phoebe said. "I have investments, and so far, they've proven profitable. Papa just suffered a bit of bad luck."

Mama shook her head. "He's lost two of them, and I believe they are with this same person. He goes on about 'him' when he's ranting about the losses."

"Who?"

"I don't know. Someone he meets at night—in Leicester Square. I only know where because I asked the coachman." Mama twisted her hands together and then set them in her lap. Then she abruptly stood and stalked toward the doors that led to the garden. Turning, she gave Phoebe a tentative look. "May I stay with you for a few days?"

"Here?" Phoebe could hardly believe her mother wanted to stay with her when she'd been so displeased that she'd purchased her own house in the first place. But it was more than that. If she stayed here, Phoebe couldn't very well have Marcus over to conduct an affair.

"If it's not too much trouble. I'm just so angry with your father. He needs to learn to take me seriously."

After over thirty years of marriage, and one in which he was most definitely in command, Phoebe wasn't sure her father was going to learn anything, but she kept her mouth closed.

Culpepper arrived with the tea. He set the tray on a table near the garden doors and asked if he should pour.

"No, thank you," Phoebe said. The butler turned to go, and Phoebe passed him as she went to sit at the table. "Culpepper, please have the spring bedroom prepared for my mother. She'll be staying with us for a few days."

He inclined his head. "Of course."

"Would you send a footman to fetch my trunk from the coach?" Mama asked.

It was a good thing Phoebe had said yes to her request. Not that she would have said no. She would always provide help and support for her parents. Frustrating as they were, she loved them. She was also keenly aware that she was their only remaining child and that she'd disappointed them gravely. While she didn't regret her choices—and wouldn't change them—she supposed she would always want to heal that rift.

Culpepper departed, and they sat down. Phoebe poured the tea.

"I interrupted you on your way out," Mama said. "I don't mean to be a bother."

"It's quite all right. I'll still go out—in a bit." Phoebe dropped sugar into their cups. "You'll need to get settled."

"Thank you for understanding, dear." She stirred her tea, then took a sip. When she looked at Phoebe next, her eyes were clouded. "I've thought a great

deal about what you told me the other day. It was...
difficult to hear."

And Phoebe hadn't even revealed the specifics,
not as she had with Marcus. "It was more difficult to
experience, I assure you."

Mama flinched. "I wanted to ask if I could tell
your father. I think he should know. It would help
him understand." She cocked her head to the side
and then straightened it again. "It might also prompt
him to violence, so perhaps we'll keep it between us."

Phoebe thought of Marcus's reaction. His anger
had been palpable. She'd gloried in its ferocity. Still,
she didn't want him to act on it. "While I would
like nothing more than for Sainsbury to suffer, I
would prefer to put the entire thing behind me. If
you think telling Papa would help do that, then
please tell him. I'd rather he stop bringing Sainsbury
up."

"I'll try to think of how to do it. When I'm no
longer angry with him." Mama scowled at her cup.
"Do you still want to go to the soiree tonight?"
They'd planned to go together.

"We don't have to." Phoebe tried not to sound
disinterested, but she was disappointed about her
plans with Marcus being ruined. She'd have to send
him a note. Or...

Phoebe took another sip of tea, then stood. "I'll
go out now. Please let Culpepper know if you need
anything. I'll see you for dinner."

Mama reached for her hand and gave it a quick
squeeze. "Thank you, Phoebe. I haven't been as supportive of you as I ought to have been. I will be
now."

"I appreciate that." Phoebe turned and left, eager
to be on her way.

She went into the entry hall and donned her hat.
"Culpepper, is the coach still outside?" She realized

she hadn't given any direction in the midst of her mother's surprise arrival.

"Yes."

"Excellent, thank you." Pulling on her gloves, she left the house. Outside, she gave the coachman her direction. "Hanover Square, please."

It wasn't very far, but she didn't want to be seen walking there. She wasn't going to Lavinia's.

A short while later, the coach stopped in front of one of the grandest homes in the square. Wide windows flanked the massive door, which stood at the top of a short flight of stone stairs.

The coachman helped her down, and she walked up to the house. She didn't have to knock, for the door opened to reveal a tall butler with a sharp nose. He was in his middle age and possessed kind eyes. She thought so because of the lines that indicated he smiled often. How peculiar for a butler, since they were often so austere. But then she imagined Marcus might give him ample opportunity to smile.

"Good afternoon. Miss Lennox to see Lord Ripley."

The butler closed the door as she stepped into the grand entry hall. Stairs climbed each side, meeting in the middle over an archway that led straight back to the rest of the house. A landscape by Joshua Reynolds hung on the right beneath the stairs.

"I'll show you to the drawing room," the butler said, gesturing toward the stairs on the right. She followed him up, taking in the paintings on the wall. An alcove halfway up held a tall Wedgwood creamware vase. She glanced across the hall to the other alcove and saw that it held the urn's twin.

She wondered who'd decorated his house. She would never have guessed the Marquess of Ripley lived in such an elegantly appointed residence.

The butler showed her into the drawing room to the right of the stairs. The room was massive, quite large enough for a ball if the furniture was moved out. She was left alone and took the opportunity to circuit the room. There were five seating areas, with ample space between each one. Two in front of the windows that overlooked the square, one near the doorway, and a large one that was in the back and center of the room, and finally a cozy gathering in front of the hearth. The space managed to be spectacular and warm at the same time.

"My God, you *are* here."

She turned from where she stood near the hearth, and her body reacted to seeing him—turning hot and tight in an instant. "Yes."

He came into the room, grinning. "Welcome to my home."

"It's stunning." Her gaze swept the room. "Did you select all the furnishings? It's so...tasteful."

He stopped just in front of her, his eyes glinting with mischief. "What did you expect, beds stretching from wall to wall?" He laughed at her expression of horrified surprise. "My apologies. I make that jest whenever someone new comes to visit, which isn't often." He leaned close. "No one dares."

Her pulse sped. "I dare."

"I'm the luckiest man alive." He took her hand and lifted it, pressing a lingering kiss to her wrist. Then he inhaled. "You smell divine. Always."

The insistent throb he'd aroused in her sex the day before returned with force, making her tremble. "I came to tell you we have to cancel our plans for this evening."

"I'm sorry to hear that," he said, tugging the edge of her glove back to kiss the heel of her hand. "Tomorrow, then."

"No." Her voice sounded a bit strangled. "No,"

she tried again. "I'm afraid that won't be possible either. My mother has come to stay for a few days."

His lips froze against her flesh, and he raised his head, frowning. "Well, that's disappointing."

His chagrin was so complete that it drew a laugh from her. What else could she do? "Quite. I hope she'll be gone by Monday or Tuesday. My father won't last that long without her. They had a disagreement over money."

"That doesn't sound good."

She shook her head. "Why did you stop?"

He glanced at her hand. "You want me to continue?"

They were alone. Their plans for later were foiled. Why not take advantage of right now? "Please. If you don't mind."

"Never." He kept his eyes on hers as he pulled the glove from her hand, then he kissed her palm, using his tongue to trace the lines there, watching her while she watched him.

Phoebe had never imagined such a simple act could be so erotic. He moved to her other hand, removing the glove, and repeating his seduction with his lips and tongue. When he'd said there were other things they could do besides intercourse, this hadn't even registered as a possibility. And yet here she was, quivering and desperate for more.

"Should I keep going?" he asked, the deep timbre of his voice sending shocks of want through her.

"Yes." She glanced toward the open doorway.

He noticed. Clasping her hand, he drew her across the room to a closed door, which he opened, and pulled her over the threshold. He closed the door with a firm click, shutting them into a much smaller, rather dim space.

"This is the music room."

She looked around and saw a pianoforte as well

as a few mismatched chairs and a chaise. "You don't come in here."

"I do not. It appears to be used for a bit of storage—the perfect place for privacy." He arched a dark brow as he pulled her against him. "Unless you'd rather I carry you up to my bedchamber?"

The pulse in her sex intensified. Before she could answer, he spoke again. "Perhaps not today. We are taking this slow, after all. Furthermore, I didn't soak a French letter. I don't suppose you brought a sponge?"

She shook her head, unable to speak. He was warm and solid against her, and her breasts tingled where they touched. She hadn't thought she would feel anything resembling pleasure when it came to her breasts, where—

No, she wouldn't think of that.

Overcome, she stood on her toes and curled her arms around his neck, then kissed him. She was a terrible novice, but hopefully what she lacked in skill, she made up for with zeal. Applying all she'd learned from him, she opened her mouth and touched her tongue to his lips. He met her with a soft moan, his arms pulling her more tightly against him.

The sensation in her breasts heightened, making them feel heavy and...aching. She wanted him to touch them. Almost as badly as she wanted him to touch her sex again.

She pressed her chest to his and tugged at his hair as she angled her head to spear her tongue deeper into his mouth. He pulled back, and she feared she'd done something wrong.

"Dear God, Phoebe," he breathed. "You are magnificent. Are you ready for the next step?"

"Yes. Please. Tell me what to do." She threw off

her hat, uncaring of where it landed. "I want to do what you did for me the other day."

His eyes darkened to nearly black, the pupils dilating. "You want to—" He gave his head a shake. "Later. This is about you first. Always."

"You're not touching me," she complained, eager for whatever this step entailed.

"My apologies." He took her hand and led her to the chaise. "Will you sit?"

She did so. "I want you to…" She faltered.

He perched on the chaise, folding one leg atop the cushion so that he faced her. "You want me to what? Don't ever be embarrassed or ashamed to ask for what you want, especially in the bedroom." He glanced about. "Or the unused music storage room."

She smiled, then worked up the courage to say what she wanted. "I can't believe I'm asking, but I want you to touch my breasts. They seem to, um, want you to."

He blinked, surprised at the request. "Well, I am not one to disappoint you or your breasts. How does this gown unfasten?"

She turned to present her back. "It's a drop front. Untie it."

He plucked at the tie, and she felt the gown loosen around the bodice. When she turned back, she opened the fabric, exposing her corset and the chemise beneath.

Slowly, he lifted his hand and drew his fingers over the upper curve of her breast. "You're certain?"

Desire trailed in the wake of his touch, stoking the fire he'd started the day before. "Yes." She lifted her hands to untie her corset below her breasts.

"May I?" He put his hands over hers, and she moved out of his way.

Picking at the laces, he untied them. He leaned forward and kissed her, his lips and tongue stealing her breath and equilibrium. She felt light again, ready to fly at any moment. He tugged her chemise down and apart, then loosed the top of her chemise. Cool air caressed her bare skin and then his fingers did the same.

He gently stroked her flesh, drawing circles around her nipple as he continued his gentle assault on her mouth. She whimpered with need as he drew closer to the tip. She clutched his shoulders, wordlessly begging him to give her what she didn't know she wanted.

His hand closed around her briefly, then cupped her from underneath, lifting the weighty globe. At last, his thumb dragged across her nipple. She gasped into his mouth and then moaned when his thumb and finger closed softly around her. When he tugged —ever so gently—she thought she might go mad.

Suddenly, his mouth was gone from hers. He was kissing her jaw and neck again. She loved the feel of him ravishing her flesh, as if he couldn't get enough of her. She moved her hands up into his hair, holding him to her and basking in his touch. He delved lower still, licking along her collarbone and then dipping over her breast.

She inhaled sharply, and he paused. Her fingers tightened around his scalp. "Don't stop."

He cupped her breast as his lips grazed her skin, leaving a path of heat and need. Then his mouth was on her nipple, wet and tantalizing as he suckled her.

Sensation overwhelmed her. She closed her eyes. Rapture bloomed and spread like a field of wildflowers opening to the sun. Desire, urgent and encompassing, pooled in her sex, growing with each lick of his tongue and caress of his fingers.

She held him against her, reveling in the pleasure building within her. It was just like the day before, her body rushing toward that magnificent release.

He guided her back on the chaise, pushing her up the cushions. Then he left her breast. She opened her eyes and saw that he was staring down at her.

"You're unbearably beautiful."

"Really? You can't bear it?" She reached for her chemise. "Should I cover myself?"

He grinned, recognizing that she was joking. "Don't you dare. I *will* bear it. I want to see more. May I?" He reached for the hem of her skirt.

She clasped the folds near her waist and pulled the fabric up in answer to his question. "Is that what you want?"

"Higher."

Kneeling between her calves, he watched her legs as she tugged the fabric. Realizing she could taunt him the way he did her, she moved slowly, revealing herself bit by bit—her knees, her thighs, higher still until the hem of her gown was at her waist.

"Open your legs." His voice had gone incredibly deep so that the words sounded like a command.

She parted her thighs, again moving slowly. When she thought she should stop, she opened them further, until she felt more exposed than she ever had in her life. The chaise wasn't wide enough, so she let her legs drape over the sides.

"Perfection," he murmured, moving between her legs, his gaze locked on her sex.

Looking at him fully dressed, a dark lock of hair hanging over his forehead, she was overcome by his masculine beauty. And the fact that she couldn't see very much of him.

Arranging the gown at her waist and pushing the weight of it to one side, she sat forward and reached for his cravat, pulling the ends from his waistcoat. He looked up at her as she untied the silk and slid it from around his neck. She brought it to her nose and inhaled. It smelled so much like him, she never wanted to return it. She clutched it in her hand and watched as he removed his coat and dropped it to the floor.

"The waistcoat too." Now she sounded like him, ordering him about.

He arched a brow but said nothing as he unbuttoned the garment. This game was almost as arousing as when he actually touched her.

The waistcoat followed his coat to the floor. He prowled up the chaise, and she reclined as he came up over her. He braced his hands on either side of her and kissed her, exploring her mouth with passion and tenderness. When he drew back, he tugged her lower lip with his teeth. "Do you trust me?"

"Yes."

"Good." He pinned her with a dark, seductive stare. "Remember that everything you feel and do is right. *Everything.*"

He kissed her again before returning his attention to her breasts. He worked at a feverish pace this time, using his lips, tongue, and fingers to tease her nipples into hard, aching buds. She cast her head back and closed her eyes, surrendering to his touch. When he pinched her, she gasped, but not from any pain. Sharp desire pulsed in her sex.

As if he knew that was precisely what had happened, his hand moved between her thighs. He grazed her heated flesh, slowly, gently, then with more purpose, his fingers tangling in the curls and finding her clitoris. When he pressed her there—like he was now—she knew she could fly.

Her hips shot up off the chaise, and she moaned.

Then something wet was against her. She opened her eyes and looked down—at the top of his head. Oh God, he was using his mouth. Was that even right?

Remember that everything you feel and do is right.

She took that to include everything he did to her. And how could anything that felt this extraordinary be wrong? She shivered with want as his tongue explored her sex, licking and teasing. Then driving right into her as his finger had done the day before.

She bucked up, unable to contain her reaction. Instinctively, she grabbed his head.

He clasped one of her thighs. "Wrap your legs around me."

She couldn't… Except she did. This couldn't possibly be right. Except it was.

Robbed of coherent thought, she arched up, wanting more of him. And he gave it to her, adding his finger to her sheath. He pumped in and out as his mouth drove her to the brink of sanity. This was familiar. The sky beckoned. She just had to let go and take flight.

He drove his finger deep inside her, and she bore down, crying out as her release flooded her senses. Her legs quivered helplessly around him as she rode the tide.

She had no idea how long it went on, but eventually, he eased her legs from him and laid them flat along the chaise. All she heard was the sound of her heart and blood pounding, a staccato rhythm of satisfaction and joy.

"I had no idea that was possible." She opened her eyes to see him standing next to the chaise. Her gaze was instantly drawn to the thick bulge of his sex pressing against his breeches.

The sight of Sainsbury's long, thin member flashed in her mind. She closed her eyes to banish the image, then opened them again.

"Do you need help with your clothing?" he asked.

Such a thoughtful man. So caring and generous. Phoebe sat up and brought her legs around to the same side of the chaise as him. Then she scooted over until she sat directly in front of him. "Not yet. I'd rather help you with yours."

He looked down at her, his brow furrowed in question. "I can manage."

"I know, but I think I'd like to unbutton your fall myself." She lifted her hand to his breeches and flicked the first button open.

"*Phoebe.*" His nostrils flared, and he put his hand over hers. "Not today."

"Yes, today." She needed to expel the Blackguard from her mind for good. "I need to do this. I showed you mine. Time for you to show me yours."

"Fine." The word was tight and hard. "But you're only looking."

He moved her hand to her lap, then finished what she'd started. With each button he freed, her heart beat faster. Shockingly, desire rippled through her again.

The fall of his breeches dropped, but his shirt covered what she was trying to see. She lifted her hand again, to move the fabric, but he did it first, lifting the lawn to expose his sex.

It looked nothing like Sainsbury's. Thick and long with a dark nest of curls at the base, the flesh appeared like velvet. She needed to know if that was true.

She glanced up at him, her voice carrying a note of apology wrapped in anticipation. "I'm afraid I'm going to have to touch you."

CHAPTER 10

*P*leasure jolted through Marcus as Phoebe's hand gently wrapped around his flesh. "You were just supposed to look." He ground the words out as if he were being tortured. And he supposed he was. He'd been working so hard to keep a rein on himself, to stifle his needs for another time.

"I did try, but you're too touchable."

He nearly laughed, but he couldn't while trying to maintain his self-control. He'd been trying so damn hard to take things slow with her. "You aren't supposed to be doing this."

"You said that already." She slid her hand down his shaft, her attention focused entirely on him.

He thought of her past experience with that blackguard Sainsbury and felt horrible for enjoying this. She shouldn't be doing it. Not yet. "Phoebe—"

"Don't tell me to stop." She paused as she brought her hand back up to the tip and looked up at him, her green eyes dark and beautiful. "Unless you really want me to. I want to touch you. I'm *enjoying* touching you. In fact, I'm considering putting my mouth on you. Is that done?"

Bloody hell. "Yes, that's done. But you don't—"

He didn't get the words out because she'd pushed

back his foreskin, and put her lips on the head of his cock, kissing him. Then they moved down the side, her softness teasing and coaxing him. As if he needed any help in getting to the edge of release.

"You should probably tell me what to do," she said between kisses. "Otherwise, I'll have to make it up."

"You're doing a fine job so far." His body, taut with lust, shuddered as she tentatively touched him with her tongue. He caressed the back of her head. "Yes."

"Yes?" She used more of her tongue, licking along his length.

He groaned, unsure of how long he would last. And he didn't want to surprise her or disgust her, given what she'd endured before. "Phoebe, at some point, I'm going to come."

She tipped her head back and looked up at him again. "In my mouth?"

Oh God, did she want him to? No, he was absolutely drawing the line there. "Not today." He saw his cravat next to her on the floor. "Hand me my cravat."

She did so, then stroked him as she dropped her head once more. "You'll tell me when?"

"Yes." The word drew out on his tongue as she took him back into her mouth. "*Phoebe.*" He gripped her scalp and took great care not to thrust. It was incredibly difficult.

Her tongue swirled over his flesh, and he nearly lost himself. Then she sucked, pulling a loud groan from his lips as her hand stroked up and down his shaft.

He was not going to last. If she took him farther into her mouth, he was done.

She took him farther into her mouth.

Holding him firm, she moved her lips down over

him, flattening her tongue. Her mouth and hand squeezed around him. His balls tightened, and he gasped. "Phoebe. Move. Just a bit." He couldn't help himself. He wanted this from her. He needed it.

She retreated to the tip, then came back down over him, engulfing his flesh. He watched her suck him, her hand wrapped around his cock, and knew the end was near.

He closed his eyes and allowed himself to just feel for a thrust or two. Three... Four... That was it. He pulled away from her and pivoted, thrusting himself into the cravat in his hand as his orgasm crashed over him. He grunted as his body trembled with the force of his release.

When he could grasp hold of his senses, he opened his eyes. Wiping himself clean, he wadded the cravat and tossed it to one of the chairs. Then he buttoned his fall before turning back to her.

Phoebe sat at the edge of the chaise, her dress back in place as she fought to tie the strings behind her back.

"Here, let me," he offered.

She stood and presented her back. He took care of setting her to rights. "All finished."

She turned to face him, her cheeks flushed, her gaze shimmering with contentment. "I hope you don't mind what I did."

"On the contrary, I would walk through fire to experience that again." Not just the physical gratification of it. More than that, it was her generosity and her sweetness that had enthralled him.

She laughed. "I can't imagine that would be necessary." Her gaze fell on the open neck of his shirt. "Next time, you should take off your shirt."

Next time... "I'll be happy to. Whenever that is."

"Hopefully, my mother won't be with me more than a few days. My father will either come to his senses and forego his investment scheme, or my mother will admit defeat and return home. I do hope it's the former."

He bent to pick up his waistcoat, then pulled it on. "Why is that? Is there something wrong with his scheme?"

"He's lost money on two prior investments with this same person." She began to button his waistcoat for him. It was a rather intimate task, and one that no other woman had performed for him. Surprisingly, he liked it. "Have you ever heard of meeting someone at night in Leicester Square for the purposes of investing?"

Marcus froze. He put his hands over hers as she fastened the last button. "Leicester Square?"

She nodded. "My mother said he goes to meet some man there. That's not how my investments are handled at all."

He took her hands in his and pressed his lips together. "Phoebe, this doesn't sound like a good strategy, particularly if he's already lost money on prior investments. You said they were with the same person?" Marcus needed to find his bloody cousin.

"I think so. Mama didn't know his name, so I can't say for certain."

Marcus looked at her intently. "You must tell him not to invest."

"I don't think he'll listen to me," she said wryly. "I tried to offer assistance when I learned they were having financial trouble. His pride won't allow it."

The bloody fool. Marcus couldn't stand by while he lost more money. "I believe this man he's meeting in Leicester Square—rather, that man's employer—is a swindler."

Phoebe sucked in a breath. "You've heard of him?" She narrowed her eyes suddenly. "Is this the same man who cheated Arabella's father and the former Duke of Halstead?"

"You know about that?" He let go of her hands and exhaled, then turned to pick up his coat. "Unfortunately, the swindler is my cousin."

She touched his arm. "The man you fought with in the park the day we met?"

"Yes." He let out an ironic chuckle. "He's an utter scoundrel, but if I hadn't fought with him that day, I wouldn't have met you."

Her lips curved into sultry smile. "Then he's not completely horrid."

"Oh, I'm afraid he is. He's gone missing. I've been trying desperately to find him—to stop him. Now, that's more important than ever."

She stepped toward him and curled her arms around his waist. "Thank you. I'll try to talk my father out of it."

Marcus hated that he'd already lost money to Drobbit. He couldn't let that happen again. Only it seemed imminent. Which meant... "If your father is planning to make another investment, he would know where to find my cousin—or at least his assistant, Osborne."

She looked up at him with a shrug. "I suppose? I could try to find out, if that would help."

"It would, thank you. I need to put a stop to Drobbit's villainy."

She pulled her hands to his front and slid them up his chest. Then she tucked them into the collar of his shirt so her bare hands were against his flesh. Desire swirled within him. He was sorry she had to go.

To punctuate that sentiment, she stood on her toes and kissed him, her lips and tongue teasing him into a half cockstand as if he hadn't just reveled in a powerful release a short time ago. It was she who ended the embrace, stepping back from him with heat and desire in her gaze.

"I must return home."

He wanted nothing more than to take her upstairs to his chamber and lock them both inside for the rest of the day. Forever, maybe.

He bent to retrieve her gloves, which he'd dropped at some point after they'd come to this room. Then he fetched her hat. "Yes. Keep me apprised of your house guest."

She laughed softly. "I will." She glanced at his coat as she took her gloves from him. "I don't suppose you can properly dress given the state of your cravat."

"No." He grinned, then turned to open the door to the drawing room. He held it for her. "After you."

She walked past him, then waited for him to follow. "Won't your retainers see your...state and conclude what we've been about?"

"Perhaps." Probably, but he didn't care. "They are incredibly discreet."

"Because you bring women here regularly." The words chilled him on their own, but she said it so pragmatically that he flinched.

He moved closer to her. "I don't."

He had, however, hosted the occasional party that often included sexual activities. Just a few weeks ago, he'd hosted a party with courtesans for the purpose of drawing Drobbit and Osborne out. It had worked. Hell, he'd do it again, but since Drobbit knew he was aware of his schemes, Marcus doubted his cousin would come within ten feet of his house.

"To be fair, you didn't bring me here either."

He took her hand. "Phoebe, I can't pretend I haven't been with other women. You know my reputation. It's not inaccurate."

"Are there any now? Other women."

"No." And there'd never been one like her. A virgin with whom he planned to have an affair. Actually, weren't they already having one? He gazed down at her, unblinking. "There is only you."

Her eyes heated with pleasure. "Good. I don't like to share."

He pulled her against his chest. "Me neither." He kissed her, a hungry claiming of her mouth that declared his intent to take her—and no one else.

After several minutes, they parted, and she rested her head against his chest with a sigh. "I really must go. My hat?" She exchanged her gloves with him for her hat, and when she had the latter fixed atop her head, she took the gloves back, swiftly donning them.

He offered her his arm and escorted her downstairs.

"I'll let you know when I've spoken to my father."

"Yes, do." He resisted the urge to kiss her again. Instead, he watched her as she departed and didn't close the door entirely until she was in her coach and it was moving away.

He turned to see Dorne watching him with a peculiar expression. "Whatever you're thinking, just keep it to yourself."

The butler inclined his head. "Of course, my lord. May I say that Miss Lennox seems charming?"

"She is." She was also intelligent, witty, delightful, kindhearted, and an utter joy to spend time with. And the things she could do with her tongue…

Marcus dashed up the stairs to fetch his abandoned clothing from the music room. Once there, he was assaulted with the musky smell of their sex. He lingered.

When at last he left, he turned his mind to Drobbit and the urgency he now had in stopping the man. It was time to tell Harry everything he knew, Drobbit be damned.

And when he got his hands on his cousin, the man was going to be very sorry he'd chosen Phoebe's father as his next victim.

~

*A*fter three days with her mother in residence, Phoebe was at her wit's end. She'd come to realize one of the things she loved best about her independent life—she didn't have to live with her parents.

Mama had taken up a position in the garden room, Phoebe's favorite place. There, she took breakfast, read the paper, ate luncheon, did her needlework, wrote correspondence, and talked. And talked. Phoebe had forgotten just how much the woman liked to talk.

And then there was the fact that Phoebe wasn't able to pursue her affair with Marcus. She'd considered paying another call and telling her mother she was visiting Lavinia. However, that idea had evaporated when Lavinia had gone into labor the day before yesterday. She and Beck were now the proud parents of a baby boy.

Then Phoebe had planned to say she would visit Jane. Before she could do so, Jane and her mother had arrived. Mama had invited them, unbeknownst to Phoebe. She'd begun to feel as if her house wasn't actually hers.

The worst part was that Mama had dragged her to church yesterday in the hope of seeing her father. He hadn't gone. Plenty of other people had, however, and Phoebe had been keenly aware of the derisive looks and whispered remarks. Mama, for her part, had seemed oblivious, and for that, Phoebe was grateful.

So here she was, back at her parents' house in the hope that she could convince her father to make amends.

Foster welcomed her and immediately asked how her mother was faring.

"She's quite well," Phoebe said. "Though, she misses Papa." While she was still angry with him, it was clear from the amount of time she spent talking about him that she was ready to come home. Even if she didn't realize it.

"I came to see if I can't find a way to smooth things between them. Will you tell my father I'm here?"

"He is in a meeting, but I will let him know," Foster said. "Do you want to wait in the sitting room?"

"I will, thank you."

Before she turned, Foster said, "I know you've been keen to determine how Harkin and Meg are faring since they were let go. Both have found positions. Harkin has become maid to Lady Knox, and Meg is working in, er, Mr. Sainsbury's household." He glanced away with a bit of discomfort as he said Sainsbury's name.

Phoebe's stomach tightened. "I'm pleased to hear about Harkin."

"But not about Meg?" Foster's brow furrowed. "Should we be concerned about her employment?"

Summoning a weak smile, Phoebe said, "I'm sure it's fine." She'd check on Meg to make sure.

Phoebe made her way toward the sitting room, her mind churning. She nearly ran into a man who'd apparently just left her father's study. He was very tall and carried a walking stick. "Pardon me," he said with a deep voice before continuing on his way.

Pausing on the threshold of the sitting room, she watched as he went to the entry hall. Then she turned and circuited the room as she waited for her father. She frowned halfway around, noticing that a few things were missing.

Papa came in, and it seemed a dark cloud followed him. Deep creases lined his forehead, and his brows were pitched at a sharp angle over his hazel eyes. "Is your mother with you?"

"No. Papa, have you sold some things, such as the silver box that sat on the mantel?"

"That's none of your concern."

Phoebe folded her arms. "Who was the man I saw leaving your study?"

"Also none of your concern."

She frowned. "I will always have concern for you. And for Mama. She needs to come home."

"Does she want to?"

"Of course." Deep down, Phoebe was certain of that. "Just as you want her to."

"Is she going to harangue me about what I do with my money?"

"Is it so terrible if she does?" Phoebe unfolded her arms and took a few steps toward him. "Papa, she's worried about losing more money to this mad investment scheme."

"She called it mad?"

"No. I was being hyperbolic." And she shouldn't. Not with him, and not now. "She has a right to be concerned. You've had two investments go poorly, you're selling things, and you've had to let retainers go. There's no shame in admitting things didn't go as planned. If you must invest, do something different. Don't use this same person."

His eyes sparked with anger. "I'll do whatever I please."

Phoebe knew the man wasn't Marcus's cousin.

She'd seen him in the park the day she'd met Marcus, and if she recalled correctly, Drobbit was short and stocky. "Was the man's name Osborne? If so, he works for a man called Drobbit. I have it on good authority that Drobbit is a swindler."

Papa's eyes widened briefly, then the sullen mask came back into place. "No. As I said, none of this is your concern. Tell your mother I am making a different kind of investment—with the man you saw. It's safer and is guaranteed not to fail."

Phoebe knew better than to believe that, but she also knew better than to argue with him any further. "All right. I'll tell her that." That would be enough to persuade her to come home. "Don't you miss her, Papa?"

He grunted, but she saw the softening in his expression. "It's quiet here."

"I'm sure it is," she said drolly. "My house, on the contrary, is not."

"Is that the real reason you live alone?"

She noted the edge of humor in the question and was so glad to hear it, she thought she might giggle with joy. "I will never say." She smiled at him and winked. "How about I ask Cook to make her favorite dessert? I'll bring her over in time for dinner."

"You'll stay too? For dinner, I mean."

She knew he wished she'd come home to stay—until she wed. But maybe, just maybe, he was beginning to accept the choices she'd made. For a brief moment, she wondered if Mama had told him about the Blackguard, but realized he would *not* have taken that well.

"Of course. I'll go speak with Cook."

He looked relieved, his shoulders dipping and his frame relaxing.

Phoebe paused as she walked past him and

lightly touched his arm. Then she continued on and went downstairs to speak with Cook.

As she climbed into her coach a short while later, she fell back onto the seat with a smile. Her mother was likely going home. That meant Marcus could come that night. She'd dispatch a note to him as soon as she got home.

She thought about the man with the cane and whether he could be Osborne. She'd ask Marcus about him that night. Phoebe could describe him— the man had been almost unnaturally tall.

Assuming he was Osborne, she could try to help Marcus find him. Presumably, Papa was able to communicate with them. She could tell him she wanted to meet with the man about investing. If it was a safe and guaranteed investment, he would have no problem helping her. And if it wasn't?

She pursed her lips as she pondered how to help Marcus. Maybe there was something in her father's study that would lead them to Drobbit or Osborne. She could surely create an opportunity to look... Yes, that seemed the best course of action. She only hoped she was able to find something that would be of use to Marcus.

He'd be so thrilled. She could hardly wait to see him.

CHAPTER 11

*E*nergy sparked through Marcus as he stepped into White's. He was a rare visitor, but for the fourth night in a row, he found himself there once again. He sincerely hoped Sainsbury finally showed up.

After Marcus accomplished his objective, he'd move on to something even better: going to Phoebe's house.

Her note that afternoon had been a welcome surprise. At last, her mother was returning home. He smiled thinking of what she'd written: *You're cordially invited to attend me at midnight for the purposes of ravishment.*

It was all he could do to focus on the matter at hand, but he was fairly motivated to his cause. He walked into the main room and looked about for his quarry. Sighting him near the center of the room, Marcus felt his pulse begin to drum. *At fucking last.*

Marcus began to thread his way through the gentlemen gathered, moving slowly to exchange pleasantries, lest it become obvious he was on a single-minded mission. He was here to punish Sainsbury in any way possible. He'd call the blackguard out if it wouldn't have further impacted Phoebe. What reason could Marcus give for demanding satisfaction aside from avenging her?

It took everything Marcus had not to march right over to Sainsbury and knock him to the ground. Hit him so hard, the man wouldn't ever be able to get up.

For a moment, Marcus froze. The busy room around him slowed to nothing, and the sound disappeared. This wasn't him. He didn't let emotion rule the day. Ever.

Everything started again, a whir of noise and light. He lingered near Sainsbury, close enough to hear him speak.

"I wish she had something better to grip, if you know what I mean." Sainsbury, a man of middling height with a small nose and pronounced chin, lifted his hands and mimicked grabbing a woman's breasts to indicate precisely what he meant, to the sniggers of those around him. "Still, she's extremely biddable, which is a far more important trait." Sainsbury brushed back a lock of dark blond hair on the side of his head.

This was met with nods in his small circle. Marcus's hands fisted. He hung back and listened.

"I agree," another man said. "My wife is well-mannered, does exactly what she must."

"Are you going to propose, then?" This came from a second man, who looked at Sainsbury expectantly.

"Not yet, but I'm considering it." He swore under his breath, then laughed. "Now you'll all spread rumors, and I'll be dragged to the altar."

Marcus sniggered to himself. That was probably the only way he could get there. If someone was stupid enough to bother.

"We would never say anything that could ensnare you in the parson's trap," the first man said, clapping his hand on Sainsbury's shoulder. "Especially after the way you were woefully mistreated last time. You must be certain you choose wisely."

The urge to strike the man for simply referring to Phoebe as an unwise choice nearly overwhelmed Marcus. Dammit, this was not who he was. Perhaps he should go. She was waiting for him—or would be soon.

"I *was* mistreated, but don't worry. I got at least a little something out of her." Sainsbury chuckled, and there was a disgusting glint of pride in his eye. Marcus longed to blacken it.

This was his moment. He pretended to trip, falling into one of Sainsbury's companions. This drew the attention of everyone in the immediate vicinity.

"My apologies," Marcus said, straightening. "Did I hear you discussing Sainsbury's upcoming betrothal?" he asked loudly.

"No," Sainsbury said, his brows darting low over his narrowing eyes.

"My mistake," Marcus said with a flat smile. "Was it your seductive prowess, then?"

One of the men snorted a laugh.

Sainsbury's thin lips twisted into a grin. "Yes, that was it."

Marcus adopted a pensive expression. "How peculiar. It's my understanding you're unable to perform at some of London's finest brothels."

Sainsbury's eyes darkened to nearly black as he glared at Marcus. "That's a bloody lie, Ripley."

"How would you even know?" one of the other men asked, turning toward Marcus. He was very young and likely didn't realize the stupidity of his question.

Laughing, Marcus slapped the buck on his upper back. "You must not be aware of my reputation. I know plenty about London's finest brothels. Who visits them and how often, as well as whether the guests are appreciated." He winked at the young man. "I'm *quite* appreciated, and therefore, I hear a great many comparisons."

Around the inner circle, men guffawed. Someone nudged Marcus on the shoulder with a laugh.

"So Sainsbury's got a broken branch?" someone asked from somewhere behind Sainsbury.

Marcus lifted a shoulder. "Seems to be the case from what I hear—from multiple sources, mind you."

Sainsbury's lips turned white and practically disappeared into his too-long chin. "Damn you, Ripley. That's a bloody lie. I ought to call you out."

Marcus took a step toward him and didn't bother to mask the malice in his gaze. "Do what you must." *Please, do it.* He held his breath.

Rather than demand satisfaction, Sainsbury came forward and put his fist in Marcus's cheek. Marcus lifted his arm in defense and turned his head, but Sainsbury was fast, and he connected with Marcus's flesh, landing a blow near his eye.

Spinning about, Marcus took the offensive and drove his fist into Sainsbury's gut, then followed with a punch to his jaw. Sainsbury tried to deflect, but Marcus was faster.

The men around them fell back, giving them a wide space. With a cry, Sainsbury flew at Marcus, wrapping his arms around his middle and taking him down to the floor.

Marcus, larger and stronger, rolled so that he was atop Sainsbury. A bulky shape beneath the man's coat pressed into Marcus's leg. Was that a bloody pistol?

Caught off guard, Marcus didn't block Sainsbury's blow. He planted his fist in Marcus's side.

Grunting, Marcus slid off him, and Sainsbury took the opportunity to land another hit on Marcus's temple.

Fury pulsed through Marcus. Baring his teeth, he pivoted and struck Sainsbury's nose. A satisfying pop sounded, and blood gushed from the man's face.

Hands hauled Marcus to his feet.

"Come on." The voice was familiar. Marcus turned his head to see Anthony staring at him grimly. He steered Marcus through the throng and out of the club. "I'm not usually the one rescuing you."

Breathing heavily, Marcus fought to regain his equilibrium as they walked up St. James's away from White's. That hadn't gone quite the way he'd planned, but he felt a sense of euphoric satisfaction. For a moment, he thought he might be fighting a duel come dawn. He was slightly disappointed that he wasn't.

"I'm glad you're speaking to me again," Marcus said. "Have I rescued you often?"

"There was the masquerade, and yes at least a couple of other occasions where you removed me from a situation that could have deteriorated."

Yes, when he'd been too far in his cups. "Seems it's your turn, then," Marcus said.

"I'm delighted to return the favor. Can I see you home?"

"No. I do need a hack, however."

"I'll fetch one." Anthony did just that, then looked to Marcus. "Where are you going?"

"Cavendish Square."

Anthony gave the direction to the driver, then climbed into the vehicle after Marcus.

"Why are you coming?" Marcus asked.

Anthony shrugged as he settled back against the seat. "I'm curious where you're going. Not really, well, yes, I am. But that's not why I'm here. What the hell was that all about?"

"Sainsbury attacked me."

"Because you maligned his masculinity. Most men would have attacked you."

The places Sainsbury had hit him began to ache, particularly the first blow near his eye. He reached up and touched the spot, wincing slightly.

"Careful, you're bleeding."

He was? Damn. Phoebe would have to tend him again. That brought back memories of when they'd met and how enchanted he'd been by her even then.

"It was just an odd thing for you to do," Anthony said, drawing Marcus's focus back to the altercation. "Actually, it's odd that you were at White's at all."

"You don't usually go there either," Marcus noted.

"Not usually, but once in a while I do." He appeared as though he might say something more, but looked out the window instead.

White's had been Anthony's father's club. Perhaps that was why he still went on occasion. Marcus wasn't going to ask—they did a good job skirting any meaningful discussion of his parents.

As they drove up Bond Street, Anthony said, "Sainsbury was bleeding far more than you. You must have broken his nose."

"I did. He deserved it." And more.

Anthony flicked him a provoking glance. "Does this have anything to do with Miss Phoebe Lennox, who was formerly betrothed to Sainsbury?" When Marcus didn't answer, he added, "Who lives in Cavendish Square?"

Marcus focused on the shops out the window as the hackney rolled along.

"And with whom you drove to Richmond for a picnic?" Anthony asked.

"Who says we did that?"

"You really don't pay attention to gossip, do you? Perhaps you should. Everyone knows you did that."

Everyone? Hell, if everyone knew that, they needed to be extra careful about their affair. Otherwise, everyone would know about that too. He fixed a demanding stare on Anthony. "Don't tell anyone where I'm going tonight."

"I would never. Are you having an affair?"

Marcus ignored the question and stared out the window.

"I won't say a word," Anthony said. "I do hope you haven't made an enemy of Sainsbury. He has a nasty temper. I saw him lose at cards a while back. It was ugly. He actually brandished a pistol before one of his chums dragged him away."

He'd had a pistol then too? The man was a menace. "He's already made an enemy of me. And since I broke his nose, I expect he'll steer quite clear of me." The coach drew to a halt in Cavendish Square. "He will if he possesses even an ounce of intelligence."

"You may be overestimating him, sadly."

Marcus opened the door of the hackney. "I can take care of myself." Once on the street, he looked up at Anthony. "Thank you for your discretion."

Anthony inclined his head, and Marcus closed the door. He heard the hackney drive away as he walked toward the mews that would lead him to the back of Phoebe's house.

As arranged, the door from the garden was not bolted. He slipped inside and closed it behind himself. He picked up a candle from atop a table and crept to the stairs, moving as silently as possible. He climbed up to the second floor and easily found her chamber, the door of which was slightly ajar, as he expected it to be.

He stepped over the threshold, and she met him immediately, her face lighting up with a brilliant smile. It fell from her face the moment she came near.

She drew in a breath and frowned, her gaze on his temple. "Why are you bleeding again?"

~

*B*lood trickled from a small cut on his head. Or had trickled. It seemed mostly dry now.

"Come and sit." She took his hand and led him through the sitting room into her bedchamber.

"This is very…pink," he said, looking around.

"It's my favorite color." She gently pushed him down into a chair near the hearth, where a few coals burned. Then she turned and went to the dresser that held a ewer of water and a basin. Grabbing a cloth from the top drawer, she wet it in the ewer and returned to him.

"Whom did you fight with now?" she asked, cleaning the dried blood away.

"No one. I hit my head getting into a hackney."

She drew back and stared at him for a moment as if she were trying to divine whether he spoke the truth. Saying nothing, she went back to tending his head.

She pressed hard, and he winced. "It started to bleed again," she said softly. "I'll just hold it here for a bit."

"You're an excellent nurse."

"You bleed too much."

He laughed. "Maybe I wound myself on purpose in order to receive your attention."

"That's preposterous, so I shan't even justify it with a response." She pulled the cloth away and surveyed his head.

"How does it look?" he asked.

"Not nearly as awful as the first time."

"Excellent. Not that I had any intention of allowing it to inhibit me this evening."

She took the cloth back to the dresser and set it beside the basin. Turning, she watched him remove his boots and set them next to the chair. His stockings followed, and she was rewarded with his bare, rather large, feet. Her pink bedchamber grew suddenly smaller. And warmer.

He stood and removed his coat, draping it over the back of the chair. Next, he unbuttoned his waistcoat, his gaze lingering on hers as he stripped the garment away and set it atop the coat. Lifting his hands, he untied his cravat, his long fingers moving with expert speed and precision. He pulled the silk off with a whoosh as it slid along the fabric of his shirt. It joined the garments on the chair.

His shirt gapped open at the neck, exposing an alluring V of his upper chest. Phoebe licked her lower lip.

"Do that again," he said. "Slower."

She did as he asked and watched his eyes narrow. Her body tingled with a heightened awareness, a hunger for the pleasure she knew he could give her.

"You said you wanted me to remove my shirt this time. Would you like to do it?"

She was before him in a trice. "Yes, please." Pulling the hem from his breeches, she pushed the fabric up his abdomen, baring inch after inch of his hard flesh. Muscles rippled beneath his taut skin, and she dragged her thumb across one.

He sucked in a breath and then tore his shirt the

rest of the way off, tossing it carelessly to the floor. She lifted her hands to his chest and flattened her palms against him, exploring his heat and strength. She traced her fingers along his collarbones and down to the hollow of his throat. Continuing downward, she swiped her fingertips over his nipples, feeling them harden beneath her touch. Feeling bold, she leaned forward and licked one, earning a gasp from him.

With a smile, she pulled him away from the chair so she could walk around him and look at his back. His wide shoulders pitched down to sharp blades, then tapered to his waist. Below that, she admired the curve of his backside. So much so that she caressed him before continuing her orbit.

"Like what you see?" he asked, his voice warm and deep.

"Yes. Very much."

"My turn," he said, reaching for the tie to her dressing gown.

Phoebe tried not to blush. But he was about to see—

"You aren't wearing anything."

The dressing gown opened, and no, she wasn't wearing anything beneath it. "I didn't think there was a point."

He pushed the garment off her shoulders and stared at her as it slipped to the floor, pooling around her feet. His dark blue gaze feasted on her, heating her along with the warmth of the hearth.

He reached for her, his fingers tangling in her hair, which she'd left loose around her shoulders. He claimed her mouth with a searing kiss. Desire leapt within her. She hadn't realized how much she'd longed for this moment, how desperately she'd craved his touch.

She clutched at him as he did with her. Hands

and fingers, their bodies touching with wild abandon.

Abruptly, he stepped back, his breath coming fast and hard.

"Why are you stopping?"

"I just—" He took a deep breath. "I need a moment."

She moved toward him and reached for the fall of his breeches. "I need you to be as naked as I am."

He groaned. "Phoebe, you're going to kill me, truly. I am a man of closely held control, of balanced composure. But you threaten my very sanity."

She finished unbuttoning his fall, his words thrilling her and making her tremble with want. "I hope this means that tonight, we will finally come together." She pushed his breeches down over his hips and reached for his cock. She wrapped her fingers around him and stood on her toes to kiss his neck. "Or do you have some other step planned?"

He tipped his head back as he clasped her to him, his hands moving around her waist and one sliding down to cup her backside. He pressed her pelvis to his, bringing his shaft against her sex. She rotated her hips, hungry for the release she knew would come and curious as to how it would feel with him inside her.

He brought his hand up to her nape and twined his fingers in her hair, gently pulling her head back so he could look into her eyes. "No more steps. Tonight, you're mine, and I am yours."

"Just tonight?" she teased.

A shadow stole over his gaze. He answered with his mouth, kissing her until she couldn't think straight. Then he picked her up in his arms and carried her to the bed, carefully laying her atop the coverlet.

He glanced toward the bedside table. "I see you soaked the French letter."

"As directed," she said. "The sponge is there too —in the other bowl—soaked and ready."

"I think it's best to use the letter for your first time." He bent his head and took her breast in his mouth. She arched up with a moan as sensation swelled through her.

While he laved one breast, he caressed the other, his fingers rolling her nipple and then pinching slightly. She cast her head back, eyes closed, and surrendered to his control. The more he touched her, the sharper the pleasure, driving straight to her sex. He skimmed his hand down her abdomen, building the anticipation in her core. When his hand pressed against her mound at last, she bucked up, desperate for him.

"Please," she moaned.

He drew on her nipple, tugging hard before leaving her entirely. He pressed her thighs apart, exposing her, which only fed her desire. Then she felt both of his hands on her sex, one pressing and massaging her clitoris while the other explored her folds, his finger ultimately sliding inside her.

She had no idea what he was actually doing, only that each caress, each stroke, each thrust felt better than the last. She opened her eyes and looked down at him just as he lowered his head and licked along her flesh, focusing his tongue on her clitoris while he pumped his finger—fingers, probably—inside her. She came up off the bed, meeting his mouth and hands, her body speeding toward release.

The storm crashed over her, and she cried out his name, closing her eyes once more. She pulled at his head, tugging his hair and pressing up into him as her muscles clenched in desperation. He guided her over the edge and down into the comforting abyss, but then he was gone.

She looked to see him kneeling between her legs as he reached for the bedside table. Fascinated, she watched as he donned the French letter, tying it around the base of his shaft. He bent down and kissed her as his fingers stroked her sex once more.

Her body still quivered from her release, and the familiar hunger he aroused in her still pulsed in her core, sparking again as she felt his sex nudge her opening. He pulled his mouth from hers and looked into her eyes. "Ready?"

She nodded. He didn't blink, holding her gaze steady with his as he moved slowly inside her. This was nothing like what they'd done before and yet similar too. He filled her, stretching her muscles and causing a bit of pain. She winced slightly, and he kissed her brow.

He stroked his thumb along her cheekbone. "My brave, beautiful Phoebe."

His.

She liked how that sounded.

"Wrap your legs around me," he whispered near her ear, his lips grazing her flesh.

She did what he asked, and the movement brought him more deeply inside her, her pelvis tipping. She gasped at the sensation, feeling a bead of pleasure amidst the discomfort.

He began to move, slowly rocking in and out of her. "Next time," he said softly, "it will feel much better. Next time, I will let go and drive so hard inside you, you'll cry out with the ecstasy of it. Next time, I'll go slow and fast and then slow again until we're both at the end of our wits. Next time, you'll explode so furiously that it will take me all night, and maybe the next day, to put you back together again."

His words thrilled her, heightening her passion. "But I want all of that now."

He chuckled softly and thrust into her. "Patience. The time after that, you may ride me, if you like, and then you can control every stroke. Fast or slow, hard or soft. Entirely your discretion." He snagged his teeth on her earlobe and began to move faster.

Phoebe moaned, her discomfort all but gone as her pleasure intensified. She tightened her legs around his hips and moved with him, clutching at his back.

Reaching between them, he pressed against her clitoris, dragging his thumb over her and sending her into a spiral of rapture. Light swirled behind her eyes as she arched up into him, her legs and muscles squeezing around him. He continued to move relentlessly, until he shouted his release. Then he kissed her again, their ragged breaths mingling as they floated from the heavens.

When they were still, Marcus rolled from her and left the bed. His back was to her, but she imagined he was removing the French letter.

She sat up against the headboard and slid under the bedclothes. "I spoke to my father today about his investment," she said as Marcus disposed of the French letter. "He is not going to invest with the same person again. In fact, there was another man there today—a tall man with a walking stick."

Marcus, who was on his way back to the bed, froze. He stared at her, his eyes glinting. "That's Osborne."

"Is it? I wondered. Papa wouldn't answer except to say he wasn't Drobbit. I worried he was perhaps not being completely honest regarding his plans, so I went into his study tonight."

Marcus climbed into the other side of the bed,

sitting up with the coverlet around his hips. He angled himself toward her. "Did you find anything?"

"I think so. He'd written something down—Tuesday evening, the Horn Tavern, Russell Street, and a name: Tibbord." She'd frowned upon seeing it. "I couldn't help noticing that is Drobbit spelled backward."

He cupped her face and kissed her, grinning. "You are brilliant, of course. Yes, that is my cousin. He's been using the name Tibbord."

"He's not exceptionally clever, is he?"

Marcus sat back from her and snorted. "Clever enough to have fleeced several people." He kissed her again, swiftly. "Thank you. Now I know where to find him—and when."

"And you can stop my father from making another doomed investment." Phoebe shook her head. "Maybe he won't go. I told him Drobbit is a swindler."

"How did he react to that?" Marcus asked, sitting back against the headboard of her bed and drawing her into the crook of his arm.

Phoebe thought back. "He didn't, actually. He seemed uncomfortable, but I suspect that's because he was embarrassed. He doesn't like my knowing he lost money, and if he lost it due to being swindled? His pride would be woefully crushed."

"He won't lose anymore, I promise. I'll take care of everything tomorrow night."

Marcus kissed her temple as his fingers stroked her arm and shoulder. Phoebe nestled into his side and put her arm around his abdomen. He smelled lovely, and his skin was so firm and warm, his muscles taut. She wanted to spend days in this bed exploring every part of him. Alas, they were not wed and he did not live there.

Wed?

That was not a word she wanted to think about. Not now, not with Marcus. She'd wanted an affair, and she had one. It was more than she'd ever expected, particularly with a man like Marcus. She tipped her head to look up at him, the strong arc of his jaw, the sensuous curve of his lips, the lines fanning around his eyes that deepened when he smiled at her, the cobalt of his eyes that sparked with desire and seduction. She couldn't believe he was hers, even for a short time.

Yes, this was more than enough.

CHAPTER 12

The Lennoxes' butler was an affable-looking gentleman in his middle age. Marcus smiled as he handed the man his card.

"Come in, my lord." The butler opened the door wide, and Marcus stepped into the small but elegant entry hall. "If you'll wait here."

Marcus inclined his head and watched as the butler walked past the stairs toward the back of the house. While he was gone, Marcus imagined a young Phoebe living here. Had she run down the stairs in her childhood, dark ringlets swinging? He smiled at the image.

A moment later, the butler returned. "Follow me, if you please."

Marcus trailed him to a doorway at which the butler announced his arrival and then stepped aside so Marcus could enter. Walking over the threshold, Marcus saw Mr. Lennox standing near a chair situated in front of the hearth. The room was clearly his study.

"Good afternoon, Mr. Lennox," Marcus greeted, offering his hand.

Lennox shook it and indicated another chair. "My lord, would you care to sit?"

"Briefly. I don't anticipate staying long. I'm sure you're wondering why I called." Marcus took his seat.

"I am." Lennox sat down opposite him.

"It's come to my attention that you've been investing with my cousin. You may know him as Tibbord, but his name is actually Drobbit. The fact that he uses an alias should tell you everything about him." Marcus crossed his legs. "To put it plainly, he's a swindler."

Lennox tried very hard to school his features, but there was no mistaking the flash of alarm in his gaze. "While I appreciate your concern, I assure you that I'm not involved with this in any way."

Marcus hadn't really known how Lennox would react, but he hadn't expected complete denial. However, Marcus couldn't call him out on the lie without saying he knew Osborne had called. And the only way he could know that was through Phoebe. Surely her father would demand to know how Marcus was privy to such information, and that was not a conversation he wished to have.

Instead, Marcus went along with him and tried to convey a warning. "That's…good to know. If you were by chance even thinking of investing with Tibbord—either with him directly or via his assistant, Osborne, I am here to tell you that is no longer an option. My cousin will not be taking money from anyone anymore. So, if you had any plans with him, don't bother keeping them. His game is done."

Hopefully, Lennox understood. Marcus didn't want to specifically mention the meeting he was perhaps going to that night. To do so could expose Phoebe, and he wouldn't do that.

"How do you know he's a swindler?" Lennox asked. "Are you a part of this?"

"No," Marcus answered coldly. "I would never participate in such a crime. He cheated some people

I know, and I am putting a stop to further misconduct. I can't allow a member of my family, no matter how estranged, to behave in this manner. Surely you understand that."

"I do. You are to be commended for your intervention. I'm sure those he's stolen from are grateful."

Was he trying to thank Marcus without actually doing so? Or was he merely being polite while trying to indicate he was not one of those who would benefit from Marcus's aid? Marcus wasn't sure.

There was nothing else he could say without being overt. He stood. "That concludes my business here, then. I wish you good fortune, Mr. Lennox."

Lennox rose. "Thank you, my lord. Good day."

Marcus departed, hoping for Lennox's sake that he wasn't lying to him—or to his daughter—about investing with Drobbit again. If he tried, the man was beyond help. Hopefully that wasn't the case since Marcus didn't wish to see Phoebe's father ruined.

As he climbed into his gig, he tried not to think about why he cared.

Because you're having an affair with his daughter.

That has nothing to do with it, he argued with himself. He wanted to stop his cousin from harming anyone else, whether they were his lover's father or not.

The word "lover" prowled through his mind as he drove back to Hanover Square. He'd never had one of those before. It made him feel slightly uneasy as well as incredibly possessive. That was a goddamned problem.

Phoebe didn't belong to him, nor did he to her. They were enjoying each other and nothing more. He was thirty-one. Perhaps he'd simply reached the stage of his life where he wanted something different. If not permanent, then at least something more than fleeting. And Phoebe was definitely that.

The question was whether she was something more. Marcus didn't have an answer—nor did he want one.

~

*J*ane stalked into Phoebe's garden room the following afternoon, a frown stamped upon her usually cheerful face. After removing her bonnet and gloves and tossing them on the settee, she joined Phoebe at the table near the door to the garden.

"I'm doomed."

Phoebe poured her a cup of tea. "Why?"

"My parents have invited Mr. Brinkley to dinner in a fortnight. I have just enough time to find someone and pay them to kidnap me to Scotland."

"Scotland? Why, are you going to wed at Gretna Green?"

"If he's handsome, intelligent, and kind, yes." She picked up her tea. "On second thought, he needn't be all that handsome if he's the other two. He cannot be boring, and he absolutely cannot be someone I've already decided I don't want to marry."

"Such as Mr. Brinkley." Phoebe sipped her tea, then set her cup down. "What is wrong with him exactly?"

Jane scowled. "My parents chose him? Oh, he's pleasant enough, I suppose. I just don't see myself married to a banker, not to mention becoming a mother overnight."

"Who do you see yourself married to?" Phoebe asked. She realized she'd never really thought about that. She just knew she'd wed whomever her parents deemed appropriate. But then it happened that their choice was anything but. "Never mind, you're right. Don't marry someone your parents chose."

"Exactly!" Jane sipped her tea and then exchanged her cup for a cake, which she nibbled for a moment. "That's the problem. I'm not sure I see myself married to anyone. The more I see you here, enjoying your independence, the more I want it for myself."

"Well, you are an official member of the Spitfire Society."

"Yes, about that. I think we should consider expanding our membership. I've met a lovely woman who's just come to town. She and her sister are already independent. She's a widow."

"The best kind of independence," Phoebe said wistfully. Then she giggled. "Such a morbid thing to say."

Jane lifted a shoulder. "You know I'm not offended. Perhaps I'll leave London for a while and return claiming to be a widow. Would anyone ever know?"

Phoebe laughed. "If anyone could do that, I'd wager it's you."

"I shall have to consider this at length." Jane sat back in her chair with a pensive expression and finished her cake. "Just think, as a widow, I could even have an affair."

"You may not even have to be a widow…" Phoebe had planned to tell Jane about Marcus. This was the perfect opportunity. She picked up her teacup and took a sip.

Jane leaned forward, her sherry-colored eyes sparkling. "Ripley?"

Phoebe nodded over the rim of her cup.

"Tell me everything."

"Maybe not *everything*." Phoebe laughed, setting her cup down. "I decided there was no point in being a spinster if I didn't take full advantage. You helped persuade me. Indeed, you're a very bad influence. It's as if you're a scandalous widow already."

Jane giggled. "Happy to oblige. Ripley! Is he wonderful?"

"As you know, I have little to compare him to. Just Sainsbury, who I am now calling the Blackguard." Her lip curled. "I can't even categorize them in the same species."

"Well, that was a given," Jane said.

"I did tell him—Marcus—about what the Blackguard did."

Surprise flashed in Jane's gaze. "Did you? Whatever did he say?"

"He was quite angry, actually. I wondered if he might do the Blackguard some harm, but that would only draw attention, and I sincerely hope he doesn't do that." Yet she gained a perverse pleasure imagining Marcus pummeling Sainsbury into oblivion.

"Speaking of Sains—I mean, the Blackguard," Jane said distastefully. "He is officially back on the Marriage Mart. He actually had the gall to ask me to dance the other night."

A tremor of disgust skipped over Phoebe. Declining to dance with someone was a noteworthy event, so she imagined Jane danced with him. "He knows you and I are good friends."

"Of course he does." Jane scoffed. "I pleaded a stomachache and even acted as though I might toss up my accounts all over him. He couldn't leave fast enough."

Phoebe smiled in relief. "I'm so glad—for your sake."

"I could never dance with him. I'd faint dead on the floor in the middle of a ballroom if I had to. My mother was annoyed, but she usually is with me of late. Fortunately, she was able to focus her attention on Anne, who continues to be more popular than I

ever was. I still don't know whom she's in love with.
In fact, she now denies that she ever was." Jane rolled
her eyes. "Fickle."

"Perhaps she changed her mind after coming to
know him better." Phoebe shuddered. "I did."
Though she'd never claimed to love Sainsbury.
Phoebe wasn't sure she'd know what that felt like.

Maybe the way you feel about Marcus?

What a preposterous thought. And one she
didn't care to ponder. Marcus excited her. He made
her feel like a desirable woman, and he honored her
opinion and choices. That wasn't love. That was
mutual admiration and respect, as well as
attraction.

What was love, then?

"It's absolutely horrid that Sainsbury, I'm sorry,
the Blackguard, can do what he did and still be invited to events to which you are not. He should be
the one who is shunned." Jane glanced at Phoebe
apologetically. "Not that you're shunned."

"I am, mostly," Phoebe said. "Or at least ignored,
which is fine with me. Let them focus their attention
on the Blackguard and whoever is foolish enough to
wed him. I pity the woman." In fact, Phoebe ought
to warn her when the time came. The thought of
someone in his clutches, as his wife, filled with
anger. That reminded her of Meg, her parents'
former maid who was *currently* in his employ.
Phoebe needed to hire her away from him immediately. She'd speak with her housekeeper as soon as
Jane left to determine the best way to accomplish
that.

"It so unfair," Jane said, flopping back against her
chair. "All of it. How we're expected to behave, our
lack of choices and control. Even our clothing is
more frustrating. Men don't wear this many under-
garments."

"Some of them do," Phoebe said with a mischievous grin. "Some men wear corsets."

Jane arched a blonde brow. "Don't tell me Ripley is one of them."

Phoebe gasped. "Good Lord, no. He's...he's perfect."

"I'm seething with jealousy," Jane said, narrowing her eyes. "I'm afraid I may have to find my own gentleman with whom to have an affair. After I declare my spinsterhood, of course."

"And when will that be?" Phoebe asked, plucking a biscuit from the tray.

"Soon." Jane reached for a biscuit too. "Soon."

The conversation turned to Lavinia's baby and then Arabella and the fact that she and Graham were leaving to visit Fanny and David the following day. By the time Jane left, Phoebe was feeling quite gratified about her life—her friends, her affair with Marcus, even things with her parents seemed to be improving.

She hoped Marcus was able to achieve whatever he intended with his cousin that night and that he prevented her father from losing any more money. Phoebe would support them, if he would let her, but knew that would be a tough fight.

She'd find out how things went later, as Marcus planned to return that night after meeting with his cousin. Phoebe smiled to herself in anticipation.

~

*R*ussell Street ran from Covent Garden to Drury Lane and was full of shops and taverns, including the Horn Tavern, which sat closer to Drury Lane. Marcus arrived at around ten o'clock and wasn't sure what to expect.

Would Drobbit be in the common room? If he

wasn't and Marcus asked for him, would he need to disclose a certain word as had been necessary in Leicester Square?

Making his way to a table in the back corner that afforded him a view of people entering as well as the staircase that led upstairs, presumably to rooms for let, Marcus sat down and ordered an ale. The serving maid who fetched it for him offered her services in plain terms, to which Marcus politely declined. "I'm otherwise engaged."

It was the reason he often used since he almost always went to Mrs. Alban's. However, tonight was different because he planned to return to Phoebe's. For the second time in the same number of nights. It was unprecedented. Not to mention the other times they'd already spent together—and it wasn't just the sex.

He'd prided himself on having no attachments. His father had drilled that into his brain from a young age, and since he'd admired his father above all others, Marcus had lived his life that way.

This wasn't an attachment. This was an affair. Phoebe didn't expect anything from him. She'd never once spoken of the future. They both seemed to want precisely the same thing, and for now, he was content to let their connection run its course.

Connection.

That word was awfully close to attachment.

Marcus snorted as he took a long pull from his tankard. He'd thought too much about her, about *them together*, today. *Enough.* He surveyed the room intently, looking for anyone he recognized. Drobbit wasn't here, nor was Osborne. Neither was Phoebe's father, thankfully.

As Marcus finished his ale, he considered his options: continue to wait and observe or try to find out if anyone here knew Drobbit. Feeling impatient, he hailed the serving maid.

He flashed her a smile. "Tilly, is it?"

She nodded, her lips parting slightly to reveal a gap between her front teeth. "Change yer mind?"

He ignored her question. "I'm looking for someone who might come here from time to time. Shorter gentleman with a stocky build. Dark hair but light gray eyes—you'd notice them if you were paying attention."

"I don't pay much attention to shorter gents. Not unless they pay me." She laughed. She bent over the table, the bodice of her dress gaping so that he had an unimpeded view of her breasts. "Ye're not short. And ye don't have to pay me."

"That's awfully generous of you, Tilly. As I said, I am otherwise engaged this evening, but if I could find this gentleman, who knows?" He slid a coin across the table to her.

She picked it up. "I'll ask Mary. She might be able to help ye." She put her hand on his thigh and slid it up to his crotch, her thumb brushing against his cock, which wasn't remotely interested in her attention. "Just remember who helped ye first."

With a wink, she took herself off. Marcus exhaled. He reached for his tankard, then realized it was empty. A moment later, a younger maid came to his table. She was rather petite, with dark blonde hair and a wide, infectious smile. "Evening, my lord. Tilly said ye're looking fer someone."

Marcus described his cousin once more and immediately saw the light of recognition in her eyes even as her smile dimmed.

"I don't think I know him, my lord. Sorry." She started to turn, but Marcus clasped her elbow. Working his hand down her forearm, he held her hand out and pressed several coins into her palm. He closed her fingers over them and encompassed her small hand with his.

"I need to see him. Is he here?" He felt her clench the coins in her hand. It was more than she made in a month.

She nodded. "Upstairs," she whispered. "But he doesn't come out. I take him supper every night and fetch his clothes from the laundry."

He took his hand from hers. "Where upstairs?"

"Last room on the right on the second floor. Please don't tell him I told ye." Her plea was quite earnest.

"He hasn't threatened you, has he?"

"He said if I told anyone he was here, he'd make sure I was tossed out."

Marcus rose, anticipation thrumming through him now that he'd finally found Drobbit. "I'm not going to tell him, Mary. I promise you."

She inclined her head. "Thank you." Then she swept his empty mug from the table, and Marcus made his way through the common room to the stairs.

He climbed up to the first floor and then to the second, where it was much quieter. There were two doors on each side of the gallery. Marcus strode to the last one on the right as Mary had described. Instead of knocking, he tried to just walk in. Unfortunately, the door was bolted.

So he rapped on the wood. When there was no response from within, he knocked more loudly. After another long moment, he pounded his fist. "I'm coming in, whether you open the door or not. And I'll not pay for any damage."

Marcus waited, listening quietly for any sign of movement. At last, there were footsteps, followed by the door creaking open. Drobbit ran a hand through his disheveled hair, further messing it.

"How the hell did you find me?"

Marcus pushed open the door, forcing Drobbit to step back, though he kept a grip on the wood. "It took quite some time. Clearly, you didn't wish to be found." He took a quick appraisal of the room. It was small and spartanly furnished, with a narrow bed in the corner and a decrepit seating area in front of a cold hearth.

"No, I did not," Drobbit snapped as he closed the door. "Shouldn't you be at a bawdy house by this time of night?"

Marcus turned. "Don't pretend to know me."

"How could I?" Drobbit grumbled. "Your father made certain you didn't associate with our side of the family." He tossed Marcus a glare as he went to a small table set beneath a window and poured a glass of brandy.

That was only a partial truth. Marcus's mother had married above her station when she'd wed a marquess, but she'd remained devoted to her family. However, her sister and her husband, Drobbit's parents, had been rife with jealousy and anger over Marcus's mother's good fortune. This had culminated in a physical altercation between Marcus's uncle and father.

"After your father attacked him. And it was my mother who asked not to associate with her sister and her husband anymore," Marcus clarified. Perhaps Drobbit hadn't known that.

Drobbit sipped his drink as he continued to glower at Marcus. "Believe the lies your father told you. I'm certain you wouldn't remember anything Aunt Helena said."

Because Marcus had been just four when his mother, Helena, died. He summoned a patronizing smile. "On the contrary, I remember many things, but nothing concerning you or your family, likely

because it wasn't important. And yes, I believe my
father, just as you, apparently, believe yours. I didn't
come here to solve the divisions of those who came
before us. I came to put a stop to your criminal
behavior."

Drobbit grunted before draining his glass. He
clacked it down on the sideboard. "You're as bloody
cold as your father was—maybe even worse. You
can't prove anything."

"I can, actually. You're actively trying to swindle
someone right now, and I'm confident he'll provide
evidence against you and Osborne. Where is he, by
the way? Weren't you expecting him?" Marcus looked
around the room, but there was nowhere to hide.

The sound of Drobbit's teeth grinding irritated
Marcus. "I'm not swindling anyone. I invest for
people."

"Invest in what?" When Drobbit didn't answer,
Marcus made a noise in his throat. "Don't bother
lying to me. I told you in the park to stop cheating
people. You ignored me, and now you'll reap what
you sowed. Bow Street will be here as soon as I tell
them."

Lines creased across Drobbit's wide forehead.
"Don't do that. Please."

Marcus walked around the room and took inven-
tory. "You stole a great deal of money from people.
Surely you should pay for that." He sent Drobbit a
taunting glance. "What did you do with all of it?"

"Nothing, because I didn't steal it," Drobbit
barked. "I lost it in an investment."

"Unlikely. You must have it hidden somewhere
—I know you like to live extravagantly." He spun
around and cocked his head to the side. "Or did,
anyway. Did you really spend it all?"

Drobbit raised his arms and his voice. "Look

around you! Where is my cache of riches? I have nothing."

Marcus strode toward him, his patience thinning. He stopped a bare foot from the smaller man. He didn't bother modulating his tone. "Don't waste both our time by pretending you're guiltless. In addition to Lennox, whom you are currently swindling, Halstead has proof. If you think a duke and a marquess—because I will help him—can't take you down, you're living in a fantasy." He fixed his gaze on Drobbit's, staring intently into the man's withering soul. "You will return whatever money you can, and you will provide me a list of those you cheated. I want the latter *now*."

"I—I can't. There really isn't any money. I've spent it all." His voice, once filling the room with its volume, dwindled to nearly nothing. He turned his head, and for the first time, Marcus saw the resemblance between his cousin and his mother—or at least the small portrait of his mother that his father had kept in his private library. The shape of her nose was the shape of Drobbit's nose. Right now, looking at his cousin, Marcus saw her. The scent of roses and tea with sugar rose from the distant past.

Marcus swore. His voice rose. "You nearly bankrupted people. Indeed, you probably did. Tell me who else you fleeced."

"Does it matter? They won't want their shame known, and there's nothing to be done now. What money I have must repay a debt." He flicked a fear-filled glance at Marcus.

Bloody hell. Marcus recalled what Harry had told him about Drobbit being involved with something dubious. "What have you gotten yourself into?"

"The less you know, the better off you'll be." Drobbit turned back to the table and poured another glass of brandy. The liquid only filled half the glass, however, because the bottle was empty.

Marcus retreated to the center of the room. "I can't imagine you've developed a sudden concern for my welfare, particularly after you tried to break my head open."

"We're family in the end, aren't we?"

They were, but Marcus didn't have sympathy to spare. Not for him. "If you tell me from whom you stole, I'll do my best to ensure you aren't punished too harshly."

"I'll give you a list—tomorrow. My head is pounding."

"You've proven yourself to be thoroughly un-trustworthy. Bow Street is around the corner. I should go fetch them now."

Sweat beaded Drobbit's forehead. "Please don't. I promise I'll come to your house in the morning." He turned and went to a dresser near the bed. Opening a drawer, he withdrew a small pouch, then came back to Marcus. "Here. This was my mother's. I swear on her grave I'll come to your house in the morning."

Marcus opened the drawstring and emptied the contents into his palm. A necklace spilled out, and he recognized it immediately. It was a cameo carved in carnelian. "This is my mother," Marcus said, skim-ming his fingertip over the raised profile.

"Yes. Do you have the one with my mother?" Drobbit asked. Their parents had given them cameos of each other when they were young.

"I do." Marcus recalled that she wore it, even after she was estranged from her sister. He remem-bered sitting on her lap and tracing the silhouette, just as he was doing now.

He shouldn't trust this man. Looking up from the cameo, he pinned Drobbit with an earnest stare.

"You swear you'll be at my house in the morning? I still intend to take you to Bow Street. These crimes cannot go unpunished. The upside is that whatever situation you've become involved in will no longer be a problem. I'm sure Bow Street would be quite happy to pursue whatever criminals have forced you to take such drastic measures."

"Thank you. Truly." Drobbit seemed to wilt before him. "I don't want to go on like this. We are family after all."

"Family who throw rocks at each other," Marcus murmured, the lingering memory of his mother floating about his head. This swindler was his family—they shared the blood that had flowed through Marcus's mother's veins. Drobbit was, in fact, the only link he had left to her. And it was a link he'd never thought much about. Maybe if he had, the man wouldn't have turned to crime. Marcus wasn't to blame for the man's transgressions, but perhaps he could now set him on the right path.

Drobbit turned toward him, his shoulders relaxing, but his jaw remaining taut. "Why do you want a list anyway?"

"Reparations must be made."

"But I told you I have no money."

Marcus, however, did. He had more than he could ever spend, and while he couldn't return everything Drobbit had stolen, he could at least ensure no one was destitute. He'd already done that for his friend, Graham, and he'd do it for whoever else needed the help.

Pocketing the cameo, Marcus turned to go.

"May I have hers?" Drobbit asked as Marcus reached the door. "The cameo with my mother on it?"

Marcus looked back over his shoulder. "Of

course. I'll give it to you in the morning—incentive to come."

"I'll see you in the morning."

Closing the door behind him, Marcus made his way downstairs and out of the tavern. He paused outside and glanced up, worried that Drobbit would disappear before morning. He realized a part of him didn't care, so long as he stopped swindling people.

Marcus made his way to his coach where it waited in Covent Garden. He worked to put the distasteful evening from his mind. Phoebe awaited him, and he looked forward to losing himself in her.

He didn't want to think of Drobbit. Of Bow Street. Of Phoebe's father. Or especially of the way he'd just capitulated to sentimentality.

CHAPTER 13

*P*hoebe wrapped her dressing gown around herself as she watched Marcus dress. The sun was barely peeking over the horizon, which meant he was a bit late leaving. Not that she cared—his tardiness was worth every moment they'd spent causing it.

Her body was still flushed from pleasure, and she knew she'd spend the day in a semigiddy state, much as she'd done the day before. Affairs, she decided, were excellent for one's well-being.

Marcus was completely dressed save his cravat and boots. As he sat down to don the latter, he asked if she might know where the former had ended up.

Phoebe thought back to the night before when he'd arrived. She'd insisted on stripping every piece of clothing from his body. "You threatened to blindfold me with it." Only it hadn't felt threatening. The suggestion had aroused her, and she looked forward to when he would. "Remember, you promised to do that next time." Discussing "next time" had become one of her favorite pastimes.

She knelt down and saw the cravat under the bed. Bending forward, she reached for the length of silk.

Marcus caressed her backside. "This is an excellent view. I think next time might also need to include shagging you from behind. Or perhaps that will be the time after."

Desire sparked in Phoebe's core as she sat back with the cravat in her hand. Marcus gave her his hand and helped her up. He tugged her gently against his chest.

"Tell me more," Phoebe said huskily as she wrapped the cravat around his neck and held onto the ends, pulling his head down to hers.

"You on all fours. Me behind you. My cock in your pussy, and my mouth on the back of your neck while you scream my name."

Heat flooded Phoebe's sex. She loved the way he talked to her when they were alone. "Can next time be now?"

He chuckled. "You're insatiable." Then he kissed her, a long, delicious exploration of her mouth that only stoked her lust.

Stepping back, he grinned as he took hold of the cravat and began to tie it.

"And you're provoking."

"No more than you." His gaze dipped over her. "Prancing around in almost nothing and putting your arse in the air."

She turned and wiggled her backside, drawing a laugh from him.

A rap on her door startled them both. Phoebe's maid knew she had a guest—it had been necessary to instruct her to stay away.

Phoebe went to the door, where a visibly concerned Page stood. "I'm so sorry to bother you, miss, but I'm afraid there's someone here."

"At this hour?" Phoebe asked, aware that Marcus, who was standing out of Page's view, had taken a step toward them.

Page nodded. "It's a *Bow Street Runner*." She sounded petrified.

"Thank you, Page. I'll be right down."

Before Phoebe could close the door, Page said, "He's not here to see you. He's here to see *him*. Lord Ripley."

Phoebe's stomach dropped to the basement. She gripped the door tightly. "I see. *We'll* be right down, then."

"Do you want me to help you dress?" Page asked.

"No, thank you." Phoebe closed the door and stared at Marcus. "How does he know you're here? Why is he looking for you in the first place?"

Marcus frowned. "It might be about my cousin. I'd asked a friend of mine who's a Runner to find him."

"But you found him."

"Yes, however, I didn't tell him to stop looking. I came here straight after seeing Drobbit last night."

"The Runner must have found him, then."

"He must have." Marcus exhaled. "Do you want to dress? He can wait a few minutes."

"I suppose."

With Marcus's assistance, she donned a simple day dress and pulled her hair up into a simple style. They were downstairs a short time later and walked together into the garden room, where the Runner was waiting.

"I'm surprised to see you here and at this hour," Marcus said. "Phoebe, allow me to present my friend, Harry Sheffield. Harry, this is Miss Phoebe Lennox."

Sheffield, a thick-chested man with auburn hair and piercing tawny eyes, bowed. "I'm pleased to make your acquaintance, Miss Lennox. Please forgive my intrusion at this impolite hour."

"I'm sure your reason for coming is important," Phoebe said. "Shall we sit?"

"That's not necessary. I'm afraid I've come with bad news." He looked to Marcus. "Your cousin was found dead a couple of hours ago."

Though Phoebe wasn't touching Marcus, he was close enough to her side that she felt him tense.

"How did he die?" Marcus's voice was calm. Unemotional.

"He was shot—square in the chest."

"Where did this happen?"

"At the Horn Tavern." Sheffield frowned briefly. "I believe you know where that is."

Something passed between the two men, an unspoken communication. Of course Marcus knew where that was—he'd been there last night. Phoebe began to grow alarmed.

Marcus inclined his head. "I do."

"You were there last night," Sheffield said. It wasn't a question. He *knew* Marcus had been there. "You saw him."

Phoebe's heart pounded as apprehension coiled inside her. She didn't like the look in Sheffield's gaze —it was rife with doubt and suspicion.

"I did, and he was alive when I left." Marcus's voice was still remarkably calm, as was his expression. He looked as if they were discussing the day's weather!

"What time was that?" Sheffield asked.

"Between eleven and midnight."

Sheffield nodded. "You didn't tell me you'd found him."

"I'd planned to today. It was rather late last night."

"And yet, the Horn is not that far from Bow Street."

Marcus smiled, but it lacked his usual charm. "As you can see, I had a far more desirable engagement."

Sheffield sent a half smile in Phoebe's direction, then looked back to Marcus. "Was Drobbit alone?"

"Yes. He was also a bit drunk."

"Did you see anyone around his room? Anything that would draw notice or suspicion?"

Marcus shook his head. "No, the floor was empty. I didn't see anyone on my way up nor on my way down."

"Did anyone see you leave?"

Marcus shrugged. "I can't say. I didn't speak to anyone on my way out."

Sheffield went silent, and Phoebe could have sworn she could hear his mind turning. She wanted to blurt that Marcus couldn't have killed Drobbit. He wouldn't have.

"You should go home," Sheffield said.

"As it happens, I am on my way there now."

"Good. Stay there. I'll be by later to ask you a few more questions."

Marcus gave him a nod. "You're welcome anytime." He sounded so smooth, so collected, while Phoebe wanted to scream.

Sheffield left, and Phoebe grabbed Marcus's hand, squeezing as she turned to him. Marcus shook his head sharply and lifted his finger to his mouth. He let go of her hand and went to the door where he stood, listening.

Phoebe also listened, and when the front door closed, Marcus visibly relaxed. He also swore violently.

Then he shot her a look of apology.

"He was alive when you left," Phoebe said.

"Yes." Marcus pulled something from his pocket and looked down at it in his palm. "He gave me this."

Phoebe went to him and saw the cameo resting in his grasp. "It's beautiful. Why did he give it to you?"

"This is my mother. It belonged to his mother. I have one of her that belonged to my mother. I was going to give it to him this morning when he came to my house." Marcus had told her of their conversation last night, that Drobbit's swindling was finished, but he hadn't mentioned the cameos.

She touched his arm, moving close to him. "I'm so sorry."

He inhaled sharply. "I'm not sad. How can I be when I scarcely knew him?"

"Wasn't he your only family?"

"Yes, but he may as well have been anyone." His voice was oddly cold, and it made her shiver. He sounded nothing like the ardent lover who came to her bed.

They were quiet a moment, then he turned to face her. "My butler must have told him where I was."

"Your retainers know you've been spending the night here?"

"Just my butler and my valet. They are incredibly discreet. Like your maid." He frowned, then took her hand. "I need to go home, and we can't see each other for a few days. I will be at the center of gossip, more than usual," he said with a grin that did nothing to ease the turmoil wreaking havoc inside Phoebe. "We mustn't do anything to draw attention."

Gossip. It would be *terrible*. Speaking of gossip... "You fought with Drobbit in the park. Worse than that, people say you threatened to kill him. Now they'll say you did."

"If anyone even knows he's dead. It's not as if Drobbit was a known member of Society."

"I think people know who he was after the incident in the park," Phoebe argued. "Weren't there wagers as to whether you would call him out?"

Marcus's face twitched, and it was the first bit of emotion she'd seen from him. "Yes, but it's just gossip. As you know, we can't let that get to us." He squeezed her hand and looked into her eyes. "Right?"

She knew that was true. It still didn't make it easier. "Right. But I don't want people thinking you're a murderer. You *aren't*."

He smiled and pressed a kiss to her hand. "So long as you don't think so—and Bow Street—that's all I care about."

"I think you're being awfully blasé about this."

"How else should I be? I didn't kill him. I'm not sad he's dead. The only thing I'm remotely bothered by is the fact that Harry had to show up here and ruin our delightful morning."

Phoebe arched a brow at him. "That's all you're concerned about?"

He drew her into his arms and kissed her soundly. "That and the fact that I can't see you for a few days."

"Can't I just steal into the back of your house like you do here?"

"As much as I would like that, we need to remain apart. It's only for a few days."

She gave him a pert look. "What if I don't care if everyone knows we're having an affair?"

"What if I do?" He laughed softly, then kissed her again. His lips lingered against hers, and when he drew back, he caressed her cheek. "I'll send word when I can return."

"You better send word before that. I want regular updates."

He stared at her for a brief moment before

kissing her cheek. "See you soon," he whispered. He turned and left.

Phoebe paced the garden room. She couldn't believe how casually he was taking this news. A Bow Street Runner had tracked him down just past dawn to question him about the murder of his cousin, a man he was known to dislike and was believed to have threatened.

She was going to be a mess until this was all behind them. She paused near the doors leading out to the garden. What did she expect, that he would go to jail? Or worse, be hanged?

The thought of either of those things filled her with a cold dread. She didn't want to lose him, not even for a few days, which was apparently necessary.

She sank down into one of the chairs at the table by the door. She couldn't think like this. They were having an affair, nothing more.

Suddenly, she thought of his expression when she'd said she wanted regular information from him. He hadn't agreed, and he'd looked…bothered. Then, when she'd suggested she maybe didn't care if people knew about their affair, he'd jokingly said that perhaps he did. Had it been a joke? He wasn't a man known for affairs. He was known for spending time with courtesans and at brothels, for *not* having a mistress.

Maybe it *would* trouble him for people to know about her. About *them*.

A disquiet ran through her. She hadn't meant to become attached, to develop feelings for him. And yet, how could she not? He understood her in ways no one ever had. Supported her, cared for her.

She could very easily fall in love with him, if she wasn't already. What if he knew that? What if this gave him the opportunity to end things before she made him uncomfortable?

What if he was asking her to stay away because he was ready to move on? Two nights with her was already one more night than she should have expected.

There was nothing she could do but wait. Or maybe she ought to put him behind her before he broke her heart.

~

For the third straight day, Marcus prowled his house. It wasn't that he couldn't leave; he didn't want to. As Anthony had told him the day before, gossip was at a fever pitch, particularly since a revolving cast of Bow Street Runners had taken up residence outside his home not long after he'd returned from Phoebe's.

He'd started inviting them in for meals yesterday.

Dorne came in, bearing a letter. "This just arrived, my lord."

Marcus wondered if it was from Phoebe. She'd written to him yesterday telling him she was thinking of him and offering words of support and encouragement that this would all be behind them soon.

It wasn't from her, however. It was an accounting from the funeral furnisher as well as confirmation that Drobbit would be buried tomorrow morning. Unless Bow Street decided they needed to review the body again.

Marcus tossed the parchment onto his desk and went to pour a glass of port. He'd drunk more than normal the past two days, but would anyone blame him? He was the bloody suspect in a murder investigation. What he really wanted to do was go out and find who'd really killed his cousin. He was close to doing so—let the Runner outside follow him.

Dorne returned and announced that Anthony was here again. Marcus said to send him in. He poured another glass of port and held it out to his friend as soon as he walked in.

Anthony accepted the drink. "Ah, you know me so well. But I thought you told me to stop drinking."

"I said to stop drinking *so much*. This is a special occasion." Marcus took a drink.

"You make it sound important instead of vexing."

"It's both." Marcus went to his favorite chair and flopped into it, stretching his legs out. "I need to get out before I go mad."

"Are you not supposed to leave?" Anthony took another chair.

"I can, but the Runner outside will follow me."

Anthony lifted a shoulder. "Does that matter? Unless you're planning to kill someone else."

Marcus glared at him.

"Too soon to jest? My apologies." Anthony sipped his port. "Where do you want to go? Hyde Park? Bond Street? Brooks's?"

Marcus shuddered. "None of those. Is the gossip not as bad as you said yesterday?"

Anthony winced. "I'm afraid it's worse. Most people are quite convinced you killed Drobbit. However, it's now getting out that he was perhaps swindling people, and there are presumptions that he was trying to cheat you and you shot him."

It shouldn't have surprised him, and really, it didn't. "Most people?" he asked. He didn't care who, except for one person. Did Phoebe think he'd killed his cousin? She didn't seem to.

He mentally shook himself. It didn't matter.

"I haven't taken an official count," Anthony said. "You don't actually care, do you?"

"No. I would prefer, however, not to be prosecuted for the murder."

"Is that a real chance?"

Marcus took another drink. He hadn't thought so, but Harry hadn't told him that he was no longer a suspect—or that there were any others. "I can't be the only person they're investigating. I can think of several gentlemen with a motive to kill him."

"Because he was cheating them. Men like Halstead." Anthony frowned. "Had he already left for Huntwell?"

"I'm not sure. I think they left Wednesday morning."

"So no."

Marcus stared at Anthony. "You can't think Graham had anything to do with this."

Anthony shook his head and settled back in his chair with a sigh. "No. Just thinking with my mouth."

"I want to go back to the Horn and poke around, ask some questions." He specifically wanted to speak with Mary since she'd been so helpful. Someone had to have seen something that night.

"Hasn't Bow Street probably already done that?" Anthony asked.

"And where are they? Harry hasn't kept me apprised of their investigation."

Dorne appeared in the doorway. "Another message has arrived for you, my lord. The lad who delivered it said it was urgent."

Marcus's gut clenched. He held up his hand, and Dorne offered the missive. Inclining his head, he turned and left.

Turning the paper over between his fingers, Marcus stared at the note.

A sensation of dread curled through Marcus. He opened the parchment and quickly read the contents, his apprehension confirmed. "This is a courtesy note from my friend the Runner, not from Bow Street. A witness has come forward to say he heard me threatening Drobbit the other night at the Horn and then a gunshot." He let his arm drop, holding the letter in his lap. "I'm going to be arrested."

Anthony's face paled. "Fuck. When?"

"I don't know, but I'm not waiting here." Marcus stood and tossed the letter on his desk, then finished his port. He set the empty glass on the sideboard. "I'm going to the Horn Tavern." It was early in the afternoon, but hopefully, Marcus would learn something. If he was stuck at Bow Street, he wouldn't be able to do anything.

Anthony tossed back the rest of his port and leapt up. "I'll go with you."

"I think it's best if I go alone. You don't need to be wrapped up in this."

"I'm your friend. Tell me what I can do to help."

"Stay here, and if Bow Street comes to arrest me, inform them I'll be back soon." Marcus wasn't trying to evade them. There would be no point in that.

"You're a marquess," Anthony said with grave confidence. "You'll be tried in the Lords, and you'll plead privilege."

"Only if they find me guilty of manslaughter." If he were found guilty of murder, he'd hang. Marcus scowled. "But I didn't do it."

Marcus called for Dorne and sent him to fetch his hat and gloves. A few minutes later, after Anthony wished him luck, Marcus made his way from the back of the house to the mews. He crept along quickly to Oxford Street, where he caught a hack to Russell Street.

The people bustling along the street during the day were quite different from late at night. Tradespeople and shoppers mingled along the thoroughfare. Marcus hurried straight to the Horn Tavern and slipped into the dim interior.

The tavern was different too, much quieter and far less crowded. Marcus went directly to the bar and motioned to the barkeeper. The older man shuffled over. "Ye want an ale?"

"Actually, I want to speak with Mary. Is she here?"

"Who wants to know?" the man asked gruffly.

Marcus dropped a few coins on the counter. "Where can I find her?"

The barkeeper scooped up the coins and nodded toward the ceiling. "Top floor. She shares a room with another of the girls."

"Thank you." Marcus strode to the stairs and took them two at a time. He hesitated briefly at the second landing, glancing down toward Drobbit's room. He really was sorry the man's life had ended that way. But who was behind it?

When he reached the top, Marcus saw several doors. Resigned to guessing, he started with the first door on the left. It took him to the third room to find her. And he hadn't had to knock because she poked her head out when he rapped on the second door.

Seeing her, Marcus hastened to her door. "May I speak with you?"

She glanced back into the room, then came out, closing the door behind her. Tucking a wayward curl behind her ear, she looked up at him with a sheen of uncertainty in her gaze. "I'm sorry I told Bow Street about you."

Marcus ground his teeth together. She was the one who'd said she'd heard him arguing? "What did you tell them?"

"That you asked about Mr. Tibbord, and that I told you where to find him."

"That's all you said?"

She nodded.

Marcus exhaled as frustration nibbled at his insides. "You didn't see anything else? No one else visited Mr. Tibbord?"

She bit her lip, and Marcus detected a note of hesitation in her demeanor as she glanced away from him.

"Mary, is there something else you can tell me about that night? Anything at all that would keep me from hanging?"

Her eyes widened just before her brow creased with worry. "There was another man, but I'm not supposed to tell people about him."

A spark of hope lit in Marcus's chest. "Why not?"

"There's some gents who come to see Mr. Tibbord, but unlike you, they know to go directly to Scog, the barkeep. They give Scog a special word, and he sends them straight up because he knows Mr. Tibbord invited them. We're supposed to ignore those gentlemen, to keep their visits secret." She took a breath, her face still etched with concern. "I don't want you to hang, my lord."

These gentlemen sounded like those who'd "invested" with Drobbit. Marcus's pulse sped at the prospect of finding another suspect. "What did this man look like?"

"Above average height, but not overly tall. Dark hair with silver in it. He wore a puce waistcoat. I remember because I thought it was pretty."

A memory flashed in Marcus's brain. Stewart Lennox had been wearing a puce waistcoat when Marcus had called on him that day. And Mary's description fit him. The idiot had come to see Drobbit even after Marcus had warned him not to. The bloody fool.

Mary touched his arm. "Please don't tell anyone I

told you." Her face fell. "But if you don't, you'll hang."

"Don't worry about that just now," Marcus said, eager for whatever information she could recall. "Did you hear the gunshot?"

"No. The common room is too loud, I think."

She had a point. Marcus wondered where this supposed witness who'd gone to Bow Street could have been in order to hear it. Not that it mattered since the witness was lying—there had been no threat and certainly no gunshot before Marcus left.

"What time did you see Lennox—" Marcus silently swore for mentioning his name. "The gentleman with the puce waistcoat?" he asked.

"Midnight, maybe?" She shrugged. "I can't be certain."

"One last thing," he said. "I wondered if you might know who told Bow Street they heard me arguing with Drobbit just before he was shot."

Mary's eyes widened with surprise once more. "Someone said that? They would have had to have been outside his door." She fell silent, her expression locked in consternation. "I don't recall seeing anyone else come up here, but I could have missed them."

"Can you think of anything else that happened that night?"

She pondered his question for a long moment. "I can't." She shook her head. "I didn't know Mr. Tibbord very well, but he was always kind to me. I hated seeing him like that."

"You saw him after he was shot?"

"I'm the one who found him. I took his supper up around one."

That was awfully late to eat supper, but perhaps she'd been busy. Or perhaps Drobbit had simply kept a very strange schedule.

That meant Drobbit had been killed sometime

after Marcus left but before one—a rather narrow window of opportunity. And Lennox had come within that timeframe. Was he the one who'd implicated Marcus? That seemed unlikely, but what did Marcus know? *Someone* wanted Marcus to take the blame.

All he needed to do was go to Bow Street and tell them Lennox had been here too. Except Marcus wouldn't do that. If Lennox had killed him, and it seemed he certainly might have, he'd hang. Marcus couldn't let that happen.

Marcus gave Mary a faint smile. "I appreciate your help." He reached into his pocket to give her another coin, but she shook her head.

"I can't take anything more from ye."

Marcus put his hand back at his side. "I think it's best if you don't tell anyone about the man in the puce waistcoat."

"But won't it help your cause if I tell Bow Street?"

"No," Marcus lied. He couldn't allow Phoebe's father to hang either. Marcus had a much better chance of surviving a trial and a conviction. "Furthermore, I don't wish to cause you any trouble. I'll be fine—I promise."

He inclined his head, then turned and started down the stairs. As he descended, his mind churned. If he tried to defend himself against Bow Street's investigation, they'd eventually find Phoebe's father. Marcus couldn't let that happen either.

Which meant he had to confess. Anthony's words vaulted into his mind: *"Claim privilege."* He could, if he were guilty of manslaughter, which he could plead. He could say he was acting in self-defense and likely escape any punishment beyond perhaps a fine. It was disgusting to think that his privilege could save him from the gallows when any other man would likely dangle from the end of a rope.

There was only one thing to be done, and the sooner he did it, the sooner he could put this entire debacle behind him.

But first, he had to pay a call.

CHAPTER 14

*M*arcus hadn't responded to the letter she'd sent the day before. In fact, he hadn't corresponded with her at all. Phoebe had to accept that their affair had met a rapid demise.

Except she wasn't ready to accept it. She wanted to fight. But for what? It was an affair with no promises, and by its very nature would be temporary. If it hadn't ended now, it would end at some point, likely in the near future.

Their time together hadn't been enough. If not for Drobbit's murder, she and Marcus would still be together. She was sure of it.

Are you?

Phoebe blinked and refocused on the book she'd been trying—and failing—to read. A shiver tripped along her shoulders. She looked over toward the door to the garden—just as Marcus was closing it.

Snapping the book shut, she jumped up and dropped it in the chair. Her heart began to pound, and her breath snagged in her lungs.

The urge to run to him and throw her arms around his neck was overwhelming. She resisted even while it felt like her body would launch of its own accord.

He glanced toward the open door to the stair vestibule. Phoebe went and closed it. Then she locked it for good measure.

When she turned back to face him, he gave her a weak smile. "Miss me?"

She strode toward him, stopping short of touching him. "Yes. I've been so worried."

He tossed his hat onto a chair and took her hands. He wasn't wearing gloves. "I can imagine, and I'm sorry. There hasn't been much to say."

She couldn't stand it anymore. Standing on her toes, she put her hands on his face, running her fingers along the familiar planes of his jaw and cheekbones. Then she kissed him.

The result was explosive and consuming. Their mouths slanted, their tongues clashed. She clutched at his shoulders, anchoring herself to him and to the sensations he wrought. Desire, elation, *need*.

He clutched her backside, drawing her to him so their hips were flush. She felt his rigid cock against her lower belly. A desperate craving flushed over her. Rotating her pelvis against him, she raked her fingers up his neck and into his hair.

Their kisses expanded, moving from mouths to jaws to necks to earlobes. She nipped at his flesh, and he groaned.

"I need you," he rasped.

She clasped his scalp. "I need *you*."

He turned her and steered them back toward the garden. She felt the table against the tops of her thighs, and then he lifted her to sit on the edge. When he shoved her skirts up, they billowed around her hips.

She brought her hands down and flicked open the buttons of his fall. Reaching inside his breeches, she encircled her fingers around his cock and tugged at his flesh. He groaned deep in his throat, a dark, gritty sound that flooded her with lust.

Marcus shoved her legs farther apart, and she positioned him at her sex. Then he drove inside her, plunging deep.

Phoebe wrapped her legs around him, digging her heels into his backside as he thrust into her. She pulled on his nape, drawing his mouth to hers. Their kisses were heady and sensual, building the passion sizzling between them. She wanted this moment, this joining, to last forever, but already, she felt her release gathering.

He cupped her head and pulled it back to expose her throat to his lips and tongue. He left a devastating trail of want and rapture from her jaw to her bodice, his mouth closing on her flesh and sucking hard before he let her go.

She broke apart, her senses splintering as pleasure engulfed her. She clung to him amidst the rapture, holding on to him as the only thing she understood, the only thing that made sense.

His hips snapped between hers, pumping into her several more times before he grunted and buried himself within her. Using her legs, she held him tightly inside, reveling in the feel of him.

She rested her forehead on his shoulder, her breath coming fast.

"Well, fuck." Marcus's words were at odds with the gentle way he stroked her back.

The question died on her lips as she realized the reason for his curse. They hadn't used a sponge or a French letter. And he hadn't pulled away before giving her his seed.

"Fuck indeed," she murmured.

He laughed softly, then more loudly. Then he kissed her temple. "You're a treasure."

Phoebe lowered her legs, and he eased back from

her. Before he went too far, she used the hem of her petticoat to wipe him off. Her eyes met the cobalt intensity of his.

"Thank you," he said simply before turning from her and fastening his breeches.

She knew he meant to give her a bit of privacy. He was an exceptionally considerate lover. He was an exceptionally considerate everything.

Taking a moment to tidy herself, she slid from the table and set herself to rights. She smoothed her hair back, unsure of what it might look like.

"I hadn't intended for that to happen," he said, pivoting to look at her again.

"Clearly. We were both unprepared."

"And utterly swept away." He sounded regretful, but there was a gleam in his eye that said otherwise —a satisfied pride in the fact that they'd been too overcome to think straight. Or maybe she was simply seeing a reflection of what she felt.

"Why did you come in through the back door?" she asked, apprehensive of his answer.

He inhaled, and the spark disappeared from his gaze. Her apprehension grew. "I wanted to take special care not to be seen. It's more crucial than ever that we not be linked too closely. I came to end our affair." He took a step toward her with a sad half smile.

The room tilted sideways for a moment. Phoebe had expected this on some level—he'd kept himself away from her entirely since Drobbit had been found.

"Two nights was one night too many?" She tried to keep her voice light. "Never mind today."

To think she would never experience that with him again... Anguish tore at her insides, and she had to clamp her jaw tightly to keep from making a sound.

He cocked his head lightly. "You aren't surprised?"

"Should I be? You aren't one to have affairs, and your absence the last few days spoke volumes."

His brow creased. "I didn't want to infect you with the disaster surrounding me. I still don't."

"Is that why you're ending it, then?" She would have preferred that excuse.

"Partly. But you're right. This is too much. For me."

Phoebe gave in to her heartache, taking a step toward him. "Why?"

He blinked and didn't immediately answer. His gaze wavered, and he looked past her to the garden. "I'm not made for this." He closed the distance between them and took her hand. "You're a beautiful, intelligent, kindhearted woman, Phoebe. I pray you will not remain alone. Unlike me, I don't think you're meant for that. You should have an adoring husband and children—if you want them. You deserve that and so much more." He kissed her wrist, his lips soft and familiar.

"I think you're being a coward." The thought sprang from her mouth before she could censor it.

His gaze flickered with surprise. "Perhaps." He let go of her hand. "I never claimed to be a hero."

And he bloody wasn't. Anger overtook her despair. "What if there is a child?"

"There won't be."

Phoebe glared at him. "How arrogant of you to say so."

"Yes, well, that is one thing I'm quite good at."

"You also excel at being ephemeral." She wanted him to go before she did something completely humiliating such as cry. "Don't let me keep you."

"I hope we'll remain friends."

Now she wanted to throw her book at his head. "Of course." Maybe. But not today.

He looked like he wanted to say something else, but in the end, he just grabbed his hat and left the way he'd come.

Phoebe stared after him until he was gone from sight. Turning, she walked woodenly to her chair and picked up her book. Slowly, she sat, holding the book on her lap.

Finally, she surrendered to emotion—to the love she just realized she felt only to have lost it already—and cried.

～

*H*arry showed Marcus into a small chamber at Bow Street. The space was starkly furnished with a small table and a few mismatched wooden chairs. A slender fireplace in the corner sat cold, and a window high on the wall allowed only a bit of light from the heavily overcast day. The dreary surroundings matched Marcus's mood.

Harry gestured toward one of the chairs. "My apologies for the lack of comfort here. This is where we typically interrogate people. I'm afraid I couldn't find anywhere for us to meet." He sat down, and as the chair beneath him creaked, Marcus wondered if it might crumble from the strain of Harry's large frame.

Marcus sat too, but his chair was quiet. "This is fine. In fact, it's probably appropriate for I've come to confess."

Harry's eyes widened and then he frowned. "To killing Drobbit?"

Marcus nodded. "Yes."

"You shot him?"

"Yes." The lie burned his throat, but it was necessary. He wasn't going to let Phoebe's father hang.

Harry took a moment before speaking again. He rubbed a hand over his deeply creased brow. "Why didn't you admit it before now?"

"I was upset—it wasn't my intent to harm him." That much was true. The intention anyway. He hadn't been upset—he was very rarely upset. Yet he was now.

He was?

Yes, he was agitated, unsettled, frustrated. Not because of Drobbit, but because of Phoebe. The look in her eyes when he'd left her a short while ago would haunt him for a long time. Forever, maybe.

Hell.

Harry shifted in his chair, causing it to moan again. "You have to know that it doesn't look good that you waited to confess until after the witness came forward about you."

"I can imagine it's not ideal. However, this is where we are." He gave Harry a weak smile. "I do appreciate you sending a note. That allowed me to arrange some things."

Surprise made Harry's auburn brows briefly dart up. "Such as?"

"Personal matters."

"Nothing to do with the murder, then? It was an odd thing to say. I have to ask."

Marcus actually chuckled. "I chose my words poorly. I needed to speak with someone, and I was able to do that."

"Miss Lennox?" Harry asked.

When Marcus didn't answer, Harry moved on. "I've learned you fought with Sainsbury at White's on Monday. Did you break his nose?"

"I didn't consult with a physician, but it seemed

so, yes." Marcus settled into his chair and crossed his legs. "What does that have to do with Drobbit?"

"It's a pattern of violent behavior. You fought with Drobbit at the park a few weeks ago too."

Fuck. That didn't look good for him either. Still, he would never regret it, and he didn't care who knew. "Sainsbury deserved what he got and more."

Harry braced his hands on his knees, leaning slightly forward. "You must realize this reflects poorly on you."

"Put together with my scandalous reputation, I can't imagine this will end well." He said this with a dose of humor, but it sounded macabre nonetheless.

Harry scowled. "I hope you aren't making light of this. The evidence will be presented to the magistrate tomorrow. There is enough that I expect he will charge you with murder."

Murder. The word echoed in Marcus's brain. The already small room closed in around him. "Where will I be jailed until tomorrow?"

"Nowhere. I'm going to allow you to return home for tonight. But there will be Runners on patrol at your house."

"So, just like the past few days, then." He couldn't keep the sarcasm from his tone, and why should he?

Harry's scowl returned but deeper. "You should be concerned at the very least. After you see the magistrate tomorrow, you'll be taken to the Tower until you stand trial."

The Tower... Wonderful. A queasy feeling worked its way through Marcus. "A trial of my peers in the House of Lords?"

"Of course. With luck, they'll acquit you, but you should prepare to be found guilty of manslaughter."

"Not murder?"

"No, because you're going to argue self-defense. You just told me you hadn't intended to harm Drobbit. The man was stealing from people, and you were trying to put a stop to it. You quarreled. Drobbit attacked you, and you shot him." Harry paused, his gaze fixing intently on Marcus. "You brought a pistol with you?"

Damn. Marcus hadn't thought about that part. "No, Drobbit had one. I threw it in the Thames."

Harry stared at him, his expression slightly dubious. He did not, perhaps, entirely trust everything Marcus said. "Assuming they find you guilty of manslaughter, you should claim privilege of peerage. You may escape this with only paying a fine. Or perhaps even acquittal—don't underestimate your number of friends."

"Or I might hang. I realize it's been a while since the Earl Ferrers was executed for murder, but not *so* long ago." Nearly sixty years, but people would remember that it wasn't unheard of for a peer to be taken to Tyburn.

"You aren't going to hang," Harry said. "Which is why you aren't going to confess."

"I *am* going to confess, but I appreciate you trying to help me—you're a good friend."

Harry sat back in his chair and crossed his arms over his wide chest. "I just wish you hadn't fought with Drobbit—or Sainsbury."

"I regret the altercation with my cousin, but he incited that. I will readily admit, however, that I provoked Sainsbury." And he'd do it again. Happily.

"I understand you defamed him?" At Marcus's nod, he continued. "Impugned his manhood is the rumor."

"That's accurate."

"What did he do to invite your wrath?"

"He insulted the wrong person." Insulted didn't

begin to describe Sainsbury's crimes, but Marcus wouldn't share the specifics.

"Are you sure you want to confess?"

"I am." Marcus's gut clenched again. He had the sense he was falling into an abyss. He cocked his head at his old friend. "You don't believe I did this."

"I don't. But I believe you want me to think you did." Harry stood. "Tomorrow, the magistrate will make a record of the murder and accusing you of committing it. If you choose to plead guilty right then, I am not sure what will happen. Please plead not guilty to give yourself a chance."

A chance for what? He really didn't know if he would hang, even if he did plead guilty to the magistrate tomorrow. There was an inherent privilege to being a marquess, which was ridiculous. He came into this world the same as any other man and would exit it the same way. Why should he benefit from something so arbitrary as blood?

Marcus slowly rose.

"I can see you're thinking about it," Harry said. "Good. I'll come fetch you in the morning. Unless I can discover what really happened before then."

That couldn't happen. He'd find out Phoebe's father had done it. Marcus took a few steps toward Harry. "Don't. *I* did this. No one else. Let it go. Please."

Harry's answering stare was dark, his jaw tight. "Do you want to sign a confession now, then? If you do, I can't let you leave."

Goddammit. The room shrank even more. Marcus tried to take a deep breath and couldn't. "Tomorrow."

"Good decision." Only Harry's gruff tone didn't sound as if he approved at all. But then, why would he if he believed Marcus was lying?

"Don't worry overmuch about me, Harry," Marcus said. "I know what I'm doing."

Harry shook his head. "I sure as hell hope so." He went to the door and opened it, gesturing with his head for Marcus to precede him.

Marcus left the building and climbed into his waiting coach. He looked down at his hands to see if they were shaking. They were not.

He'd count that as a victory.

The truth was that while he knew what he was doing, he wasn't at all sure how it would turn out. Furthermore, he wasn't sure he cared. For the first time in his life, he felt truly despondent. And dammit if that didn't scare him to death.

CHAPTER 15

*C*ollecting herself after Marcus had left had taken Phoebe some time. She'd gone out to the yard and viciously pruned a pair of shrubs. When she'd finished, she hoped she hadn't stunted them forever.

Eager to clean up after her exertions, Phoebe awaited the arrival of fresh water in her chamber. She was delighted to see that Meg, the maid her father had terminated and who had ended up working for Sainsbury, was the one to deliver it.

"Meg, you're here!" In the cloud of her sadness about Marcus, Phoebe had forgotten she would be coming today. The housekeeper had arranged it the day before yesterday.

Meg, a young maid, perhaps not even quite twenty, grinned as she poured the steaming water into the basin. She was already garbed in the clothing Phoebe provided, something she did whenever anyone came to work in her household. The dark peach color of her gown brought out the warm hues of her dark blonde hair. "I am, miss. Thank you for the new dress."

"I'm so glad it seems to fit well enough."

"Indeed it does. I can't thank you enough for

hiring me away from Mr. Sainsbury." She flinched as she stepped back from the basin and went to set the empty bucket near the door.

"I'm so glad to have you. I'm just sorry you ended up in Sainsbury's household at all." Phoebe had learned from the housekeeper that Meg had leapt upon the opportunity to leave. She'd said she was miserable working for Sainsbury, which hadn't surprised Phoebe, of course.

"I own I'm worried about those who are left," Meg said, clasping her hands as her brow puckered.

Phoebe turned her back to Meg. "Would you mind unfastening my gown? Page is out this afternoon."

Meg loosened the ties and then helped Phoebe to undress.

"Are you concerned for their safety?" Phoebe asked, wondering if Sainsbury had abused any of his female servants the way he had her. She stood at the basin and washed her arms, face, and neck.

"Yes, I think so. He didn't physically harm any of us—not in the way one would think, anyway."

Phoebe, clad in just her corset and chemise, turned to look at Meg. "I understand. You recall that I was betrothed to Sainsbury. He didn't physically hurt me either, not in the traditional sense where one might be bloody or bruised. But he did take physical advantage, and he did cause harm."

Tears formed in Meg's eyes, but she blinked them away before they fell. Phoebe clasped her hands and gave them a squeeze. "You're safe now. And let's see what we can do to deliver the others to safety too."

Meg nodded. "Thank you, miss. You're so very kind. I do worry that Mr. Sainsbury might start actually hurting someone. He's quite fond of his pistols, always cleaning them, shooting them, bandying them about. He carries one on his person nearly all the time. It makes us nervous. I was so relieved when Mrs. Tarcove came to see me, especially since he'd arrived home early Wednesday morning with gunpowder on his clothing. We speculated that he'd perhaps fought a duel, but we didn't hear of one. Did you?" Meg winced slightly. "Begging your pardon, miss. I don't mean to gossip."

Phoebe was intrigued by all this information about the man she'd escaped marrying. She'd never felt more fortunate—he sounded even worse than she'd thought him to be. "I am not aware of a duel." But that didn't mean it hadn't happened. She could well imagine Sainsbury getting into such trouble.

"We wondered because he came home Monday night in a rage with blood all over him, said his nose had been broken in a fight." Meg went to the wardrobe to fetch a fresh petticoat.

A fight? On Monday… That night was emblazoned in her mind forever, because it was the first night she and Marcus had lain together. Marcus had also been bleeding—supposedly from hitting his head on the hack. "Do you know whom he fought with?" Phoebe asked.

Meg returned and dropped the garment over Phoebe's head before tying it in place. "Mr. Sainsbury didn't say, but I do recall him muttering the name Ripley several times. He seemed quite angry when he did so. Perhaps that's who he fought?"

Of course it was—Phoebe had absolutely no doubt. Her heart tripped, and she sucked in a breath. Why hadn't Marcus told her he'd fought with Sainsbury? What had happened to provoke the conflict? She'd told him what Sainsbury had done… Had Marcus started a fight with him? Worse, had they fought a duel?

No, that couldn't have happened. Sainsbury would likely be dead. She'd heard that Marcus was an excellent shot—it was part of his scandalous reputation.

She longed to ask Marcus about their fight, but how could she do that now? Her anger at him resurfaced. Oh, he was a frustrating man!

Calming her emotions while Meg fastened her into a gown, Phoebe focused on the problem at hand: Sainsbury and the gunpowder on his clothing. Something about that tugged at her thoughts, and it wasn't because she thought he and Marcus had somehow fought a duel from which they'd both escaped unscathed. Unless Sainsbury *had* been wounded? "When Sainsbury came home with gunpowder on his clothing, was he hurt?"

Meg shook her head. "Not at all. In fact, he was in a rather cheerful mood. It was very strange. Whatever happened, he was quite pleased about it. We determined he must have won the duel."

Phoebe's blood went cold. Had he—? No, it couldn't be possible. And yet she was fixated on the possibility that Sainsbury had killed Marcus's cousin. But why would he do that?

To make it look as though Marcus had done it.

She wasn't sure she believed that. Sainsbury was despicable, but why would he seek to completely ruin Marcus? Not just ruin him, but potentially see him hanged, since that was the punishment for murder.

It made some sense. Or maybe Phoebe was simply trying to find a way to save Marcus. Discovering Sainsbury to be the villain in this scenario would be particularly satisfying, which meant it likely wasn't true.

Phoebe summoned a feeble smile for Meg. "Thank you for your help. I'm so glad you're here."

Meg dipped a curtsey before she picked up the basin of water. "I am too, miss." As she went to pour the used water into the bucket, Phoebe donned her shoes and tidied her hair. All the while, her mind turned at the possibility of Sainsbury's involvement in Drobbit's death.

Meg departed and then returned almost immediately. "There's someone here to see you. Mr. Harry Sheffield from Bow Street."

Phoebe's blood turned colder still. "Thank you, Meg. Please let Culpepper know I'll meet Mr. Sheffield in the garden room."

Taking a final look in the glass, Phoebe smoothed her hair, then hurried downstairs. She composed herself and slowed as she entered the garden room. Mr. Sheffield stood near the glass doors that led to the garden. He was a massive presence, both taller and wider across the shoulders than Marcus, which seemed an impossible feat to Phoebe.

"Good afternoon, Mr. Sheffield." It was nearly evening, actually.

He bowed. "Good afternoon, Miss Lennox. I do hope I am not intruding upon you."

"Not at all. Would you care to sit?"

"Thank you." He took her favorite chair near the hearth, prompting her to find another chair nearby. "I do hope you won't think me too forward—and I want you to know that I will do my best to protect anything you tell me here with regard to your reputation."

Phoebe's curiosity was intrigued, but her thoughts were agitated after what she'd just learned from Meg. "I appreciate you saying that."

"Pardon the indelicacy of my inquiry, but is it acceptable—to you—for me to assume that when I visited here early Wednesday that Lord Ripley had spent the night here?"

She didn't want to lie, not about anything to do with what happened to Marcus's cousin. "Yes."

"What time did he arrive that night?"

"About…one, I think. Maybe shortly before."

Sheffield clasped his hands in his lap. "How did he seem?"

Phoebe wasn't sure how to answer that question. She thought back to that night. He'd come into her chamber, and she'd poured him a glass of port. He barely drank any of it because she'd stripped her dressing gown away almost immediately. There was little conversation.

"Fine," she answered.

"He didn't seem agitated or upset?"

She shook her head. "Not at all. He was as he always is—utterly in possession of his control and desires." She blushed at her embarrassing choice of words. Plus, it wasn't entirely true. He'd nearly lost control, and she'd had to remind him to don the French letter. "Why do you ask?" She wanted to know, and she didn't want to leave the last word she'd said hanging in the air.

Sheffield frowned. "He came to Bow Street earlier and confessed to killing his cousin."

"*What?*" The word spilled from her mouth without thought. "That's ridiculous."

The Runner's expression was grim. "I think so too, and yet he insists he did it. I couldn't determine why he would lie to me so I went back to the Horn Tavern. I learned that someone else visited Drobbit that night."

There was an expectant weight to his words. "Who?" Phoebe asked.

"Your father."

Phoebe clutched the arms of her chair, her insides somersaulting. She wanted to ask why, but she knew. Drobbit had been cheating her father. Marcus also knew that. "Did Marcus know my father was there?"

"Yes. One of the Horn's employees, a maid, said she told Ripley about your father—she didn't know his identity until Ripley referred to him as Lennox. That conversation happened just before Ripley confessed to me."

The room swam before Phoebe. Marcus had confessed to this crime after learning her father may have committed it… "You don't believe Marcus did this."

"I do not. And neither does Mary—the maid I spoke with. Ripley told her he was trying to avoid hanging, which was why she told him about your father visiting. She'd withheld that information from me before because of some arrangement between Drobbit and her employer, Mr. Scoggins. Gentlemen who came to see Drobbit were to be kept secret. Mary feared for her job, so she didn't say anything until she realized Ripley could be charged with a crime he didn't commit."

If Marcus hadn't done this—and she was certain he hadn't. Did that mean her father had? Phoebe couldn't believe that either, and yet her father had been so angry of late. Angry enough to kill someone? No, she couldn't imagine it.

She did, however, have an idea of someone who could. Someone who apparently always carried a pistol and had come home with gunpowder on his clothing that night.

"Are you all right, Miss Lennox?" Sheffield looked to her with an expression of genuine concern.

She was not, but she had to maintain her composure. She turned, breathing deep in an effort to slow her racing pulse. "I can't believe that either Marcus or my father did this. The culprit has to be someone else. And I think I might know who."

The Runner blinked in surprise. "Why didn't you say so immediately?"

"I didn't realize until right now. I mean, I suspected, but it seemed far-fetched. And it may still be." She shook her head. "I'm confusing you. Let me start at the beginning. Apparently, Marcus fought with Mr. Laurence Sainsbury on Monday night. I believe he broke Sainsbury's nose."

"I'd heard about this fight. It doesn't bode well for Ripley since it shows he has a violent side."

"It also shows that Sainsbury does too," Phoebe said, warming to her theory. "Did you know that Sainsbury carries a pistol?"

Sheffield's auburn brows pitched into a V as he leaned slightly forward. "No, and how do you know this?"

"I've just hired a maid who was in his employ until this morning. She told me he returned home early Wednesday with gunpowder on his clothing. They'd assumed he'd gotten into a duel and that he'd won, for he was uncharacteristically happy. As opposed to the night before, when he'd arrived home in a rage with a bloodied nose, muttering about Marcus."

The Runner abruptly stood and paced a few steps. He was quiet, clearly pondering what she'd told him. Then, just as suddenly as he'd gotten to his feet, he turned to face her. "You think Sainsbury killed Drobbit?"

"I think Sainsbury is a vengeful blackguard." He'd done plenty to denounce Phoebe after she'd jilted him. "What if he went after Marcus the night after their fight and then, with the convenience of his pistol, found an opportunity to blame a murder on him?"

"That's possible…" Sheffield took a few steps to the side and then returned to the same spot. "May I speak with your maid?"

"Of course." Phoebe sent for Meg, who came to

the garden room and timidly repeated to the Runner what she'd told Phoebe.

"I don't suppose anyone in Mr. Sainsbury's household saved the gunpowder-stained clothing?"

"I don't know," Meg said hesitantly.

Sheffield gave her a reassuring smile. "It's all right. I'd like to go and speak with your former coworkers. Do you think they would talk to me?"

Meg wrung her hands. "Maybe, but only if Mr. Sainsbury wouldn't be angry. He has a powerfully bad temper, sir."

"I understand," Sheffield said soothingly. "I will ensure the safety and well-being of everyone."

"They can all come work here," Phoebe offered. "I mean that. Until they can find employment elsewhere. And I'll help them do that too." It wasn't as if Phoebe had anything else to do. Without Marcus, her life seemed incredibly empty, which was strange because it hadn't felt that way before he'd come into it.

"You're very kind, miss," Meg said, her brown eyes warm with gratitude.

Phoebe turned to the Runner. "Is there anything else you need from Meg?"

"No." He pivoted toward Meg. "Thank you for your assistance."

Meg presented a quick curtsey and took herself off.

When she was gone, Phoebe asked, "So you think it's possible Sainsbury could have killed Drobbit?"

"It *is* possible. I just wish Sainsbury had the same history of violence as Ripley."

Phoebe put her hand on her hip. "Marcus fought with Drobbit for good reason. If you think that's a history of violence compared to what Sainsbury has done—" She stopped herself before she revealed too much.

Sheffield narrowed his eyes at her. "What has Sainsbury done?"

Phoebe realized she had to reveal too much. To save Marcus. So she recounted, in less specific terms than she'd shared with Marcus, what Sainsbury had done to her. Instead of making her feel weak and horrid, the revelation steeled her with strength and something she'd once thought she'd lost: power. She concluded by saying, "When you question Sainsbury's maids, ask them what he's done. I believe you'll find he has behaved consistently in terms of violence and reprehensible behavior."

He nodded grimly. "He certainly sounds capable of killing Drobbit, whereas I don't think Ripley is. However, after hearing what Sainsbury did, I am surprised the man survived his altercation with Ripley."

"Why would you say that?" Phoebe asked.

"Because Ripley said the man deserved what he'd gotten and more." Sheffield's gaze softened slightly. "Ripley is the kind of man who protects the people he cares about. I've known him a very long time. You may think he's incapable of emotion—sometimes I think *he* thinks he's incapable of it—but he is not."

His words warmed Phoebe, but then it was as if a bucket of frigid water had been tossed upon her. Marcus might care for Phoebe, but not enough to forge a future together. Especially since he'd just confessed to a crime he didn't commit.

To save my father.

That wasn't the action of a man who didn't care, who didn't feel emotion. Phoebe wasn't sure what emotion he felt, but she knew her own heart, and she knew she loved him.

She longed to go to him, but she was also worried about her father. What if her theory about

Sainsbury wasn't true? "Are you going to Sainsbury's now?" she asked.

"First, I'm going to visit your father. I would like to speak with him about his visit to Drobbit."

"I'm sure he left the man alive," Phoebe said with conviction.

"Hopefully, he can provide information that will corroborate that."

"Do you mind if I go with you? I can leave immediately." When he nodded, she went to the hall and asked Culpepper to send someone for her hat and gloves. Returning to the garden room, she asked, "What will happen to Marcus if we can't prove Sainsbury—or someone else—is the real culprit?"

"Ripley is due before the magistrate tomorrow, and that's without a confession, which I convinced him not to provide yet. After that, he'll go to the Tower of London to await a trial in the House of Lords. If he confesses, there will be no trial, just punishment." Sheffield didn't elaborate on what that could be, but Phoebe could well imagine.

The world turned to gray around her. She fought to keep herself together.

Sheffield gave her a look that was surely meant to buoy her spirits. "Have faith. Even if he pleads guilty to manslaughter—which is what I will recommend the charge should be—he can claim privilege of peerage and, with luck, escape the worst of punishments."

Luck. Phoebe prayed they had enough of that to go around.

CHAPTER 16

*T*he pencil flew across the paper as Marcus detailed yet another drawing of Phoebe. He'd drawn several of her over the past few days and had no intention of slowing down or even stopping. He saw her in his mind's eye in a myriad states and positions, and he wanted to commit them all to parchment.

Perhaps he'd cover the walls of his cell at the Tower with them.

Marcus's hand didn't slow, even with that maudlin thought. He supposed he should tell his retainers that as of tomorrow, he would no longer be a resident. After this drawing, he'd do so.

Except when he finished the drawing, he couldn't move. He sat there staring at her image, her familiar dimples winking at him. She looked particularly mischievous in this one, her expression inviting and teasing at once.

An ache, dark and desperate, ate at him as he stared at her. He ran his finger over the paper, as if he could actually touch her face. How he wished that were possible.

"That's beautiful."

Marcus's head shot up. Shock and elation jolted

through him, driving him to his feet. "Where did you come from?"

Phoebe gestured to the entry to his private sitting room. "The door. You were rather focused on your work."

He drank in her form, her sable hair gathered atop her head, a dark green cloak draped around her. "How long have you been here?"

"A few minutes, actually. As I said, you were rather focused."

He couldn't believe he'd missed her arrival, not when he'd been fantasizing about her. He wanted to rush over to her, to take her in his arms. But he'd put an end to his ability to do that. "How did you get up here?"

She lifted a shoulder as she removed her cloak, draping it over a chair. "Dorne was kind enough to tell me where to find you."

"He didn't announce you." Why he was stuck on the hows of her presence was beyond Marcus, but his brain seemed arrested. There was really only one question he wanted answered. "Why?"

"Because I asked him not to." She opened the front of her gown, and the bodice fell to her waist, exposing her underclothes.

Words tangled in Marcus's mouth for a moment. "No, not why did Dorne not announce you. Why are you *here*?"

Her gown loosened, and she stepped out of the garment, laying it over her cloak. Then she sat in the chair and began to remove her boots. "Why is a very good question. Let me ask you. Why did you end things between us?"

What the hell was she doing? Disrobing, obviously. But *why*? Yes, that was definitely the most important question. "I explained why."

She exposed her knees and calves as she peeled

away her stockings, and his body reacted, quivering with desire. "I know what you said, but I'm here to confirm what you meant." She set her boots to the side, then stood, her hands going to the tie of her petticoat. "Did you end our affair because you can't commit to anything at all or because you expect to hang?" She removed the petticoat, and the garment joined the others on the chair.

Marcus swore. Somehow, she knew he was going to be arrested tomorrow. "You're aware I'm going in front of the magistrate tomorrow?"

"I am." She sounded so calm, as if his entire life wasn't about to change drastically. As if he hadn't already ruined what they'd shared. And all while, she unlaced her corset. "I'm also aware you're trying to protect my father, which is unnecessary. He didn't kill Drobbit any more than you did."

She fucking *knew*. "How—"

Having removed her corset, she now wore nothing but her chemise. She walked toward him with a feminine confidence that nearly destroyed what was left of his control. His hands shook when she stopped in front of him. She pulled the hem of his shirt from his breeches—he wore only the two garments.

"Harry is taking care of everything. He doesn't think you'll need to go to the magistrate tomorrow. I, however, still need an answer to my question. Why did you end things? If it's because you can't endure any kind of connection, tell me now, please, and I'll go."

"That is why, yes."

Her gaze, so bold and seductive the entire time she'd been there, wavered with doubt. Something inside him shattered. He grabbed her waist and slammed her against him. "But I've changed my mind."

She arched a dark, slender, ridiculously gorgeous brow and gave him a thoroughly sardonic look that pushed his already heated blood to boiling. "Because I'm here in my chemise?"

"Because when I think about the rest of my life without you in it, even for one more night, I can't breathe."

Phoebe put her hands on his face. "Breathe, my love. I'm here, and I'm not leaving."

She stood on her toes and kissed him. It was more than he expected and so much more than he deserved. He swept her up against him and gloried in the taste and feel of her. How had he thought he could walk away from her? As if she were no different from the nameless women who'd warmed his bed for years? She was absolutely different. She was exceptional. She was everything.

She was Phoebe.

She was *his*.

He turned and carried her to the bed and was about to lay her upon it, but she put her feet down and pulled away from him.

"I came here. I'm in charge." She pushed his shirt up, and he drew the garment over his head. Her hands skimmed over him, blazing a path of need with every stroke of her fingers. She unfastened his fall and pushed his breeches down over his hips, her palms caressing his backside and sending a jolt of lust straight to his cock.

He wriggled his hips, sending the garment to the floor, and kicked it aside. He looked into her eyes. "I'm yours to command."

Her lips curved up, and her gaze sparked with heat. "On the bed. On your back."

Eager to comply, he did as she bade and watched as she climbed up next to him. She kissed him again, her tongue driving deep into his mouth and pulling a groan from his throat. After leaving him breathless, she moved down his jaw and neck, using her teeth and tongue to devastating effect.

She took her time, exploring every bit of his chest and abdomen. As her tongue swirled over his hip, her hand curled around his cock, then lower to cup his balls. Marcus thrust, unable to stop himself, and let out a low groan.

Moving her hands around him, she took his tip into her mouth, licking his flesh. Ragged desire tore at him as he clasped her head. He told her in plain, filthy terms what he wanted from her.

She did them all, taking him deep into her mouth while she squeezed his balls with one hand and his hip with the other. He rose up, sliding along her tongue and filling her until he felt her throat.

Then she was gone, pulling back, only to engulf him once more. Over and over, she sucked him. He pulled the pins from her hair and tangled his fingers in the dark, silky mass, holding her while he pumped into her, captive to her.

"Phoebe, I'm going to come. In your mouth."

She released him and came up over him with a sultry smile. "Next time."

Straddling him, she pulled the chemise over her head, exposing her delectable body inch by inch. He reached for her, but she shook her head. "Just watch for a moment. And listen."

She clasped his cock and positioned it at her pussy. He clung desperately to what was left of his control. "Next time, you can come in my mouth. This time, I'm riding you because I rather liked that the other morning, and as I said, I'm in charge. Understand?"

He nodded, unable to speak through his cloud of staggering lust. She pushed down over him, taking his cock into her with ease. She was so wet, so hot, so unbelievably tight around him.

She just sat there for a moment, her eyes narrowing to slits. Then she wiggled her hips, and he moaned again, his eyes closing briefly. But only briefly. He couldn't bear not to look at her.

She began to move on him, slowly at first, her body undulating with elegant grace. Her breasts, so round and pert, beckoned him.

"May I touch you yet?" He clutched at the bed-clothes in desperation.

"Yes."

He put his hands on her breasts, cupping and kneading them, then tugging on her nipples and drawing a cry from her lips. She cast her head back, and he was certain he'd never seen anything so erotic. He would draw her like this—the line of her throat, the curve of her breast with his hand around her.

He flattened his palm at the top of her breast, his fingers grazing the hollow of her throat, his touch memorizing the planes of her flesh so he could translate them to parchment. If he could.

She put her hand over his and dragged it down between her breasts and straight to her sex. With his thumb, he teased her there, coaxing whimpers from her mouth as she rode him faster. She pitched forward slightly as her movements increased.

Marcus cupped the back of her head and brought her toward him so he could capture her breast in his mouth. He feasted on her flesh, welcoming the distraction of pleasuring her lest he explode before he was ready.

Fuck, once again, they'd neglected to plan. This time, he'd pull out.

He pressed on her clitoris and rubbed her flesh until he felt her muscles clench around him. She cried out, over and over, as her body shuddered. Her movements became stilted under the onslaught of her orgasm.

Marcus held on to her until the storm passed and her eyes opened. She blinked, bracing her hands on his chest.

"May I roll you over?" he asked.

She nodded, and he flipped her to her back. Settling himself between her legs, he thrust into her, then came up on his elbows. He stroked her face with his hands and kissed her.

"I love you," she said between kisses.

He froze, staring down at her. She looked up at him with her beautiful green eyes and moved her hips. Her dimples flashed, and he was overcome.

"Don't stop," she rasped, wrapping her legs around his waist.

Marcus kissed her again, pushing his hands into her hair as he pumped into her. He didn't want this moment, this perfect bliss, to end. But his balls tightened, and he knew he was going to spend.

"Phoebe, I need—"

She dug her heels into his backside and squeezed his hips with her hands. "Don't leave me."

Groaning, Marcus drove hard and deep, giving her everything he had. He held on to her as he poured himself into her, body and soul. She came again with him, her pussy clenching around him and sending him into a void of sheer mindlessness.

When he was spent, he rolled to his back, panting, and still so overcome, he could barely think. Had she said she loved him?

She pressed herself to his side and rose over him. "Did you hear me, Marcus? I love you. I don't expect you to say the same in return. I just want to make sure you know it. I love you. You might be a scandalous rakehell, but you're *my* scandalous rakehell. I don't know what the future holds, but so long as I have you for now—for a time—I will count myself lucky. Please don't throw away what we share because of fear."

Was he scared? Not of her, of losing her, of what she'd just said—not knowing what the future held. He'd always lived for now—for the absolute present. It wasn't enough.

Marcus sat up and clasped her head in his hands. "I am afraid. Terrified of a life without you in it. Now that I have you, I don't ever want to let you go."

She grinned, her dimples cutting deep. "You don't ever have to. Let's be terrified and then blissfully happy together."

Together. He'd been alone, truly alone, for so long. "I don't know how to be a family." He stroked his hand down her cheek and along her jaw. "But I love you, Phoebe. Somehow, impossibly, I am in love with you."

She arched her brow in that damnably provocative way again. "*Impossibly?*"

He laughed. "I don't love anything. Hell, I don't feel anything strongly. At least, I didn't until you." He stared at her, baffled. "I don't know how you did it, but please don't stop."

"Never." She kissed him, twining her arms around his neck and moving onto his lap.

After several moments, she settled into his embrace and rested her head on his shoulder.

Marcus smoothed her hair back from her face. "You said Harry—whom you are apparently on a first-name basis with now—is taking care of things. Just what is he doing?"

She moved off his lap, disappointingly, and sat at his side, turning toward him. "Oh! I should tell you about that. Harry—and yes, we have become close friends already due to our shared goal of proving your innocence—has a new suspect."

It couldn't be her father, not with the glee she displayed. Marcus couldn't think of who it might be. "Who, and however did you find this person?"

"You won't believe it." She hesitated the barest moment, during which his anxiety climbed. "Sainsbury."

Marcus gaped at her. "Of all the—"

"It was a stroke of good fortune of sorts when my father let one of his maids go." Marcus looked at her in abject confusion, and thankfully, she quickly explained. "Meg was hired by Sainsbury's household. He was as terrible an employer as you can imagine, but Meg was there to see him return home early Wednesday morning in fine spirits and sporting gunpowder on his clothing." Phoebe's brow darkened briefly. "That reminds me, you neglected to tell me that Sainsbury was the cause of your wound on Monday or that you broke his nose." She smiled widely. "Thank you for that—for breaking his nose, not for keeping it from me."

Marcus kissed her. "I'd break him in two if I could." He leaned back. "So he killed Drobbit?"

"Harry is still investigating, but we both agree that he had the motive to do so. He was angry after you humiliated him at White's and then quite cheerful after Drobbit was murdered."

"He would have had to have been following me that night," Marcus said, thinking of the events that had transpired. "No one knew where to find Drobbit until you discovered that note on your father's desk." Marcus frowned. "How would Sainsbury even know to kill Drobbit, unless he overheard our conversation?"

"There was a rumor that you threatened him that

day in the park," Phoebe reminded him. "Sainsbury was likely aware of that too."

It was a bloody diabolical scheme. "If this is true, Sainsbury is a truly horrible human being." Another thought struck him. "What about the witness who came forward to say he heard me arguing with Drobbit just before the gunshot?"

Phoebe quickly nodded, demonstrating she was well versed in this entire situation. Perhaps more versed than Marcus. "Harry was going to interview him again. He went to see Sainsbury—after he came to tell me what you'd done. Not just that, actually, he also questioned me about your behavior when you came to my house that night. I told him the truth—you didn't behave like a man who'd committed a murder."

"Any man would be hard-pressed to behave like anything but a besotted fool in your arms."

She pursed her lips. "You are not a fool. But I will accept besotted." Her dimples emerged again, and he fell even more in love with her. Would he always feel like this? He wanted to. Every damn minute of every day.

Marcus wrapped her in his arms and kissed her soundly, taking them both down so they lay side by side. They stared at each other, a kind of wonder arcing between them.

"What do we do now?" she whispered.

"Wait to see what happens with Harry's investigation, I suppose. As far as I know, I'm still going to see the magistrate tomorrow, and then I'll be thrown in the Tower." He'd been resigned to that, but now he would move heaven and earth to avoid it—to stay with Phoebe.

Forever.

The permanence frightened him, but the alternative was unacceptable.

"You are not going to be thrown anywhere," she said fiercely. "It's all going to work out—you'll see. What happens after that is up to you." Her tone turned soft, shy almost.

"Us. It's up to us. Can I assume we both want to continue our affair?"

"At least."

"I suppose the potential for a child is even greater now, since you lured me to remain inside you tonight."

"I *lured* you." She rolled her eyes. "I asked, you complied. Do not act as though you played no part in that. I will not accept responsibility for your choices."

She was right. If he'd really wanted to, he would have left her. But he hadn't. He'd known then, just as he'd known the other night, that he loved her, that he was committed to her in every way. "I knew," he said softly, smiling. "I knew you were mine and we were meant to be together, even if I was too foolish to recognize it until tonight."

"I said you aren't a fool, so you can't be foolish. You were…unilluminated."

He laughed. "Well, you have brought brightness and clarity to my world. Thank you." He leaned his forehead against hers. "Thank you."

"I love you, Marcus." She yawned. "I'm staying here. I hope you don't mind."

"I love you too." He gathered her in his arms and kissed her temple. "Stay."

CHAPTER 17

*D*espite her assurances to Marcus the night before, Phoebe was filled with a mixture of anticipation and dread as they took breakfast in the morning room of Marcus's town house. At least she didn't feel self-conscious about staying the night and arriving downstairs this morning. Marcus's retainers were kind, considerate, and they behaved as if she belonged there.

How easy it would be to make that mistake.

And it would be a mistake because she no more belonged here today than she had last night or last week. While it was clear her affair with Marcus had been rekindled, he'd made no promises for the future. No firm indication that he wanted their relationship to be permanent.

She looked at him from beneath her lids, sitting across the table perusing the newspaper that sat next to his plate. She sipped her tea, trying to focus on just putting Drobbit's murder behind them.

"You've barely eaten anything," Marcus noted.

She glanced at his plate. "You haven't exactly devoured yours."

He made a sound in his throat and went back to reading.

"Are you nervous?" she asked. "I am."

"A bit," he said, his gaze meeting hers. "But someone I admire very much told me everything would work out."

Her heart did a somersault just as the clock chimed the ten o'clock hour. Marcus closed his eyes briefly, then dipped his head.

"Is everything all right?" Phoebe asked.

"My cousin is being buried this morning. I thought to go, but that was before I learned I would be visiting the magistrate today."

"I need to go home and change my clothing," Phoebe said, suddenly feeling as though she had to do something beyond sitting here staring at the remnants of a breakfast she had no plans to eat.

Marcus gave her a dark stare. "You're not coming with me."

"I am, and you can't stop me—I'll wait in your coach. Don't you know I'm an independent spinster?"

"You're a bloody spitfire," he muttered, a smile teasing his lips.

Dorne appeared in the doorway and announced the arrival of Mr. Harry Sheffield.

Marcus sprang from his chair. "We'll meet him in the drawing room."

Phoebe was on her feet before Marcus could aid her. Clasping his arm, she walked upstairs with him to the drawing room.

Harry stood inside already, his large frame imposing even in the spacious chamber. His gaze lit with surprise as it landed on Phoebe. "Good morning."

"Don't bother with nonsense," Marcus said. "What news?"

Phoebe took her hand from Marcus's arm, then

promptly wished she hadn't. She needed his support and wanted to give it in return. She edged closer to his side.

"I've been very busy. Do you mind if I sit down?" Harry asked, moving to a wide chair.

Marcus scowled slightly, then escorted Phoebe to a settee near Harry. "If you're trying to increase our anticipation to a boiling point, I'd say you're succeeding rather well."

"Indeed," Phoebe murmured. She wanted to yell at him to tell them what he'd learned.

Harry grinned. "My apologies. I'm just delighted to see you here together. Particularly after what I've discovered." He looked to Phoebe. "As you know, I went to find the witness who informed us that Marcus had quarreled with Drobbit just before he was shot. I'm pleased to say that I found him, and when he was presented with the dangers of being found guilty of perjury, he completely recanted."

Phoebe took Marcus's hand between hers and squeezed, her insides singing with joy. "Did he say why he lied?"

"Sainsbury paid him to."

Marcus sagged beside her. "Was that to cover up his crime?"

"It seems so, though he hasn't confessed. We caught him trying to escape to the continent, however, and that won't recommend him to the magistrate when he appears before him in," Harry withdrew a timepiece from his pocket and glanced at the face, "two hours."

"Marcus doesn't need to go, then?" Phoebe thought she already knew the answer, but she wanted to hear it from Harry.

Harry smiled at them both. "Marcus is no longer a suspect."

Phoebe gave in to her joy and threw her arms around Marcus's neck, laughing. He clasped her tightly and kissed her cheek.

Harry's cough drew them apart. Phoebe let Marcus go and turned to see that Harry had stood. Marcus also rose, holding his hand for Phoebe to join him. She clasped his fingers with hers and didn't let go.

"I hope you'll invite me to the wedding," Harry said. "Or at least the wedding breakfast, unless it's just for Society types."

"Whether you like it or not, you're a Society type," Marcus said with a chuckle. "Or have you forgotten that your father is an earl?"

"No, I haven't forgotten, nor that my older brother has a courtesy title—he likes to remind me often."

"Did you know that Harry is a twin?" Marcus stage-whispered to Phoebe. "He's the younger by what, eleven minutes?"

"Twelve, but I appreciate you giving me the slight benefit." Harry smiled again. "I'll expect an invitation, then."

"Don't hold your breath," Phoebe said. "We do not have any plans to wed."

Harry stared at Marcus, his jaw dipping open. "You're an idiot."

Marcus inclined his head. "You aren't the first one to call me that, and you probably won't be the last."

"If you let her get away, I will *definitely* not be the last." He went to Phoebe and bowed. "It's been my pleasure to make your acquaintance, and I do hope you'll invite me to your nuptials, because I have to believe this," he glared at Marcus, "*imbecile* will come to his senses."

"Thank you for all your help, Harry." Phoebe let

go of Marcus's hand and dipped a brief curtsey, then Harry left.

"I suppose I should go too," she announced, taking a step toward the door.

Marcus grabbed her hand, and led her back upstairs to his sitting room. He stood her near the hearth and said, "Don't move."

He disappeared into his bedchamber for a moment. She waited patiently, wondering what the devil he was about. When he came back and knelt before her, his plan became evident and, in response, her heart vaulted into her throat. "Don't go. Not now. Not ever, actually." He reached into his pocket and pulled forth a ring.

He took her hand again and looked up at her. "Now that the threat of going to jail or worse isn't hanging over us" —Phoebe noted his use of the word *us*—"I would be humbly honored if you would be my wife."

"You truly want to marry me?" Phoebe wanted to be sure—she knew how far he'd come in such a short time. "It wasn't so long ago that we both turned our noses up at marriage."

"And I still would with anyone else. This is more than a marriage, however. Certainly more than most marriages we see. This is what we were meant to do, who are meant to be. You are the only woman who can be my wife."

Phoebe's spirit soared. "Just as you're the only man who could be my husband."

His eyes glinted with humor. "Is that a yes?"

"The most emphatic one I can give."

Marcus slipped the ring on her finger. "This was my mother's. I never thought I'd give it to someone."

She held her hand up, and the emerald glittered in the light from the windows. "It fits perfectly."

He stood and pulled her into his arms. "Of course it does. Because we fit perfectly."

She smiled widely, never more happy than at that moment. "As though we were made for each other."

EPILOGUE

$\mathcal{T}$he following Friday, Marcus stared at the beautiful woman standing in the middle of his drawing room and couldn't believe she was his wife. Not because he'd never intended to wed, but because he was astonished that she'd chosen *him*. Adorned in an aqua gown decorated with crystals that sparkled like the night sky when she moved, Phoebe took his breath away. Thankfully, she also gave it back every time she looked at him.

The wedding by special license had concluded a short while ago, and they would shortly move to the dining room for an elaborate breakfast. Then he would politely kick every single one of their guests out of his house so he could have his bride to himself.

It was notable that Phoebe's friend Jane Pemberton had arrived alone. She stood speaking animatedly with Phoebe. Curiosity got the better of him, and he moved to join them.

Miss Pemberton smiled at him as he arrived. "You are the luckiest of men, my lord."

"I am. Please call me Rip, or Marcus, if you prefer."

"Then you must call me Jane."

Phoebe brushed her arm against Marcus's. "Jane is now an official spinster."

That explained, he supposed, why she'd arrived alone. "Is there a decree that must be signed? A notice published in the paper?"

"Oh, that's a marvelous idea," Jane said with a laugh. "Though my parents would likely be even more furious. They forbade me from attending your wedding, *and* they gave me an ultimatum—I am to marry Mr. Brinkley or leave their household and make my own way." She shrugged. "The choice was simple, particularly since my sister is now betrothed." That had happened just two days ago.

"I've invited Jane to live at my house in Cavendish Square," Phoebe said.

Marcus blinked in surprise. They hadn't yet decided which house they would keep. His was larger, but she loved her garden and her garden room.

Phoebe smiled up at him, her eyes glowing. "Yes, my love, that means I've decided we should live here. If you don't mind? I'm rather looking forward to redoing your garden."

Marcus slipped his arm around her waist. "*Your* garden."

"I think I shall convene an official meeting of the Spitfire Society," Jane said.

Phoebe looked to Jane, her brows drawing together. "Who will be there? I will be at Brixton Park for the next fortnight."

Alone together away from the bustle of town—Marcus could hardly wait.

"I plan to invite the ladies I mentioned to you recently—the sisters who are new to town."

Phoebe nodded. "I recall. I look forward to meeting them. We shall include Arabella when she returns, of course."

"Of course. Do you mind if I move my things there this afternoon?"

"Not at all." Phoebe squeezed her friend's hand. "Are you certain this is what you want? You won't receive the same invitations."

"Oh, good." Jane grinned, her eyes twinkling, then she turned and went to speak with Anthony, who leaned against the mantel, a glass of champagne dangling from his fingers.

Marcus pivoted toward her. "You're sure you want to live here?"

She put her hands on his chest, smiling up at him adoringly so that his heart threatened to explode from his chest. "I honestly don't care where we live, so long as we're together."

Being this happy would never cease to astound him.

Phoebe's parents came toward them. Her mother beamed, and her father looked…less uncomfortable than when Marcus had first met him.

"Look at how happy you are," Mrs. Lennox said.

"Look at how happy *you* are," Phoebe murmured with just an edge of humor—not enough for her parents to catch it, probably, but Marcus did. He'd come to know her so well. Despite not wedding until that morning, they'd spent every day and night together over the past week. He wasn't sure he'd ever get enough of her. Indeed, he was sometimes annoyed that it had taken so long for them to find each other.

"I wanted to thank you again for restoring what Drobbit stole," Lennox said gruffly.

Marcus nodded in response. "My family's honor demanded it." And he was glad Lennox had accepted it. Convincing Graham to do the same when Marcus insisted on returning Brixton Park would prove more difficult. Still, Marcus would see it done—even going so far as to lie to Graham and tell him that Drobbit had returned some of the money before he'd died. Marcus had also made reparations to the Stokes and to a few other people his cousin had fleeced.

Osborne had come to see him and provided a partial list of Drobbit's victims. It had only been partial because Osborne admitted he hadn't always kept proper records. Then he'd promised to leave London for good. Marcus had warned him Bow Street would be watching.

Making restitution with those he could was the least Marcus could do. He hoped it went a small way to healing the damage Drobbit's thievery and deviousness had caused.

They chatted with Phoebe's parents for a while longer until Marcus saw Anthony take yet another glass of champagne and then stumble on his way back to propping up the mantel.

Marcus excused himself and went to speak with Anthony. "Should you go upstairs and sleep for a while?" he asked with a half smile.

Anthony snorted before he took a sip of the champagne. "It's your fault for serving such delicious wine."

"Perhaps. I could always stop serving it, if that would help."

Anthony scowled at him. "Don't be a bore now that you're married."

"I'm offended you would think so," Marcus said. He moved closer and lowered his voice. "I think it's time you pulled yourself together. I can't imagine I'll become a bore, but I *am* married now, and I can't keep as close an eye on you as I have been."

"I don't need to be watched over." Anthony sniffed. "I am, however, disappointed that you'll be abandoning me. I befriended you entirely because I thought you could be trusted to keep me eternally amused. And now look at you—absolutely besotted. You're lost to me completely."

Marcus heard the sadness beating beneath the sarcasm. "This gives you time to sort yourself out," he said quietly. "To face what you need to face."

Anthony glared at him. "And what's that?"

"The pain of the loss of your parents."

The glass in Anthony's hand shattered, splashing champagne on him and all over the floor. A footman rushed toward them as Anthony shook out his hand, swearing.

"Are you all right?" Marcus asked, trying to see if Anthony's hand was cut.

"Don't pretend to care," Anthony said through his teeth. "Go back to your wife. I'll be fine." He strode from the drawing room.

Before he could follow, Phoebe arrived at his side. She placed her hand on his arm. "Do you want to go after him?"

He did, but also didn't think it would do any good. In fact, it could worsen matters. Anthony was going to do what he wanted, and the more Marcus tried to pull him back from the abyss, the more he would barrel straight into the darkness.

"I do, but he won't like it." He exhaled before giving Phoebe his heartfelt attention. "Besides, I'm not leaving you on our wedding day."

"I wouldn't mind, not if you think he needs you. He's...troubled."

"I thought so too, but I'm beginning to realize that's an understatement. I'll see what I can do to help him. I wish that Felix and Sarah were here." Anthony's sister was due to give birth to her first child in the next few weeks.

"We'll help him." Phoebe gave him a reassuring smile. "Together. Who knows, maybe he'll be as happy as we are sooner than he expects. That happened to you."

"That happened to both of us, and I daresay the odds are one in a million. "

"Oh, come now," she scoffed. "Think of all the happy couples we know—Felix and Sarah, Beck and Lavinia, Arabella and Graham. And that's just a start."

"Are you saying it's an epidemic and Anthony could be the next to fall victim?" he asked wryly.

"I can think of worse things to happen," she said, taking his hand.

He lifted their joined hands and kissed the back of her wrist. "It may surprise you to hear that I can think of nothing better. You've given me a joy I never imagined."

She gave him a seductive look and darted her tongue over her lower lip, launching a shock of stark arousal through him. "Maybe later, you can return that joy."

"Just as soon as everyone leaves, my love." He squeezed her hand. "And then you're mine."

Her eyes glowed with love as she looked up at him. "For always."

Can an intrepid spitfire heal a broken viscount or will the sins of his past ruin them both?
Find out what happens with Anthony, Viscount Colton and Jane Pemberton in *A Duke Will Never Do*, coming May 19, 2020!

THANK YOU!

Thank you so much for reading A Duke is Never Enough! It's the second book in The Spitfire Society series. I hope you enjoyed it!

Would you like to know when my next book is available and to hear about sales and deals? Sign up for my VIP newsletter at https://www.darcyburke. com/readergroup, follow me on social media:
Facebook: https://facebook.com/DarcyBurkeFans
Twitter at @darcyburke
Instagram at darcyburkeauthor
Pinterest at darcyburkewrite

And follow me on Bookbub to receive updates on pre-orders, new releases, and deals!

Want to read about some of the characters in this book such as Lavinia and Beck, the Marchioness and Marqeuss of Northam, and Arabella and Graham, the Duke and Duchess of Halstead? Grab The Duke of Seduction and Never Have I Ever with a Duke! To read more about Anthony Colton, don't miss The Duke of Distraction.

Need more Regency romance? Check out my other historical series:

The Untouchables - Swoon over twelve of Society's most eligible and elusive bachelor peers and the bluestockings, wallflowers, and outcasts who bring them to their knees!

Wicked Dukes Club - six books written by me and my BFF, NYT Bestselling Author Erica Ridley. Meet the unforgettable men of London's most notorious tavern, The Wicked Duke. Seductively handsome, with charm and wit to spare, one night with these rakes and rogues will never be enough...

Love is All Around - heartwarming Regency-set retellings of classic Christmas stories (written after the Regency!) featuring a cozy village, three siblings, and the best gift of all: love.

Secrets and Scandals - six epic stories set in London's glittering ballrooms and England's lush countryside, and the first one, Her Wicked Ways, is free!

Legendary Rogues - Four intrepid heroines and adventurous heroes embark on exciting quests across Regency England and Wales!

If you like contemporary romance, I hope you'll check out my Ribbon Ridge series available from Avon Impulse, and the continuation of Ribbon Ridge in So Hot.

I hope you'll consider leaving a review at your favorite online vendor or networking site!

I appreciate my readers so much. Thank you, thank you, *thank you.*

Joy to the Duke

The Untouchables Series

THE FORBIDDEN DUKE

"I LOVED this story!!" 5 Stars

-Historical Romance Lover

"This is a wonderful read and I can't wait to see what comes next in this amazing series..." 5 Stars

-Teatime and Books

THE DUKE of DARING

"You will not be able to put it down once you start. Such a good read."

-Books Need TLC

"An unconventional beauty set on life as a spinster meets the one man who might change her mind, only to find his painful past makes it impossible to love. A wonderfully emotional journey from attraction, to friendship, to a love that conquers all."

-Bronwen Evans, *USA Today* Bestselling Author

THE DUKE of DECEPTION

"...an enjoyable, well-paced story ... Ned and Aquilla are an engaging, well-matched couple – strong, caring and compassionate; and ...it's easy to believe that they will continue to be happy together long after the book is ended."

"This is my favorite so far in the series! They had chemistry from the moment they met...their passion leaps off the pages."

THE DUKE of DESIRE

"Masterfully written with great characterization...with a flourish toward characters, secrets, and romance... Must read addition to "The Untouchables" series!"

"If you are looking for a truly endearing story about two people who take the path least travelled to find the other, with a side of 'YAH THAT'S HOT!' then this book is absolutely for you!"

THE DUKE of DEFIANCE

"This story was so beautifully written, and it hooked me from page one. I couldn't put the book down and just had to read it in one sitting even though it meant reading into the wee hours of the morning."

"I loved the Duke of Defiance! This is the kind of book you hate when it is over and I had to make myself stop reading just so I wouldn't have to leave the fun of Knighton's (aka Bran) and Joanna's story!"

-Behind Closed Doors Book Review

THE DUKE of DANGER

"The sparks fly between them right from the start... the HEA is certainly very hard-won, and well-deserved."

-All About Romance

"Another book hangover by Darcy! Every time I pick a favorite in this series, she tops it. The ending was perfect and made me want more."

-Sassy Book Lover

THE DUKE of ICE

"Each book gets better and better, and this novel was no exception. I think this one may be my fave yet! 5 out 5 for this reader!"

-Front Porch Romance

"An incredibly emotional story...I dare anyone to stop reading once the second half gets under way because this is intense!"

-Buried Under Romance

THE DUKE of RUIN

"This is a fast paced novel that held me until the last page."

" ...everything I could ask for in a historical romance... impossible to stop reading."

THE DUKE of LIES

"THE DUKE OF LIES is a work of genius! The characters are wonderfully complex, engaging; there is much mystery, and so many, many lies from so many people; I couldn't wait to see it all uncovered."

"..the epitome of romantic [with]...a bit of danger/action. The main characters are mature, fierce, passionate, and full of surprises. If you are a hopeless romantic and you love reading stories that'll leave you feeling like you're walking on clouds then you need to read this book or maybe even this entire series."

THE DUKE of SEDUCTION

"There were tears in my eyes for much of the last 10% of this book. So good!"

"An absolute joy to read... I always recommend Darcy!"

-Brittany and Elizabeth's Book Boutique

THE DUKE of KISSES

"Don't miss this magnificent read. It has some comedic fun, heartfelt relationships, heartbreaking moments, and horrifying danger."

-*The Reading Café*

"...my favorite story in the series. Fans of Regency romances will definitely enjoy this book."

-*Two Ends of the Pen*

THE DUKE of DISTRACTION

"Count on Burke to break a heart as only she can. This couple will get under the skin before they steal your heart."

-*Hopeless Romantic*

"Darcy Burke never disappoints. Her storytelling is just so magical and filled with passion. You will fall in love with the characters and the world she creates!"

-*Teatime and Books*

Secrets & Scandals Series

HER WICKED WAYS

"A bad girl heroine steals both the show and a highwayman's heart in Darcy Burke's deliciously wicked debut."

–Courtney Milan, *NYT* Bestselling Author

"...fast paced, very sexy, with engaging characters."

–*Smexybooks*

HIS WICKED HEART

"Intense and intriguing. Cinderella meets *Fight Club* in a historical romance packed with passion, action and secrets."

–Anna Campbell, *Seven Nights in a Rogue's Bed*

"A romance...to make you smile and sigh...a wonderful read!"

–*Rogues Under the Covers*

TO SEDUCE A SCOUNDREL

"Darcy Burke pulls no punches with this sexy, romantic page-turner. Sevrin and Philippa's story grabs you from the first scene and doesn't let go. *To Seduce a Scoundrel* is simply delicious!"

–Tessa Dare, *NYT* Bestselling Author

"I was captivated on the first page and didn't let go until this glorious book was finished!"

–*Romancing the Book*

TO LOVE A THIEF

"With refreshing circumstances surrounding both the hero and the heroine, a nice little mystery, and a touch of heat, this novella was a perfect way to pass the day."

—The Romanceaholic

"A refreshing read with a dash of danger and a little heat. For fans of honorable heroes and fun heroines who know what they want and take it."

-The Luv NV

NEVER LOVE A SCOUNDREL

"I loved the story of these two misfits thumbing their noses at society and finding love." Five stars.

—A Lust for Reading

"A nice mix of intrigue and passion...wonderfully complex characters, with flaws and quirks that will draw you in and steal your heart."

—BookTrib

SCOUNDREL EVER AFTER

"There is something so delicious about a bad boy, no matter what era he is from, and Ethan was definitely delicious."

-A Lust for Reading

"I loved the chemistry between the two main characters...Jagger/Ethan is not what he seems at all and neither is sweet society Miss Audrey. They are believably compatible."

-Confessions of a College Angel

Legendary Rogues Series

LADY of DESIRE

"A fast-paced mixture of adventure and romance, very much in the mould of *Romancing the Stone* or *Indiana Jones*."

-*All About Romance*

"...gave me such a book hangover! ...addictive...one of the most entertaining stories I've read this year!"

-*Adria's Romance Reviews*

ROMANCING the EARL

"Once again Darcy Burke takes an interesting story and...turns it into magic. An exceptionally well-written book."

-*Bodice Rippers, Femme Fatale, and Fantasy*

"...A fast paced story that was exciting and interesting. This is a definite must add to your book lists!"

-*Kilts and Swords*

LORD of FORTUNE

"I don't think I know enough superlatives to describe this book! It is wonderfully, magically delicious. It sucked me in from the very first sentence and didn't turn me loose—not even at the end ..."

"If you love a deep, passionate romance with a bit of mystery, then this is the book for you!"

CAPTIVATING the SCOUNDREL

"I am in absolute awe of this story. Gideon and Daphne stole all of my heart and then some. This book was such a delight to read."

"Darcy knows how to end a series with a bang! Daphne and Gideon are a mix of enemies and allies turned lovers that will have you on the edge of your seat at every turn."

Contemporary Romance

Ribbon Ridge Series

A contemporary family saga featuring the Archer family of sextuplets who return to their small Oregon wine country town to confront tragedy and find love...

The "multilayered plot keeps readers invested in the story line, and the explicit sensuality adds to the excitement that will have readers craving the next Ribbon Ridge offering."

-Library Journal Starred Review on YOURS TO HOLD

"Darcy Burke writes a uniquely touching and heart-warming series about the love, pain, and joys of family as well as the love that feeds your soul when you meet "the one."

-The Many Faces of Romance

I can't tell you how much I love this series. Each book gets better and better.

-Romancing the Readers

"Darcy Burke's Ribbon Ridge series is one of my all-time favorites. Fall in love with the Archer family, I know I did."

-Forever Book Lover

Ribbon Ridge: So Hot

SO GOOD

" ...worth the read with its well-written words, beau-tiful descriptions, and likeable characters...they are flirty, sexy and a match made in wine heaven."

-Harlequin Junkie Top Pick

"I absolutely love the characters in this book and the families. I honestly could not put it down and fin-ished it in a day."

SO RIGHT

"This is another great story by Darcy Burke. Painting pictures with her words that make you want to sit and stare at them for hours. I love the banter between the characters and the general sense of fun and friendliness."

-*The Ardent Reader*

" ...the romance is emotional; the characters are spirited and passionate... "

-*The Reading Café*

SO WRONG

"As usual, Ms. Burke brings you fun characters and witty banter in this sweet hometown series. I loved the dance between Crystal and Jamie as they fought their attraction."

-*The Many Faces of Romance*

"I really love both this series and the Ribbon Ridge series from Darcy Burke. She has this way of taking your heart and ripping it right out of your chest one second and then the next you are laughing at something the characters are doing."

-*Romancing the Readers*

ABOUT THE AUTHOR

Darcy Burke is the USA Today Bestselling Author of sexy, emotional historical and contemporary romance. Darcy wrote her first book at age 11, a happily ever after about a swan addicted to magic and the female swan who loved him, with exceedingly poor illustrations. Join her Reader Club at http://www.darcyburke.com/readerclub.

A native Oregonian, Darcy lives on the edge of wine country with her guitar-strumming husband, their two hilarious kids who seem to have inherited the writing gene. They're a crazy cat family with two Bengal cats, a small, fame-seeking cat named after a fruit, and an older rescue Maine Coon who is the master of chill and five a.m. serenading. In her "spare" time Darcy is a serial volunteer enrolled in a 12-step program where one learns to say "no," but she keeps having to start over. Her happy places are Disneyland and Labor Day weekend at the Gorge. Visit Darcy online at http://www.darcyburke.com and follow her social media: Facebook at http://www.facebook.com/darcyburkefans, Twitter @darcyburke at http://www.twitter.com/darcyburke, Instagram at http://www.instagram/darcyburkeauthor, and Pinterest at http://www.pinterest.com/darcyburkewrite.